The Best
Short Stories of
GUY
DE MAUPASSANT

The Best
Short Stories of
GUY
DE MAUPASSANT

Amereon
House

TO THE READER

It is our pleasure to keep available uncommon titles and to this end, at the time of publication, we have used the best available sources. To aid catalogers and collectors, this title is printed in an edition limited to 300 copies. —— **Enjoy!**

AMEREON HOUSE
the publishing division of
Amereon Ltd.
PO Box 1200
Mattituck, New York 11952-9500

Republished 1976 by special arrangement

THE BEST SHORT STORIES OF GUY DE MAUPASSANT

GUY DE MAUPASSANT

INTRODUCTION

The name of Guy de Maupassant has become synonymous with short story writing at its very best. Few writers in any language have rivalled him, and none has surpassed him. Maupassant was able to maintain a high level of excellence in all his works. Thus his reputation has a firm and wide base, for he was a prolific author and produced over three hundred short stories in slightly more than one decade. Most of those who have read Maupassant remember only those stories that have become standard fare for the high school anthology. Presented here is a wider sampling of Maupassant's incomparable art.

Guy de Maupassant was born in Normandy, France, in 1850. His parents separated when he was about six and he went to live with his mother on her country estate. At age thirteen, he was sent to a Catholic school, but was expelled. He continued his education at a school in Rouen and there won a prize for one of his poems. Thus his writing began at an early age. Outbreak of the Franco-Prussian War (1870) created a temporary pause in his literary career, but, after the war, he went to Paris to seek a civil service job, which he hoped would leave him time free to write. It was in Paris that Maupassant came under the tutelage of one of the masters of French prose, Gustave Flaubert. [Flaubert had a personal interest in Guy because Maupassant's mother was the sister of one of Flaubert's best friends and the same friend was married to Maupassant's paternal aunt.] In Flaubert, Guy de Maupassant had a stern critic and an insightful one from whom he was able to learn much. Flaubert was also instrumental in introducing Maupassant to the great literary figures of the day: Turgenev, Zola, Daudet and Goncourt, to name a few. Only a few of the writings which Maupassant did for Flaubert are still available, but they give a definite indication of good things to come.

Besides his writing, Maupassant found time to devote himself to rowing. According to popular story, he is reputed to have rowed as many as fifty miles in one day. His other interest was women and he became the center figure in many whispered tales of conquest. It was at this time in his life that the first hint appeared of his later bouts with serious illness. He complained of various illnesses and spent much time in doctor's offices. The tragic truth was that Maupassant had contracted syphilis. He went to take the cure at various thermal baths, but there was no absolute remedy for the disease at that time. The best that could be hoped for was that the disease would enter into a period of remission from time to time before continuing on its deadly course.

It is understandable that a man such as Maupassant would find life in the civil service restricting, although he did find material for many stories while working as a clerk. But he turned more and more away from the office work and toward a full-time literary career. His short story "Ball-of-Fat" was accepted for publication in a volume of short stories prepared by Zola and his circle. The story is of a prostitute traveling across Normandy during its occupation by German soldiers. Her companions in the stagecoach are respectable citizens of Rouen who don't want to muddle their own moral purity by mixing with one of her kind. They remain painfully aloof until it becomes obvious that the prostitute is the only one who is carrying any food. In this story Maupassant makes full use of his talent. His feelings are not difficult to discern.

He has nothing but contempt for the "solid citizens" of Rouen, nor has he any illusions about the nature of war. The story illustrates well Maupassant's ability to draw the reader into his stories. The reader experiences a definite sense of uneasiness as the plot unfolds. The uneasiness is created by our recognition of the truth of Maupassant's point—that society professes one set of values, but practices quite another. The only characters who emerge morally unscathed are the humble whose common sense and basic values keep them from the corruption of hypocrisy.

The story is representative of the later works of Maupassant, not only because of the view expressed on war, but because of the theme of appearance and reality. This was Maupassant's first great story, and the highest praise of it came from Flaubert himself, who called it "a masterpiece of writing, of comedy, and of observation."

Shortly after this first triumph, Maupassant did leave the civil service in order to spend full time on his writing. By the age of thirty-four, he had a well-established reputation. During this time, Maupassant did some of his best-known and best work, including "The Diamond Necklace," probably one of the most famous short stories in the world. The force of the ending never loses its appeal. Some critics have compared the character of Mme. Loisel to that of Emma Bovary in Flaubert's *Madame Bovary,* for both of their downfalls stem from their pride and social aspirations. While there is some truth in that comparison, it should not be carried too far. Maupassant's development of character is necessarily more limited for within the confines of the short story it is the simplicity and compelling quality of the plot which are of greatest importance. If one were to generalize, it might be said that the outstanding aspect of Maupassant's stories is their detached spareness in which each detail moves the reader inexorably along towards the conclusion.

Many of Maupassant's remarkable stories were written in between bouts of growing illness, for Maupassant's incurable affliction was gaining ground. He struggled to continue writing and occasionally, with tremendous will-power, he was able to produce a story which met his own exacting standards. Added to his physical and mental suffering, he had increased trouble with publishers who frequently had the misfortune of dealing with him at some of his most depressed moments which did little to recommend Maupassant to them.

For Maupassant, the end was as tragic as for some of his protagonists. He became steadily worse, was admitted to a sanitorium, and finally failed to even recognize the friends who came to visit him. He died on July 6, 1893.

CONTENTS

BALL-OF-FAT

For many days now the fag-end of the army had been strag-gling through the town. They were not troops, but a dis-banded horde. The beards of the men were long and filthy, their uniforms in tatters, and they advanced at an easy pace without flag or regiment. All seemed worn-out and back-broken, incapable of a thought or a resolution, march-ing by habit solely, and falling from fatigue as soon as they stopped. In short, they were a mobilized, pacific people, bending under the weight of the gun; some little squads on the alert, easy to take alarm and prompt in enthusiasm, ready to attack or to flee; and in the midst of them, some red breeches, the remains of a division broken up in a great battle; some somber artillery men in line with these varied kinds of foot soldiers; and, sometimes the brilliant helmet of a dragoon on foot who followed with difficulty the short-est march of the lines.

Some legions of free-shooters, under the heroic names of "Avengers of the Defeat," "Citizens of the Tomb," "Par-takers of Death," passed in their turn with the air of ban-dits.

Their leaders were former cloth or grain merchants, ex-merchants in tallow or soap, warriors of circumstance, elected officers on account of their escutcheons and the length of their mustaches, covered with arms and with braid, speaking in constrained voices, discussing plans of campaign, and pretending to carry agonized France alone on their swaggering shoulders, but sometimes fearing their own soldiers, prison-birds, that were often brave at first and later proved to be plunderers and debauchees.

It was said that the Prussians were going to enter Rouen. The National Guard who for two months had been care-

11

fully reconnoitering in the neighboring woods, shooting sometimes their own sentinels, and ready for a combat whenever a little wolf stirred in the thicket, had now returned to their firesides. Their arms, their uniforms, all the murderous accoutrements with which they had lately struck fear into the national heart for three leagues in every direction, had suddenly disappeared.

The last French soldiers finally came across the Seine to reach the Audemer bridge through Saint-Sever and Bourg-Achard; and, marching behind, on foot, between two officers of ordnance, the General, in despair, unable to do anything with these incongruous tatters, himself lost in the breaking-up of a people accustomed to conquer, and disastrously beaten, in spite of his legendary bravery.

A profound calm, a frightful, silent expectancy had spread over the city. Many of the heavy citizens, emasculated by commerce, anxiously awaited the conquerors, trembling lest their roasting spits or kitchen knives be considered arms.

All life seemed stopped; shops were closed, the streets dumb. Sometimes an inhabitant, intimidated by this silence, moved rapidly along next the walls. The agony of waiting made them wish the enemy would come.

In the afternoon of the day which followed the departure of the French troops, some uhlans, coming from one knows not where, crossed the town with celerity. Then, a little later, a black mass descended the side of St. Catharine, while two other invading bands appeared by the way of Darnetal and Boisguillaume. The advance guard of the three bodies joined one another at the same moment in Hotel de Ville square and, by all the neighboring streets, the German army continued to arrive, spreading out its battalions, making the pavement resound under their hard, rhythmic step.

Some orders of the commander, in a foreign, guttural voice, reached the houses which seemed dead and deserted, while behind closed shutters, eyes were watching these victorious men, masters of the city, of fortunes, of lives, through the "rights of war." The inhabitants, shut up in their rooms, were visited with the kind of excitement that a cataclysm, or some fatal upheaval of the earth, brings to us, against which all force is useless. For the same sensation is produced each time that the established order of things is overturned, when security no longer exists, and all that protect the laws of man and of nature find themselves at the mercy of unreasoning, ferocious brutality. The trembling of the earth crushing the houses and burying an entire people; a river overflowing its banks and carrying in its course the drowned peasants, carcasses of beeves, and girders snatched from roofs, or a glorious army massacring those trying to defend themselves, leading others prisoners, pillaging in the name of the sword and thanking God to the sound of the cannon, all are alike frightful scourges which disconnect all belief in eternal justice, all the confidence that we have in the protection of Heaven and the reason of man.

Some detachments rapped at each door, then disappeared into the houses. It was occupation after invasion. Then the duty commences for the conquered to show themselves gracious toward the conquerors.

After some time, as soon as the first terror disappears, a new calm is established. In many families, the Prussian officer eats at the table. He is sometimes well bred and, through politeness, pities France, and speaks of his repugnance in taking part in this affair. One is grateful to him for this sentiment; then, one may be, some day or other, in need of his protection. By treating him well, one has, perhaps, a less number of men to feed. And why should we wound anyone on whom we are entirely dependent? To act thus would be less bravery than temerity. And temerity is no longer a fault of the commoner of Rouen, as it was at the time of the heroic defense, when their city became famous. Finally, each told himself that the highest judgment of French urbanity required that they be allowed to be polite to the strange soldier in the house, provided they did not show themselves familiar with him in public. Outside they would not make themselves known to each other, but at home they could chat freely, and the German might remain longer each evening warming his feet at their hearthstones.

The town even took on, little by little, its ordinary aspect. The French scarcely went out, but the Prussian soldiers grumbled in the streets. In short, the officers of the Blue Hussars, who dragged with arrogance their great weapons of death up and down the pavement, seemed to have no more grievous scorn for the simple citizens than the officers or the sportsmen who, the year before, drank in the same *cafés*.

There was nevertheless, something in the air, something subtle and unknown, a strange, intolerable atmosphere like a penetrating odor, the odor of invasion. It filled the dwellings and the public places, changed the taste of the food, gave the impression of being on a journey, far away, among barbarous and dangerous tribes.

The conquerors exacted money, much money. The inhabitants always paid and they were rich enough to do it. But the richer a trading Norman becomes the more he suffers at every outlay, at each part of his fortune that he sees pass from his hands into those of another.

Therefore, two or three leagues below the town, following the course of the river toward Croisset, Dieppedalle, or Biessart mariners and fishermen often picked up the swollen corpse of a German in uniform from the bottom of the river, killed by the blow of a knife, the head crushed with a stone, or perhaps thrown into the water by a push from the high bridge. The slime of the river bed buried these obscure vengeances, savage, but legitimate, unknown heroisms, mute attacks more perilous than the battles of broad day, and without the echoing sound of glory.

For hatred of the foreigner always arouses some intrepid ones, who are ready to die for an idea.

Finally, as soon as the invaders had brought the town quite under subjection with their inflexible discipline, without having been guilty of any of the horrors for which they were famous along their triumphal line of march, people began to take courage, and the need of trade put new heart into the commerce of the country. Some had large interests at Havre, which the French army occupied, and they wished to try and reach this port by going to Dieppe by land and there embarking.

They used their influence with the German soldiers with whom they had an acquaintance, and finally, an authorization of departure was obtained from the General-in-chief.

Then, a large diligence, with four horses, having been engaged for this journey, and ten persons having engaged seats in it, it was resolved to set out on Tuesday morning before daylight, in order to escape observation.

For some time before, the frost had been hardening the earth and on Monday, toward three o'clock, great black clouds coming from the north brought the snow which fell without interruption during the evening and all night.

At half past four in the morning, the travelers met in the courtyard of Hotel Normandie, where they were to take the carriage.

They were still full of sleep, and shivering with cold under their wraps. They could only see each other dimly in the obscure light, and the accumulation of heavy winter garments made them all resemble fat curates in long cassocks. Only two of the men were acquainted; a third accosted them and they chatted: "I'm going to take my wife," said one. "I too," said another. "And I," said the third. The first added: "We shall not return to Rouen, and if the Prussians approach Havre, we shall go over to England." All had the same projects, being of the same mind.

As yet the horses were not harnessed. A little lantern, carried by a stable boy, went out one door from time to time, to immediately appear at another. The feet of the horses striking the floor could be heard, although deadened by the straw and litter, and the voice of a man talking to the beasts, sometimes swearing, came from the end of the building. A light tinkling of bells announced that they were taking down the harness; this murmur soon became a clear and continuous rhythm by the movement of the animal, stopping sometimes, then breaking into a brusque shake which was accompanied by the dull stamp of a sabot upon the hard earth.

The door suddenly closed. All noise ceased. The frozen citizens were silent; they remained immovable and stiff.

A curtain of uninterrupted white flakes constantly sparkled in its descent to the ground. It effaced forms, and powdered everything with a downy moss. And nothing could be heard in the great silence. The town was calm, and buried under the wintry frost, as this fall of snow, unnamable and floating, a sensation rather than a sound (trembling atoms which only seem to fill all space), came to cover the earth.

The man reappeared with his lantern, pulling at the end of a rope a sad horse which would not come willingly. He placed him against the pole, fastened the traces, walked about a long time adjusting the harness, for he had the use of but one hand, the other carrying the lantern. As he went for the second horse, he noticed the travelers, motionless, already white with snow, and said to them: "Why not get into the carriage? You will be under cover, at least."

They had evidently not thought of it, and they hastened to do so. The three men installed their wives at the back and then followed them. Then the other forms, undecided and veiled, took in their turn the last places without exchanging a word.

The floor was covered with straw, in which the feet ensconced themselves. The ladies at the back having brought little copper foot stoves, with a carbon fire, lighted them and, for some time, in low voices, enumerated the advantages of the appliances, repeating things that they had known for a long time.

Finally, the carriage was harnessed with six horses instead of four, because the traveling was very bad, and a voice called out:

"Is everybody aboard?"

And a voice within answered: "Yes."

They were off. The carriage moved slowly, slowly for a little way. The wheels were imbedded in the snow; the whole body groaned with heavy cracking sounds; the horses glistened, puffed, and smoked; and the great whip of the driver snapped without ceasing, hovering about on all sides, knotting and unrolling itself like a thin serpent, lashing brusquely some horse on the rebound, which then put forth its most violent effort.

Now the day was imperceptibly dawning. The light flakes, which one of the travelers, a Rouenese by birth, said looked like a shower of cotton, no longer fell. A faint light filtered through the great dull clouds, which rendered more brilliant the white of the fields, where appeared a line of great trees clothed in whiteness, or a chimney with a cap of snow.

In the carriage, each looked at the others curiously, in the sad light of this dawn.

At the back, in the best places, Mr. Loiseau, wholesale merchant of wine, of Grand-Pont street, and Mrs. Loiseau were sleeping opposite each other. Loiseau had bought out his former patron who failed in business, and made his fortune. He sold bad wine at a good price to small retailers in the country, and passed among his friends and acquaintances as a knavish wag, a true Norman full of deceit and joviality.

His reputation as a sharper was so well established that one evening at the residence of the prefect, Mr. Tournel, author of some fables and songs, of keen, satirical mind, a local celebrity, having proposed to some ladies, who seemed to be getting a little sleepy, that they make up a game of "Loiseau tricks," the joke traversed the rooms of the prefect, reached those of the town, and then, in the months to come, made many a face in the province expand with laughter.

Loiseau was especially known for his love of farce of every kind, for his jokes, good and bad; and no one could ever talk with him without thinking: "He is invaluable, this Loiseau." Of tall figure, his balloon-shaped front was surmounted by a ruddy face surrounded by gray whiskers.

His wife, large, strong, and resolute, with a quick, decisive manner, was the order and arithmetic of this house of commerce, while he was the life of it through his joyous activity.

Beside them, Mr. Carré-Lamadon held himself with great dignity, as if belonging to a superior caste; a considerable man, in cottons, proprietor of three mills, officer of the Legion of Honor, and member of the General Council. He had remained, during the Empire, chief of the friendly opposition, famous for making the Emperor pay dearer for rallying to the cause than if he had combated it with blunted arms, according to his own story. Madame Carré-Lamadon, much younger than her husband, was the consolation of officers of good family sent to Rouen in garrison. She sat opposite her husband, very dainty, petite, and pretty, wrapped closely in furs and looking with sad eyes at the interior of the carriage.

Her neighbors, the Count and Countess Hubert de Breville, bore the name of one of the most ancient and noble families of Normandy. The Count, an old gentleman of good figure, accentuated, by the artifices of his toilette, his resemblance to King Henry IV., who, following a glorious legend of the family, had impregnated one of the De Breville ladies, whose husband, for this reason, was made a count and governor of the province.

A colleague of Mr. Carré-Lamadon in the General Council, Count Hubert represented the Orléans party in the Department.

The story of his marriage with the daughter of a little captain of a privateer had always remained a mystery. But as the Countess had a grand air, received better than anyone, and passed for having been loved by the son of Louis Philippe, all the nobility did her honor, and her salon remained the first in the country, the only one which preserved the old gallantry, and to which the *entrée* was difficult. The fortune of the Brevilles amounted, it was said, to five hundred thousand francs in income, all in good securities.

These six persons formed the foundation of the carriage company, the society side, serene and strong, honest, established people, who had both religion and principles.

By a strange chance, all the women were upon the same seat; and the Countess had for neighbors two sisters who picked at long strings of beads and muttered some *Paters* and *Aves*. One was old and as pitted with smallpox as if she had received a broadside of grapeshot full in the face. The other, very sad, had a pretty face and a disease of the lungs, which, added to their devoted faith, illumined them and made them appear like martyrs.

Opposite these two devotees were a man and a woman who attracted the notice of all. The man, well known, was Cornudet the democrat, the terror of respectable people. For twenty years he had soaked his great red beard in the

bocks of all the democratic *cafés*. He had consumed with
his friends and *confrères* a rather pretty fortune left him
by his father, an old confectioner, and he awaited the es-
tablishing of the Republic with impatience, that he might
have the position he merited by his great expenditures. On
the fourth of September, by some joke perhaps, he believed
himself elected prefect, but when he went to assume the
duties, the clerks of the office were masters of the place
and refused to recognize him, obliging him to retreat.
Rather a good bachelor, on the whole, inoffensive and serv-
iceable, he had busied himself, with incomparable ardor,
in organizing the defense against the Prussians. He had
dug holes in all the plains, cut down young trees from
the neighboring forests, sown snares over all routes and,
at the approach of the enemy, took himself quickly back
to the town. He now thought he could be of more use in
Havre where more entrenchments would be necessary.

The woman, one of those called a coquette, was celebrated for her *embonpoint,* which had given her the nickname of "Ball-of-Fat." Small, round, and fat as lard, with
puffy fingers choked at the phalanges, like chaplets of
short sausages; with a stretched and shining skin, an enormous bosom which shook under her dress, she was, nevertheless, pleasing and sought after, on account of a certain
freshness and breeziness of disposition. Her face was a
round apple, a peony bud ready to pop into bloom, and inside that opened two great black eyes, shaded with thick
brows that cast a shadow within; and below, a charming mouth, humid for kissing, furnished with shining, mi-
croscopic baby teeth. She was, it was said, full of admirable
qualities.

As soon as she was recognized, a whisper went around
among the honest women, and the words "prostitute" and
"public shame" were whispered so loud that she raised
her head. Then she threw at her neighbors such a provok-
ing, courageous look that a great silence reigned, and everybody looked down except Loiseau, who watched her with an
exhilarated air.

And immediately conversation began among the three
ladies, whom the presence of this girl had suddenly ren-

dered friendly, almost intimate. It seemed to them they should bring their married dignity into union in opposition to that sold without shame; for legal love always takes on a tone of contempt for its free *confrère*.

The three men, also drawn together by an instinct of preservation at the sight of Cornudet, talked money with a certain high tone of disdain for the poor. Count Hubert talked of the havoc which the Prussians had caused, the losses which resulted from being robbed of cattle and from destroyed crops, with the assurance of a great lord, ten times millionaire whom these ravages would scarcely cramp for a year. Mr. Carré-Lamadon, largely experienced in the cotton industry, had had need of sending six hundred thousand francs to England, as a trifle in reserve if it should be needed. As for Loiseau, he had arranged with the French administration to sell them all the wines that remained in his cellars, on account of which the State owed him a formidable sum, which he counted on collecting at Havre.

And all three threw toward each other swift and amicable glances.

Although in different conditions, they felt themselves to be brothers through money, that grand free-masonry of those who possess it, and make the gold rattle by putting their hands in their trousers' pockets.

The carriage went so slowly that at ten o'clock in the morning they had not gone four leagues. The men had got down three times to climb hills on foot. They began to be disturbed because they should be now taking breakfast at Tôtes and they despaired now of reaching there before night. Each one had begun to watch for an inn along the route, when the carriage foundered in a snowdrift, and it took two hours to extricate it.

Growing appetites troubled their minds; and no eating-house, no wine shop showed itself, the approach of the Prussians and the passage of the troops having frightened away all these industries.

The gentlemen ran to the farms along the way for provisions, but they did not even find bread, for the defiant peasant had concealed his stores for fear of being pillaged by the soldiers who, having nothing to put between their teeth, took by force whatever they discovered.

Toward one o'clock in the afternoon, Loiseau announced that there was a decided hollow in his stomach. Everybody suffered with him, and the violent need of eating, ever increasing, had killed conversation.

From time to time some one yawned; another immediately imitated him; and each, in his turn, in accordance with his character, his knowledge of life, and his social position, opened his mouth with carelessness or modesty, placing his hand quickly before the yawning hole from whence issued a vapor.

Ball-of-Fat, after many attempts, bent down as if seeking something under her skirts. She hesitated a second, looked at her neighbors, then sat up again tranquilly. The faces were pale and drawn. Loiseau affirmed that he would give a thousand francs for a small ham. His wife made a gesture, as if in protest; but she kept quiet. She was always troubled when anyone spoke of squandering money, and could not comprehend any pleasantry on the subject. "The fact is," said the Count, "I cannot understand why I did not think to bring some provisions with me." Each reproached himself in the same way.

However, Cornudet had a flask full of rum. He offered it; it was refused coldly. Loiseau alone accepted two swallows, and then passed back the flask saying, by way of thanks: "It is good all the same; it is warming and checks the appetite." The alcohol put him in good-humor and he proposed that they do as they did on the little ship in the song, eat the fattest of the passengers. This indirect allusion to Ball-of-Fat choked the well-bred people. They said nothing. Cornudet alone laughed. The two good sisters had ceased to mumble their rosaries and, with their hands enfolded in their great sleeves, held themselves immovable, obstinately lowering their eyes, without doubt offering to Heaven the suffering it had brought upon them.

Finally at three o'clock, when they found themselves in the midst of an interminable plain, without a single village in sight, Ball-of-Fat bending down quickly drew from under the seat a large basket covered with a white napkin.

At first she brought out a little china plate and a silver cup; then a large dish in which there were two whole chickens, cut up and imbedded in their own jelly. And one could still see in the basket other good things, some *pâtés*, fruits, and sweetmeats, provisions for three days if they should not see the kitchen of an inn. Four necks of bottles were seen among the packages of food. She took a wing of a chicken and began to eat it delicately, with one of those little biscuits called "Regence" in Normandy.

All looks were turned in her direction. Then the odor spread, enlarging the nostrils and making the mouth water, besides causing a painful contraction of the jaw behind the ears. The scorn of the women for this girl became ferocious, as if they had a desire to kill her and throw her out of the carriage into the snow, her, her silver cup, her basket, provisions and all.

But Loiseau with his eyes devoured the dish of chicken. He said: "Fortunately Madame had more precaution than we. There are some people who know how to think ahead always."

She turned toward him, saying: "If you would like some of it, sir? It is hard to go without breakfast so long."

He saluted her and replied: "Faith, I frankly cannot refuse; I can stand it no longer. Everything goes in time of war, does it not, Madame?" And then casting a comprehensive glance around, he added: "In moments like this, one can but be pleased to find people who are obliging."

He had a newspaper which he spread out on his knees, that no spot might come to his pantaloons, and upon the point of a knife that he always carried in his pocket, he took up a leg all glistening with jelly, put it between his teeth and masticated it with a satisfaction so evident that there ran through the carriage a great sigh of distress.

Then Ball-of-Fat, in a sweet and humble voice, proposed that the two sisters partake of her collation. They both accepted instantly and, without raising their eyes, began to eat very quickly, after stammering their thanks. Cornudet no longer refused the offers of his neighbor, and they formed with the sisters a sort of table, by spreading out some newspapers upon their knees.

The mouths opened and shut without ceasing, they masticated, swallowed, gulping ferociously. Loiseau in his corner was working hard and, in a low voice, was trying to induce his wife to follow his example. She resisted for a long time; then, when a drawn sensation ran through her body, she yielded. Her husband, rounding his phrase, asked their "charming companion" if he might be allowed to offer a little piece to Madame Loiseau.

She replied: "Why, yes, certainly, sir," with an amiable smile, as she passed the dish.

An embarrassing thing confronted them when they opened the first bottle of Bordeaux: they had but one cup. Each passed it after having tasted. Cornudet alone, for politeness without doubt, placed his lips at the spot left humid by his fair neighbor.

Then, surrounded by people eating, suffocated by the odors of the food, the Count and Countess de Breville, as well as Madame and M. Carré-Lamadon, were suffering that odious torment which has preserved the name of Tantalus. Suddenly the young wife of the manufacturer gave forth such a sigh that all heads were turned in her direction; she was as white as the snow without; her eyes closed, her head drooped; she had lost consciousness. Her husband, much excited, implored the help of everybody. Each lost his head completely, until the elder of the two sisters, holding the head of the sufferer, slipped Ball-of-Fat's cup between her lips and forced her to swallow a few drops of wine. The pretty little lady revived, opened her eyes, smiled, and declared in a dying voice that she felt very well now. But, in order that the attack might not return, the sister urged her to drink a full glass of Bordeaux, and added: "It is just hunger, nothing more."

Then Ball-of-Fat, blushing and embarrassed, looked at the four travelers who had fasted and stammered: "Goodness knows! if I dared to offer anything to these gentlemen and ladies, I would—" Then she was silent, as if fearing an insult. Loiseau took up the word: "Ah! certainly, in times like these all the world are brothers and ought to aid each other. Come, ladies, without ceremony; why the devil not accept? We do not know whether we shall even find a

house where we can pass the night. At the pace we are going now, we shall not reach Tôtes before noon to-morrow—"

They still hesitated, no one daring to assume the respon-
sibility of a "Yes." The Count decided the question. He
turned toward the fat, intimidated girl and, taking on a
grand air of condescension, he said to her:

"We accept with gratitude, Madame."

It is the first step that counts. The Rubicon passed, one
lends himself to the occasion squarely. The basket was
stripped. It still contained a *pâté de foie gras, a pâté* of
larks, a piece of smoked tongue, some preserved pears, a
loaf of hard bread, some wafers, and a full cup of pickled
gherkins and onions, of which crudities Ball-of-Fat, like all
women, was extremely fond.

They could not eat this girl's provisions without speaking to her. And so they chatted, with reserve at first; then,
as she carried herself well, with more abandon. The ladies
De Breville and Carré-Lamadon, who were acquainted with
all the ins and outs of good-breeding, were gracious with a
certain delicacy. The Countess, especially, showed that
amiable condescension of very noble ladies who do not
fear being spoiled by contact with anyone, and was charming. But the great Madame Loiseau, who had the soul of a
plebeian, remained crabbed, saying little and eating much.

The conversation was about the war, naturally. They
related the horrible deeds of the Prussians, the brave acts of
the French; and all of them, although running away, did
homage to those who stayed behind. Then personal stories
began to be told, and Ball-of-Fat related, with sincere emotion, and in the heated words that such girls sometimes use·
in expressing their natural feelings, how she had left Rouen:

"I believed at first that I could remain," she said. "I had
my house full of provisions, and I preferred to feed a few
soldiers rather than expatriate myself, to go I knew not
where. But as soon as I saw them, those Prussians, that was
too much for me! They made my blood boil with anger,
and I wept for very shame all day long. Oh! if I were only a
man! I watched them from my windows, the great porkers
with their pointed helmets, and my maid held my hands to

keep me from throwing the furniture down upon them. Then one of them came to lodge at my house; I sprang at his throat the first thing; they are no more difficult to strangle than other people. And I should have put an end to that one then and there had they not pulled me away by the hair. After that, it was necessary to keep out of sight. And finally, when I found an opportunity, I left town and— here I am!"

They congratulated her. She grew in the estimation of her companions, who had not shown themselves so hot-brained, and Cornudet, while listening to her, took on the approving, benevolent smile of an apostle, as a priest would if he heard a devotee praise God, for the long-bearded democrats have a monopoly of patriotism, as the men in cassocks have a religion. In his turn he spoke, in a doctrinal tone, with the emphasis of a proclamation such as we see pasted on the walls about town, and finished by a bit of eloquence whereby he gave that "scamp of a Badinguet" a good lashing.

Then Ball-of-Fat was angry, for she was a Bonapartist. She grew redder than a cherry and, stammering with indignation, said:

"I would like to have seen you in his place, you other people. Then everything would have been quite right; oh, yes! It is you who have betrayed this man! One would never have had to leave France if it had been governed by blackguards like you!"

Cornudet, undisturbed, preserved a disdainful, superior smile, but all felt that the high note had been struck, until the Count, not without some difficulty, calmed the exasperated girl and proclaimed with a manner of authority that all sincere opinions should be respected. But the Countess and the manufacturer's wife, who had in their souls an unreasonable hatred for the people that favor a Republic, and the same instinctive tenderness that all women have for a decorative, despotic government, felt themselves drawn, in spite of themselves, toward this prostitute so full of dignity, whose sentiments so strongly resembled their own.

The basket was empty. By ten o'clock they had easily exhausted the contents and regretted that there was not more. Conversation continued for some time, but a little more coldly since they had finished eating.

The night fell, the darkness little by little became profound, and the cold, felt more during digestion, made Ball-of-Fat shiver in spite of her plumpness. Then Madame de Breville offered her the little footstove, in which the fuel had been renewed many times since morning; she accepted it immediately, for her feet were becoming numb with cold. The ladies Carré-Lamadon and Loiseau gave theirs to the two religious sisters.

The driver had lighted his lanterns. They shone out with a lively glimmer showing a cloud of foam beyond, the sweat of the horses; and, on both sides of the way, the snow seemed to roll itself along under the moving reflection of the lights.

Inside the carriage one could distinguish nothing. But a sudden movement seemed to be made between Ball-of-Fat and Cornudet; and Loiseau, whose eye penetrated the shadow, believed that he saw the big-bearded man start back quickly as if he had received a swift, noiseless blow.

Then some twinkling points of fire appeared in the distance along the road. It was Tôtes. They had traveled eleven hours, which, with the two hours given to resting and feeding the horses, made thirteen. They entered the town and stopped before the Hotel of Commerce.

The carriage door opened! A well-known sound gave the travelers a start; it was the scabbard of a sword hitting the ground. Immediately a German voice was heard in the darkness.

Although the diligence was not moving, no one offered to alight, fearing some one might be waiting to murder them as they stepped out. Then the conductor appeared, holding in his hand one of the lanterns which lighted the carriage to its depth, and showed the two rows of frightened faces, whose mouths were open and whose eyes were wide with surprise and fear.

Outside beside the driver, in plain sight, stood a German officer, an excessively tall young man, thin and blond, squeezed into his uniform like a girl in a corset, and wearing on his head a flat, oilcloth cap which made him resemble the porter of an English hotel. His enormous mustache, of long straight hairs, growing gradually thin at each side and terminating in a single blond thread so fine that one could not perceive where it ended, seemed to weigh heavily on the corners of his mouth and, drawing down the cheeks, left a decided wrinkle about the lips.

In Alsatian French, he invited the travelers to come in, saying in a suave tone: "Will you descend, gentlemen and ladies?"

The two good sisters were the first to obey, with the docility of saints accustomed ever to submission. The Count and Countess then appeared, followed by the manufacturer and his wife; then Loiseau, pushing ahead of him his larger half. The last-named, as he set foot on the earth, said to the officer: "Good evening, sir," more as a measure of prudence than politeness. The officer, insolent as all powerful people usually are, looked at him without a word.

Ball-of-Fat and Cornudet, although nearest the door, were the last to descend, grave and haughty before the enemy. The fat girl tried to control herself and be calm. The democrat waved a tragic hand and his long beard seemed to tremble a little and grow redder. They wished to preserve their , dignity, comprehending that in such meetings as these they represented in some degree their great country, and somewhat disgusted with the docility of her companions, the fat girl tried to show more pride than her neighbors, the honest women, and, as she felt that some one should set an example, she continued her attitude of resistance assumed at the beginning of the journey.

They entered the vast kitchen of the inn, and the German, having demanded their traveling papers signed by the General-in-chief (in which the name, the description, and profession of each traveler was mentioned), and having examined them all critically, comparing the people and their signatures, said: "It is quite right," and went out.

Then they breathed. They were still hungry and supper was ordered. A half hour was necessary to prepare it, and while two servants were attending to this they went to their rooms. They found them along a corridor which terminated in a large glazed door.

Finally, they sat down at table, when the proprietor of
the inn himself appeared. He was a former horse merchant,
a large, asthmatic man, with a constant wheezing and rattling in his throat. His father had left him the name of Follenvie. He asked:

"Is Miss Elizabeth Rousset here?"

Ball-of-Fat started as she answered: "It is I."

"The Prussian officer wishes to speak with you immediately."

"With me?"

"Yes, that is, if you are Miss Elizabeth Rousset."

She was disturbed, and reflecting for an instant, declared
flatly:

"That is my name, but I shall not go."

A stir was felt around her; each discussed and tried to
think of the cause of this order. The Count approached her,
saying:

"You are wrong, Madame, for your refusal may lead to
considerable difficulty, not only for yourself, but for all
your companions. It is never worth while to resist those in
power. This request cannot assuredly bring any danger; it
is, without doubt, about some forgotten formality."

Everybody agreed with him, asking, begging, beseech-
ing her to go, and at last they convinced her that it was best;
they all feared the complications that might result from
disobedience. She finally said:

"It is for you that I do this, you understand."

The Countess took her by the hand, saying: "And we are
grateful to you for it."

She went out. They waited before sitting down at table.

Each one regretted not having been sent for in the place
of this violent, irascible girl, and mentally prepared some
platitudes, in case they should be called in their turn.

But at the end of ten minutes she reappeared, out of
breath, red to suffocation, and exasperated. She stammered:
"Oh! the rascal; the rascal!"

All gathered around to learn something, but she said
nothing; and when the Count insisted, she responded with
great dignity: "No, it does not concern you; I can say nothing."

Then they all seated themselves around a high soup tureen, whence came the odor of cabbage. In spite of alarm, the supper was gay. The cider was good, the beverage Loiseau and the good sisters took as a means of economy. The others called for wine; Cornudet demanded beer. He had a special fashion of uncorking the bottle, making froth on the liquid, carefully filling the glass and then holding it before the light to better appreciate the color. When he drank, his great beard, which still kept some of the foam of his beloved beverage, seemed to tremble with tenderness; his eyes were squinted, in order not to lose sight of his tipple, and he had the unique air of fulfilling the function for which he was born. One would say that there was in his mind a meeting, like that of affinities, between the two great passions that occupied his life—Pale Ale and Revolutions; and assuredly he could not taste the one without thinking of the other.

Mr. and Mrs. Follenvie dined at the end of the table. The man, rattling like a crackled locomotive, had too much trouble in breathing to talk while eating, but his wife was never silent. She told all her impressions at the arrival of the Prussians, what they did, what they said, reviling them because they cost her some money, and because she had two sons in the army. She addressed herself especially to the Countess, flattered by being able to talk with a lady of quality.

When she lowered her voice to say some delicate thing; her husband would interrupt, from time to time, with: "You had better keep silent, Madame Follenvie." But she paid no attention, continuing in this fashion:

"Yes, Madame, those people there not only eat our potatoes and pork, but our pork and potatoes. And it must not be believed that they are at all proper—oh, no! such filthy things they do, saving the respect I owe to you! And if you could see them exercise for hours in the day! they are all there in the field, marching ahead, then marching back, turning here and turning there. They might be cultivating the land, or at least working on the roads of their own country! But no, Madame, these military men are profitable to no one. Poor people have to feed them, or perhaps be murdered! I am only an old woman without education, it is true, but when I see some endangering their constitutions by raging from morning to night, I say: "When there are so many people found to be useless, how unnecessary it is for others to take so much trouble to be nuisances! Truly, is it not an abomination to kill people, whether they be Prussian, or English, or Polish, or French? If one man revenges himself upon another who has done him some injury, it is wicked and he is punished; but when they exterminate our boys, as if they were game, with guns, they give decorations, indeed, to the one who destroys the most! Now, you see, I can never understand that, never!"

Cornudet raised his voice: "War is a barbarity when one attacks a peaceable neighbor, but a sacred duty when one defends his country."

The old woman lowered her head:

"Yes, when one defends himself, it is another thing; but why not make it a duty to kill all the kings who make these wars for their pleasure?"

Cornudet's eyes flashed. "Bravo, my country-woman!" said he.

Mr. Carré-Lamadon reflected profoundly. Although he was prejudiced as a Captain of Industry, the good sense of this peasant woman made him think of the opulence that would be brought into the country were the idle and consequently mischievous hands, and the troops which were now maintained in unproductiveness, employed in some great industrial work that it would require centuries to achieve.

Loiseau, leaving his place, went to speak with the innkeeper in a low tone of voice. The great man laughed, shook, and squeaked, his corpulence quivered with joy at the jokes of his neighbor, and he bought of him six cases of wine for spring, after the Prussians had gone.

As soon as supper was finished, as they were worn out with fatigue, they retired.

However, Loiseau, who had observed things, after getting his wife to bed, glued his eye and then his ear to a hole in the wall, to try and discover what are known as "the mysteries of the corridor."

At the end of about an hour, he heard a groping, and, looking quickly, he perceived Ball-of-Fat, who appeared still more plump in a blue cashmere negligee trimmed with white lace. She had a candle in her hand and was directing her steps toward the great door at the end of the corridor. But a door at the side opened, and when she returned at the end of some minutes Cornudet, in his suspenders, followed her. They spoke low, then they stopped. Ball-of-Fat seemed to be defending the entrance to her room with energy. Loiseau, unfortunately, could not hear all their words, but finally, as they raised their voices, he was able to catch a few. Cornudet insisted with vivacity. He said:

"Come, now, you are a silly woman; what harm can be done?"

She had an indignant air in responding: "No, my dear, there are moments when such things are out of place. Here it would be a shame."

He doubtless did not comprehend and asked why. Then she cried out, raising her voice still more:

"Why? you do not see why? When there are Prussians in the house, in the very next room, perhaps?"

He was silent. This patriotic shame of the harlot, who would not suffer his caress so near the enemy, must have awakened the latent dignity in his heart, for after simply kissing her, he went back to his own door with a bound.

Loiseau, much excited, left the aperture, cut a caper in his room, put on his pajamas, turned back the clothes that covered the bony carcass of his companion, whom he awakened with a kiss, murmuring: "Do you love me, dearie?"

Then all the house was still. And immediately there arose somewhere, from an uncertain quarter, which might be the cellar but was quite as likely to be the garret, a powerful snoring, monotonous and regular, a heavy, prolonged sound, like a great kettle under pressure. Mr. Follenvie was asleep.

As they had decided that they would set out at eight o'clock the next morning, they all collected in the kitchen. But the carriage, the roof of which was covered with snow, stood undisturbed in the courtyard, without horses and without a conductor. They sought him in vain in the stables, in the hay, and in the coach-house. Then they resolved to scour the town, and started out. They found themselves in a square, with a church at one end, and some low houses on either side, where they perceived some Prussian soldiers. The first one they saw was paring potatoes. The second, further off, was cleaning the hairdresser's shop. Another, bearded to the eyes, was tending a troublesome brat, cradling it and trying to appease it; and the great peasant women, whose husbands were "away in the army," indicated by signs to their obedient conquerors the work they wished to have done: cutting wood, cooking the soup, grinding the coffee, or what not. One of them even washed the linen of his hostess, an impotent old grandmother.

The Count, astonished, asked questions of the beadle who came out of the rectory. The old man responded:

"Oh! those men are not wicked; they are not the Prussians we hear about. They are from far off, I know not where; and they have left wives and children in their country; it is not amusing to them, this war, I can tell you! I am sure they also weep for their homes, and that it makes as much sorrow among them as it does among us. Here, now, there is not so much unhappiness for the moment, because the soldiers do no harm and they work as if they were in their own homes. You see, sir, among poor people it is necessary that they aid one another. These are the great traits which war develops."

Cornudet, indignant at the cordial relations between the conquerors and the conquered, preferred to shut himself up in the inn. Loiseau had a joke for the occasion: "They will repeople the land."

Mr. Carré-Lamadon had a serious word: "They try to make amends."

But they did not find the driver. Finally, they discovered him in a *café* of the village, sitting at table fraternally with the officer of ordnance. The Count called out to him:

"Were you not ordered to be ready at eight o'clock?"

"Well, yes; but another order has been given me since."

"By whom?"

"Faith! the Prussian commander."

"What was it?"

"Not to harness at all."

"Why?"

"I know nothing about it. Go and ask him. They tell me not to harness, and I don't harness. That's all."

"Did he give you the order himself?"

"No, sir, the innkeeper gave the order for him."

"When was that?"

"Last evening, as I was going to bed."

The three men returned, much disturbed. They asked for Mr. Follenvie, but the servant answered that that gentleman, because of his asthma, never rose before ten o'clock. And he had given strict orders not to be wakened before that, except in case of fire.

They wished to see the officer, but that was absolutely impossible, since, while he lodged at the inn, Mr. Follenvie alone was authorized to speak to him upon civil affairs. So they waited. The women went up to their rooms again and occupied themselves with futile tasks.

Cornudet installed himself near the great chimney in the kitchen, where there was a good fire burning. He ordered one of the little tables to be brought from the *café*, then a can of beer; he then drew out his pipe, which plays among democrats a part almost equal to his own, because in serving Cornudet it was serving its country. It was a superb pipe, an admirably colored meerschaum, as black as the teeth of its master, but perfumed, curved, glistening, easy to the hand, completing his physiognomy. And he remained motionless, his eyes as much fixed upon the flame of the fire as upon his favorite tipple and its frothy crown; and each time that he drank, he passed his long, thin fingers through his scanty, gray hair, with an air of satisfaction, after which he sucked in his mustache fringed with foam.

Loiseau, under the pretext of stretching his legs, went to place some wine among the retailers of the country. The Count and the manufacturer began to talk politics. They could foresee the future of France. One of them believed in an Orléans, the other in some unknown savior for the country, a hero who would reveal himself when all were in despair: a Guesclin, or a Joan of Arc, perhaps, or would it be another Napoleon First? Ah! if the Prince Imperial were not so young!

Cornudet listened to them and smiled like one who holds the word of destiny. His pipe perfumed the kitchen.

As ten o'clock struck, Mr. Follenvie appeared. They asked him hurried questions; but he could only repeat two or three times without variation, these words:

"The officer said to me: 'Mr. Follenvie, you see to it that the carriage is not harnessed for those travelers tomorrow. I do not wish them to leave without my order. That is sufficient.' "

Then they wished to see the officer. The Count sent him his card, on which Mr. Carré-Lamadon wrote his name and all his titles. The Prussian sent back word that he would meet the two gentlemen after he had breakfasted, that is to say, about one o'clock.

The ladies reappeared and ate a little something, despite their disquiet. Ball-of-Fat seemed ill and prodigiously troubled.

They were finishing their coffee when the word came that the officer was ready to meet the gentlemen. Loiseau joined them; but when they tried to enlist Cornudet, to give more solemnity to their proceedings, he declared proudly that he would have nothing to do with the Germans; and he betook himself to his chimney corner and ordered another liter of beer.

The three men mounted the staircase and were introduced to the best room of the inn, where the officer received them, stretched out in an armchair, his feet on the mantelpiece, smoking a long, porcelain pipe, and enveloped in a flamboyant dressing-gown, appropriated, without doubt, from some dwelling belonging to a common citizen of bad taste. He did not rise, nor greet them in any way, not even looking at them. It was a magnificent display of natural blackguardism transformed into the military victor.

At the expiration of some moments, he asked: "What is it you wish?"

The Count became spokesman: "We desire to go on our way, sir."

"No."

"May I ask the cause of this refusal?"

"Because I do not wish it."

"But, I would respectfully observe to you, sir, that your General-in-chief gave us permission to go to Dieppe; and I know of nothing we have done to merit your severity."

"I do not wish it—that is all; you can go."

All three having bowed, retired.

The afternoon was lamentable. They could not understand this caprice of the German; and the most singular ideas would come into their heads to trouble them. Everybody stayed in the kitchen and discussed the situation endlessly, imagining all sorts of unlikely things. Perhaps they would be retained as hostages—but to what end?—or taken prisoners—or rather a considerable ransom might be demanded. At this thought a panic prevailed. The richest were the most frightened, already seeing themselves constrained to pay for their lives with sacks of gold poured into the hands of this insolent soldier. They racked their brains to think of some acceptable falsehoods to conceal their riches and make them pass themselves off for poor people, very poor people. Loiseau took off the chain to his watch and hid it away in his pocket. The falling night increased their apprehensions. The lamp was lighted, and as there was still two hours before dinner, Madame Loiseau proposed a game of Thirty-one. It would be a diversion. They accepted. Cornudet himself, having smoked out his pipe, took part for politeness.

The Count shuffled the cards, dealt, and Ball-of-Fat had thirty-one at the outset; and immediately the interest was great enough to appease the fear that haunted their minds. Then Cornudet perceived that the house of Loiseau was given to tricks.

As they were going to the dinner table, Mr. Follenvie again appeared, and, in wheezing, rattling voice, announced:

"The Prussian officer orders me to ask Miss Elizabeth Rousset if she has yet changed her mind."

Ball-of-Fat remained standing and was pale; then suddenly becoming crimson, such a stifling anger took possession of her that she could not speak. But finally she flashed out: "You may say to the dirty beast, that idiot, that carrion of a Prussian, that I shall never change it; you understand, never, never, never!"

The great innkeeper went out. Then Ball-of-Fat was immediately surrounded, questioned, and solicited by all to disclose the mystery of his visit. She resisted, at first, but soon becoming exasperated, she said: "What does he want? You really want to know what he wants? He wants to sleep with me."

Everybody was choked for words, and indignation was rife. Cornudet broke his glass, so violently did he bring his fist down upon the table. There was a clamor of censure against this ignoble soldier, a blast of anger, a union of all for resistance, as if a demand had been made on each one of the party for the sacrifice exacted of her. The Count declared with disgust that those people conducted themselves after the fashion of the ancient barbarians. The women, especially, showed to Ball-of-Fat a most energetic and tender commiseration. The good sisters who only showed themselves at mealtime, lowered their heads and said nothing.

They all dined, nevertheless, when the first furore had abated. But there was little conversation; they were thinking.

The ladies retired early, and the men, all smoking, organized a game at cards to which Mr. Follenvie was invited, as they intended to put a few casual questions to him on the subject of conquering the resistance of this officer. But he thought of nothing but the cards and, without listening or answering, would keep repeating: "To the game, sirs, to the game." His attention was so taken that he even forgot to expectorate, which must have put him some points to the good with the organ in his breast. His whistling lungs ran the whole asthmatic scale, from deep, profound tones - to the sharp rustiness of a young cock essaying to crow.

He even refused to retire when his wife, who had fallen asleep previously, came to look for him. She went away alone, for she was an "early bird," always up with the sun, while her husband was a "night owl," always ready to pass the night with his friends. He cried out to her: "Leave my creamed chicken before the fire!" and then went on with his game. When they saw that they could get nothing from him, they declared that it was time to stop, and each sought his bed.

They all rose rather early the next day, with an undefined hope of getting away, which desire the terror of passing another day in that horrible inn greatly increased.

Alas! the horses remained in the stable and the driver was invisible. For want of better employment, they went out and walked around the carriage.

The breakfast was very doleful; and it became apparent that a coldness had arisen toward Ball-of-Fat, and that the night, which brings counsel, had slightly modified their judgments. They almost wished now that the Prussian had secretly found this girl, in order to give her companions a pleasant surprise in the morning. What could be more simple? Besides, who would know anything about it? She could save appearances by telling the officer that she took pity on their distress. To her, it would make so little difference!

No one had avowed these thoughts yet.

In the afternoon, as they were almost perishing from ennui, the Count proposed that they take a walk around the village. Each wrapped up warmly and the little party set out, with the exception of Cornudet, who preferred to remain near the fire, and the good sisters, who passed their time in the church or at the curate's.

The cold, growing more intense every day, cruelly pinched their noses and ears; their feet became so numb that each step was torture; and when they came to a field it seemed to them frightfully sad under this limitless white, so that everybody returned immediately, with hearts hard pressed and souls congealed.

The four women walked ahead, the three gentlemen followed just behind. Loiseau, who understood the situation, asked suddenly if they thought that girl there was going to keep them long in such a place as this. The Count, always courteous, said that they could not exact from a woman a sacrifice so hard, unless it should come of her own will. Mr. Carré-Lamadon remarked that if the French made their return through Dieppe, as they were likely to, a battle would surely take place at Tôtes. This reflection made the two others anxious.

"If we could only get away on foot," said Loiseau.

The Count shrugged his shoulders: "How can we think

of it in this snow? and with our wives?" he said. "And then,
we should be pursued and caught in ten minutes and led
back prisoners at the mercy of these soldiers."

It was true, and they were silent.

The ladies talked of their clothes, but a certain constraint
seemed to disunite them. Suddenly at the end of the street,
the officer appeared. His tall, wasp-like figure in uniform
was outlined upon the horizon formed by the snow, and he
was marching with knees apart, a gait particularly military,
which is affected that they may not spot their carefully
blackened boots.

He bowed in passing near the ladies and looked disdainfully at the men, who preserved their dignity by not seeing
him, except Loiseau, who made a motion toward raising his
hat.

Ball-of-Fat reddened to the ears, and the three married
women resented the great humiliation of being thus met by
this soldier in the company of this girl whom he had treated
so cavalierly.

But they spoke of him, of his figure and his face. Madame
Carré-Lamadon who had known many officers and considered herself a connoisseur of them, found this one not
at all bad; she regretted even that he was not French, because he would make such a pretty hussar, one all the
women would rave over.

Again in the house, no one knew what to do. Some sharp
words, even, were said about things very insignificant. The
dinner was silent, and almost immediately after it, each one
went to his room to kill time in sleep.

They descended the next morning with weary faces and
exasperated hearts. The women scarcely spoke to Ball-of-Fat.

A bell began to ring. It was for a baptism. The fat girl had
a child being brought up among the peasants of Yvetot. She
had not seen it for a year, or thought of it; but now the idea
of a child being baptized threw into her heart a sudden
and violent tenderness for her own, and she strongly wished
to be present at the ceremony.

As soon as she was gone, everybody looked at each other,
then pulled their chairs together, for they thought that
finally something should be decided upon. Loiseau had an

inspiration: it was to hold Ball-of-Fat alone and let the others go.

Mr. Follenvie was charged with the commission, but he returned almost immediately, for the German, who understood human nature, had put him out. He pretended that he would retain everybody so long as his desire was not satisfied.

Then the commonplace nature of Mrs. Loiseau burst out with:

"Well, we are not going to stay here to die of old age. Since it is the trade of this creature to accommodate herself to all kinds, I fail to see how she has the right to refuse one more than another. I can tell you she has received all she could find in Rouen, even the coachmen! Yes, Madame, the prefect's coachman! I know him very well, for he bought his wine at our house. And to think that to-day we should be drawn into this embarrassment by this affected woman, this minx! For my part, I find that this officer conducts himself very well. He has perhaps suffered privations for a long time; and doubtless he would have preferred us three; but no, he is contented with common property. He respects married women. And we must remember too that he is master. He has only to say 'I wish,' and he could take us by force with his soldiers."

The two women had a cold shiver. Pretty Mrs. Carré-Lamadon's eyes grew brilliant and she became a little pale, as if she saw herself already taken by force by the officer.

The men met and discussed the situation. Loiseau, furious, was for delivering "the wretch" bound hand and foot to the enemy. But the Count, descended through three generations of ambassadors, and endowed with the temperament of a diplomatist, was the advocate of ingenuity.

"It is best to decide upon something," said he. Then they conspired.

The women kept together, the tone of their voices was lowered, each gave advice and the discussion was general. Everything was very harmonious. The ladies especially found delicate shades and charming subtleties of expression for saying the most unusual things. A stranger would have understood nothing, so great was the precaution of language observed. But the light edge of modesty, with which every woman of the world is barbed, only covers the surface; they blossom out in a scandalous adventure of this kind, being deeply amused and feeling themselves in their element, mixing love with sensuality as a greedy cook prepares supper for his master.

Even gaiety returned, so funny did the whole story seem to them at last. The Count found some of the jokes a little off color, but they were so well told that he was forced to smile. In his turn, Loiseau came out with some still bolder tales, and yet nobody was wounded. The brutal thought, expressed by his wife, dominated all minds: "Since it is her trade, why should she refuse this one more than another?" The genteel Mrs. Carré-Lamadon seemed to think that in her place, she would refuse this one less than some others.

They prepared the blockade at length, as if they were about to surround a fortress. Each took some rôle to play, some arguments he would bring to bear, some maneuvers that he would endeavor to put into execution. They decided on the plan of attack, the ruse to employ, the surprise of assault, that should force this living citadel to receive the enemy in her room.

Cornudet remained apart from the rest, and was a stranger to the whole affair.

So entirely were their minds distracted that they did not hear Ball-of-Fat enter. The Count uttered a light "Ssh!" which turned all eyes in her direction. There she was. The abrupt silence and a certain embarrassment hindered them from speaking to her at first. The Countess, more accustomed to the duplicity of society than the others, finally inquired:

"Was it very amusing, that baptism?"

The fat girl, filled with emotion, told them all about it, the faces, the attitudes, and even the appearance of the church. She added: "It is good to pray sometimes."

And up to the time for luncheon these ladies continued to be amiable toward her, in order to increase her docility and her confidence in their counsel. At the table they commenced the approach. This was in the shape of a vague conversation upon devotion. They cited ancient examples:

Judith and Holophernes, then, without reason, Lucrece and Sextus, and Cleopatra obliging all the generals of the enemy to pass by her couch and reducing them in servility to slaves. Then they brought out a fantastic story, hatched in the imagination of these ignorant millionaires, where the women of Rome went to Capua for the purpose of lulling Hannibal to sleep in their arms, and his lieutenants and phalanxes of mercenaries as well. They cited all the women who have been taken by conquering armies, making a battlefield of their bodies, making them also a weapon, and a means of success; and all those hideous and detestable beings who have conquered by their heroic caresses, and sacrificed their chastity to vengeance or a beloved cause. They even spoke in veiled terms of that great English family which allowed one of its women to be inoculated with a horrible and contagious disease in order to transmit it to Bonaparte, who was miraculously saved by a sudden illness at the hour of the fatal rendezvous.

And all this was related in an agreeable, temperate fashion, except as it was enlivened by the enthusiasm deemed proper to excite emulation.

One might finally have believed that the sole duty of woman here below was a sacrifice of her person, and a continual abandonment to soldierly caprices.

The two good sisters seemed not to hear, lost as they were in profound thought. Ball-of-Fat said nothing.

During the whole afternoon they let her reflect. But, in the place of calling her "Madame" as they had up to this time, they simply called her "Mademoiselle" without knowing exactly why, as if they had a desire to put her down a degree in their esteem, which she had taken by storm, and make her feel her shameful situation.

The moment supper was served, Mr. Follenvie appeared with his old phrase: "The Prussian officer orders me to ask if Miss Elizabeth Rousset has yet changed her mind."

Ball-of-Fat responded dryly: "No, sir."

But at dinner the coalition weakened. Loiseau made three unhappy remarks. Each one beat his wits for new examples but found nothing; when the Countess, without premeditation, perhaps feeling some vague need of rendering homage to religion, asked the elder of the good sisters to tell them some great deeds in the lives of the saints. It appeared that many of their acts would have been considered crimes in our eyes; but the Church gave absolution of them readily, since they were done for the glory of God, or for the good of all. It was a powerful argument; the Countess made the most of it.

Thus it may be by one of those tacit understandings, or the veiled complacency in which anyone who wears the ecclesiastical garb excels, it may be simply from the effect of a happy unintelligence, a helpful stupidity, but in fact the religious sister lent a formidable support to the conspiracy. They had thought her timid, but she showed herself courageous, verbose, even violent. She was not troubled by the chatter of the casuist; her doctrine seemed a bar of iron; her faith never hesitated; her conscience had no scruples. She found the sacrifice of Abraham perfectly simple, for she would immediately kill father or mother on an order from on high. And nothing, in her opinion, could displease the Lord, if the intention was laudable. The Countess put to use the authority of her unwitting accomplice, and added to it the edifying paraphrase and axiom of Jesuit morals: "The need justifies the means."

Then she asked her: "Then, my sister, do you think that God accepts intentions, and pardons the deed when the motive is pure?"

"Who could doubt it, Madame? An action blamable in itself often becomes meritorious by the thought it springs from."

And they continued thus, unraveling the will of God, foreseeing his decisions, making themselves interested in things that, in truth, they would never think of noticing. All this was guarded, skillful, discreet. But each word of the saintly sister in a cap helped to break down the resistance of the unworthy courtesan. Then the conversation changed a little, the woman of the chaplet speaking of the houses of her order, of her Superior, of herself, of her dainty neighbor, the dear sister Saint-Nicephore. They had been called to the hospitals of Havre to care for the hundreds of soldiers stricken with smallpox. They depicted these miserable creatures, giving details of the malady. And while they were stopped, *en route,* by the caprice of this Prussian officer, a great number of Frenchmen might die, whom perhaps they could have saved! It was a specialty with her, caring for soldiers. She had been in Crimea, in Italy, in Austria, and, in telling of her campaigns, she revealed herself as one of those religious aids to drums and trumpets, who seem made to follow camps, pick up the wounded in the thick of battle, and, better than an officer, subdue with a word great bands of undisciplined recruits. A true, good sister of the rataplan, whose ravaged face, marked with innumerable scars, appeared the image of the devastation of war.

No one could speak after her, so excellent seemed the effect of her words.

As soon as the repast was ended they quickly went up to their rooms, with the purpose of not coming down the next day until late in the morning.

The luncheon was quiet. They had given the grain of seed time to germinate and bear fruit. The Countess proposed that they take a walk in the afternoon. The Count, being agreeably inclined, gave an arm to Ball-of-Fat and walked behind the others with her. He talked to her in a familiar, paternal tone, a little disdainful, after the manner of men having girls in their employ, calling her "my dear child," from the height of his social position, of his undisputed honor. He reached the vital part of the question at once:

"Then you prefer to leave us here, exposed to the violences which follow a defeat, rather than consent to a favor which you have so often given in your life?"

Ball-of-Fat answered nothing.

Then he tried to reach her through gentleness, reason, and then the sentiments. He knew how to remain "The Count," even while showing himself gallant or complimentary, or very amiable if it became necessary. He exalted the service that she would render them, and spoke of her appreciation; then suddenly became gaily familiar, and said:

"And you know, my dear, it would be something for him to boast of that he had known a pretty girl; something it is difficult to find in his country."

Ball-of-Fat did not answer but joined the rest of the party. As soon as they entered the house she went to her room and did not appear again. The disquiet was extreme. What were they to do? If she continued to resist, what an embarrassment!

The dinner hour struck. They waited in vain. Mr. Follenvie finally entered and said that Miss Rousset was indisposed, and would not be at the table. Everybody pricked up his ears. The Count went to the innkeeper and said in a low voice:

"Is he in there?"

"Yes."

For convenience, he said nothing to his companions, but made a slight sign with his head. Immediately a great sigh of relief went up from every breast and a light appeared in their faces. Loiseau cried out:

"Holy Christopher! I pay for the champagne, if there is any to be found in the establishment." And Mrs. Loiseau was pained to see the proprietor return with four quart bottles in his hands.

Each one had suddenly become communicative and buoyant. A wanton joy filled their hearts. The Count suddenly perceived that Mrs. Carré-Lamadon was charming, the manufacturer paid compliments to the Countess. The conversation was lively, gay, full of touches.

Suddenly Loiseau, with anxious face and hand upraised, called out: "Silence!" Everybody was silent, surprised, already frightened. Then he listened intently and said: "S-s-sh!" his two eyes and his hands raised toward the ceiling, listening, and then continuing, in his natural voice: "All right! All goes well!"

They failed to comprehend at first, but soon all laughed. At the end of a quarter of an hour he began the same farce again, renewing it occasionally during the whole afternoon. And he pretended to call to some one in the story above, giving him advice in a double meaning, drawn from the fountain-head—the mind of a commercial traveler. For some moments he would assume a sad air, breathing in a whisper: "Poor girl!" Then he would murmur between his teeth, with an appearance of rage: "Ugh! That scamp of a Prussian." Sometimes, at a moment when no more was thought about it, he would say, in an affected voice, many times over: "Enough! enough!" and add, as if speaking to himself, "If we could only see her again, it isn't necessary that he should kill her, the wretch!"

Although these jokes were in deplorable taste, they amused all and wounded no one, for indignation, like other things, depends upon its surroundings, and the atmosphere which had been gradually created around them was charged with sensual thoughts.

At the dessert the women themselves made some delicate and discreet allusions. Their eyes glistened; they had drunk much. The Count, who preserved, even in his flights, his grand appearance of gravity, made a comparison, much relished, upon the subject of those wintering at the pole, and the joy of ship-wrecked sailors who saw an opening toward the south.

Loiseau suddenly arose, a glass of champagne in his hand, and said: "I drink to our deliverance." Everybody was on his feet; they shouted in agreement. Even the two good sisters consented to touch their lips to the froth of the wine which they had never before tasted. They declared that it tasted like charged lemonade, only much nicer.

Loiseau resumed: "It is unfortunate that we have no piano, for we might make up a quadrille."

Cornudet had not said à word, nor made a gesture; he appeared plunged in very grave thoughts, and made sometimes a furious motion, so that his great beard seemed to wish to free itself. Finally, toward midnight, as they were separating, Loiseau, who was staggering, touched him suddenly on the stomach and said to him in a stammer: "You are not very funny, this evening; you have said nothing, citizen!" Then Cornudet raised his head brusquely and, casting a brilliant, terrible glance around the company, said: "I tell you all that you have been guilty of infamy!" He rose, went to the door, and again repeated: "Infamy, I say!" and disappeared.

This made a coldness at first. Loiseau, interlocutor, was stupefied; but he recovered immediately and laughed heartily as he said: "He is very green, my friends. He is very green." And then, as they did not comprehend, he told them about the "mysteries of the corridor." Then there was a return of gaiety. The women behaved like lunatics. The Count and Mr. Carré-Lamadon wept from the force of their laughter. They could not believe it.

"How is that? Are you sure?"

"I tell you I saw it."

"And she refused—"

"Yes, because the Prussian officer was in the next room."

"Impossible!"

"I swear it!"

The Count was stifled with laughter. The industrial gentleman held his sides with both hands. Loiseau continued:

"And now you understand why he saw nothing funny this evening! No, nothing at all!" And the three started out half ill, suffocated.

They separated. But Mrs. Loiseau, who was of a spiteful nature, remarked to her husband as they were getting into bed, that "that *grisette*" of a little Carré-Lamadon was yellow with envy all the evening. "You know," she continued, "how some women will take to a uniform, whether it be French or Prussian! It is all the same to them! Oh! what a pity!"

And all night, in the darkness of the corridor, there were to be heard light noises, like whisperings and walking in bare feet, and imperceptible creakings. They did not go to sleep until late, that is sure, for there were threads of light shining under the doors for a long time. The champagne had its effect; they say it troubles sleep.

The next day a clear winter's sun made the snow very brilliant. The diligence, already harnessed, waited before the door, while an army of white pigeons, in their thick plumage, with rose-colored eyes, with a black spot in the center, walked up and down gravely among the legs of the six horses, seeking their livelihood in the manure there scattered.

The driver, enveloped in his sheepskin, had a lighted

pipe under the seat, and all the travelers, radiant, were rapidly packing some provisions for the rest of the journey. They were only waiting for Ball-of-Fat. Finally she appeared.

She seemed a little troubled, ashamed. And she advanced timidly toward her companions, who all, with one motion, turned as if they had not seen her. The Count, with dignity, took the arm of his wife and removed her from this impure contact.

The fat girl stopped, half stupefied; then, plucking up courage, she approached the manufacturer's wife with "Good morning, Madame," humbly murmured. The lady made a slight bow of the head which she accompanied with a look of outraged virtue. Everybody seemed busy, and kept themselves as far from her as if she had had some infectious disease in her skirts. Then they hurried into the carriage, where she came last, alone, and where she took the place she had occupied during the first part of the journey.

They seemed not to see her or know her; although Madame Loiseau, looking at her from afar, said to her husband in a half-tone: "Happily, I don't have to sit beside her."

The heavy carriage began to move and the remainder of the journey commenced. No one spoke at first. Ball-of-Fat dared not raise her eyes. She felt indignant toward all her neighbors, and at the same time humiliated at having yielded to the foul kisses of this Prussian, into whose arms they had hypocritically thrown her.

Then the Countess, turning toward Mrs. Carré-Lamadon, broke the difficult silence:

"I believe you know Madame d'Etrelles?"

"Yes, she is one of my friends."

"What a charming woman!"

"Delightful! A very gentle nature, and well educated, besides; then she is an artist to the tips of her fingers, sings beautifully, and draws to perfection."

The manufacturer chatted with the Count, and in the midst of the rattling of the glass, an occasional word escaped such as "coupon—premium—limit—expiration."

. Loiseau, who had pilfered the old pack of cards from the

inn, greasy through five years of contact with tables badly cleaned, began a game of bezique with his wife.

The good sisters took from their belt the long rosary which hung there, made together the sign of the cross, and suddenly began to move their lips in a lively murmur, as if they were going through the whole of the "Oremus." And from time to time they kissed a medal, made the sign anew, then recommenced their muttering, which was rapid and continued.

Cornudet sat motionless, thinking.

At the end of three hours on the way, Loiseau put up the cards and said: "I am hungry."

His wife drew out a package from whence she brought a piece of cold veal. She cut it evenly in thin pieces and they both began to eat.

"Suppose we do the same," said the Countess.

They consented to it and she undid the provisions prepared for the two couples. It was in one of those dishes whose lid is decorated with a china hare, to signify that a *pâté* of hare is inside, a succulent dish of pork, where white rivers of lard cross the brown flesh of the game, mixed with some other viands hashed fine. A beautiful square of Gruyère cheese, wrapped in a piece of newspaper, preserved the imprint "divers things" upon the unctuous plate.

The two good sisters unrolled a big sausage which smelled of garlic; and Cornudet plunged his two hands into the vast pockets of his overcoat, at the same time, and drew out four hard eggs and a piece of bread. He removed the shells and threw them in the straw under his feet; then he began to eat the eggs, letting fall on his vast beard some bits of clear yellow, which looked like stars caught there.

Ball-of-Fat, in the haste and distraction of her rising, had not thought of anything; and she looked at them exasperated, suffocating with rage, at all of them eating so placidly. A tumultuous anger swept over her at first, and she opened her mouth to cry out at them, to hurl at them a flood of injury which mounted to her lips; but she could not speak, her exasperation strangled her.

No one looked at her or thought of her. She felt herself drowned in the scorn of these honest scoundrels, who had first sacrificed her and then rejected her, like some improper or useless article. She thought of her great basket full of good things which they had greedily devoured, of her two chickens shining with jelly, of her *pâtés,* her pears, and the four bottles of Bordeaux; and her fury suddenly falling, as a cord drawn too tightly breaks, she felt ready to weep. She made terrible efforts to prevent it, making ugly faces, swallowing her sobs as children do, but the tears came and glistened in the corners of her eyes, and then two great drops, detaching themselves from the rest, rolled slowly down like little streams of water that filter through rock, and, falling regularly, rebounded upon her breast. She sits erect, her eyes fixed, her face rigid and pale, hoping that no one will notice her.

But the Countess perceives her and tells her husband by a sign. He shrugs his shoulders, as much as to say:

"What would you have me do, it is not my fault."

Mrs. Loiseau indulged in a mute laugh of triumph and murmured:

"She weeps for shame."

The two good sisters began to pray again, after having wrapped in a paper the remainder of their sausage.

Then Cornudet, who was digesting his eggs, extended his legs to the seat opposite, crossed them, folded his arms, smiled like a man who is watching a good farce, and began to whistle the "Marseillaise."

All faces grew dark. The popular song assuredly did not please his neighbors. They became nervous and agitated, having an appearance of wishing to howl, like dogs, when they hear a barbarous organ. He perceived this but did not stop. Sometimes he would hum the words:

> "Sacred love of country
> Help, sustain th' avenging arm;
> Liberty, sweet Liberty
> Ever fight, with no alarm."

They traveled fast, the snow being harder. But as far as Dieppe, during the long, sad hours of the journey, across the jolts in the road, through the falling night, in the profound darkness of the carriage, he continued his vengeful, monotonous whistling with a ferocious obstinacy, contraining his neighbors to follow the song from one end to the other, and to recall the words that belonged to each measure.

And Ball-of-Fat wept continually; and sometimes a sob, which she was not able to restrain, echoed between the two rows of people in the shadows.

THE DIAMOND NECKLACE

She was one of those pretty, charming young ladies, born, as if through an error of destiny, into a family of clerks. She had no dowry, no hopes, no means of becoming known, appreciated, loved, and married by a man either rich or distinguished; and she allowed herself to marry a petty clerk in the office of the Board of Education.

She was simple, not being able to adorn herself; but she was unhappy, as one out of her class; for women belong to no caste, no race; their grace, their beauty, and their charm serving them in the place of birth and family. Their inborn finesse, their instinctive elegance, their suppleness of wit are their only aristocracy, making some daughters of the people the equal of great ladies.

She suffered incessantly, feeling herself born for all delicacies and luxuries. She suffered from the poverty of her apartment, the shabby walls, the worn chairs, and the faded stuffs. All these things, which another woman of her station would not have noticed, tortured and angered her. The sight of the little Breton, who made this humble home, awoke in her sad regrets and desperate dreams. She thought of quiet antechambers, with their Oriental hangings, lighted by high, bronze torches, and of the two great footmen in short trousers who sleep in the large armchairs, made sleepy by the heavy air from the heating apparatus. She thought of large drawing-rooms, hung in old silks, of graceful pieces of furniture carrying bric-à-brac of inestimable value, and of the little perfumed coquettish apartments, made for five o'clock chats with most intimate friends, men known and sought after, whose attention all women envied and desired.

When she seated herself for dinner, before the round table where the tablecloth had been used three days, opposite her husband who uncovered the tureen with a delighted air, saying: "Oh! the good potpie! I know nothing better than that—" she would think of the elegant dinners, of the shining silver, of the tapestries peopling the walls with ancient personages and rare birds in the midst of fairy forests; she thought of the exquisite food served on marvelous dishes, of the whispered gallantries, listened to with the smile of the sphinx, while eating the rose-colored flesh of the trout or a chicken's wing.

She had neither frocks nor jewels, nothing. And she loved only those things. She felt that she was made for them. She had such a desire to please, to be sought after, to be clever, and courted.

She had a rich friend, a schoolmate at the convent, whom she did not like to visit, she suffered so much when she returned. And she wept for whole days from chagrin, from regret, from despair, and disappointment.

One evening her husband returned elated bearing in his hand a large envelope.

"Here," he said, "here is something for you."

She quickly tore open the wrapper and drew out a printed card on which were inscribed these words:

"The Minister of Public Instruction and Madame George Ramponneau ask the honor of Mr. and Mrs. Loisel's company Monday evening, January 18, at the Minister's residence.

Instead of being delighted, as her husband had hoped, she threw the invitation spitefully upon the table murmuring:

"What do you suppose I want with that?"

"But, my dearie, I thought it would make you happy. You never go out, and this is an occasion, and a fine one! I had a great deal of trouble to get it. Everybody wishes one, and it is very select; not many are given to employees. You will see the whole official world there."

She looked at him with an irritated eye and declared impatiently:

"What do you suppose I have to wear to such a thing as that?"

He had not thought of that; he stammered:

"Why, the dress you wear when we go to the theater. It seems very pretty to me——"

He was silent, stupefied, in dismay, at the sight of his wife weeping. Two great tears fell slowly from the corners of his eyes toward the corners of his mouth; he stammered:

"What is the matter? What is the matter?"

By a violent effort, she had controlled her vexation and responded in a calm voice, wiping her moist cheeks:

"Nothing. Only I have no dress and consequently I cannot go to this affair. Give your card to some colleague whose wife is better fitted out than I."

He was grieved, but answered:

"Let us see, Matilda. How much would a suitable costume cost, something that would serve for other occasions, something very simple?"

She reflected for some seconds, making estimates and thinking of a sum that she could ask for without bringing with it an immediate refusal and a frightened exclamation from the economical clerk.

Finally she said, in a hesitating voice:

"I cannot tell exactly, but it seems to me that four hundred francs ought to cover it."

He turned a little pale, for he had saved just this sum to buy a gun that he might be able to join some hunting parties the next summer, on the plains at Nanterre, with some friends who went to shoot larks up there on Sunday. Nevertheless, he answered:

"Very well. I will give you four hundred francs. But try to have a pretty dress."

The day of the ball approached and Mme. Loisel seemed sad, disturbed, anxious. Nevertheless, her dress was nearly ready. Her husband said to her one evening:

"What is the matter with you? You have acted strangely for two or three days."

And she responded: "I am vexed not to have a jewel,

not one stone, nothing to adorn myself with. I shall have such a poverty-laden look. I would prefer not to go to this party."

He replied: "You can wear some natural flowers. At this season they look very *chic*. For ten francs you can have two or three magnificent roses."

She was not convinced. "No," she replied, "there is nothing more humiliating than to have a shabby air in the midst of rich women."

Then her husband cried out: "How stupid we are! Go and find your friend Mrs. Forestier and ask her to lend you her jewels. You are well enough acquainted with her to do this."

She uttered a cry of joy: "It is true!" she said. "I had not thought of that."

The next day she took herself to her friend's house and related her story of distress. Mrs. Forestier went to her closet with the glass doors, took out a large jewel-case, brought it, opened it, and said: "Choose, my dear."

She saw at first some bracelets, then a collar of pearls, then a Venetian cross of gold and jewels and of admirable workmanship. She tried the jewels before the glass, hesitated, but could neither decide to take them nor leave them. Then she asked:

"Have you nothing more?"

"Why, yes. Look for yourself. I do not know what will please you."

Suddenly she discovered, in a black satin box, a superb necklace of diamonds, and her heart beat fast with an immoderate desire. Her hands trembled as she took them up. She placed them about her throat against her dress, and remained in ecstasy before them. Then she asked, in a hesitating voice, full of anxiety:

"Could you lend me this? Only this?"

"Why, yes, certainly."

She fell upon the neck of her friend, embraced her with passion, then went away with her treasure.

The day of the ball arrived. Mme. Loisel was a great success. She was the prettiest of all, elegant, gracious, smiling, and full of joy. All the men noticed her, asked her name, and wanted to be presented. All the members of the Cabinet wished to waltz with her. The Minister of Education paid her some attention.

She danced with enthusiasm, with passion, intoxicated with pleasure, thinking of nothing, in the triumph of her beauty, in the glory of her success, in a kind of cloud of happiness that came of all this homage, and all this admiration, of all these awakened desires, and this victory so complete and sweet to the heart of woman.

She went home toward four o'clock in the morning. Her husband had been half asleep in one of the little saloñs since midnight, with three other gentlemen whose wives were enjoying themselves very much.

He threw around her shoulders the wraps they had carried for the coming home, modest garments of everyday wear, whose poverty clashed with the elegance of the ball costume. She felt this and wished to hurry away in order not to be noticed by the other women who were wrapping themselves in rich furs.

Loisel retained her: "Wait," said he. "You will catch cold out there. I am going to call a cab."

But she would not listen and descended the steps rapidly. When they were in the street, they found no carriage; and they began to seek for one, hailing the coachmen whom they saw at a distance.

They walked along toward the Seine, hopeless and shivering. Finally they found on the dock one of those old, nocturnal *coupés* that one sees in Paris after nightfall, as if they were ashamed of their misery by day.

It took them as far as their door in Martyr street, and they went wearily up to their apartment. It was all over for her. And on his part, he remembered that he would have to be at the office by ten o'clock.

She removed the wraps from her shoulders before the glass, for a final view of herself in her glory. Suddenly she uttered a cry. Her necklace was not around her neck.

Her husband, already half undressed, asked: "What is the matter?"

She turned toward him excitedly:

"I have—I have—I no longer have Mrs. Forestier's necklace."

He arose in dismay: "What! How is that? It is not possible."

And they looked in the folds of the dress, in the folds of the mantle, in the pockets, everywhere. They could not find it.

He asked: "You are sure you still had it when we left the house?"

"Yes, I felt it in the vestibule as we came out."

"But if you had lost it in the street, we should have heard it fall. It must be in the cab."

"Yes. It is probable. Did you take the number?"

"No. And you, did you notice what it was?"

"No."

They looked at each other utterly cast down. Finally, Loisel dressed himself again.

"I am going," said he, "over the track where we went on foot, to see if I can find it."

And he went. She remained in her evening gown, not having the force to go to bed, stretched upon a chair, without ambition or thoughts.

Toward seven o'clock her husband returned. He had found nothing.

He went to the police and to the cab offices, and put an advertisement in the newspapers, offering a reward; he did everything that afforded them a suspicion of hope.

She waited all day in a state of bewilderment before this frightful disaster. Loisel returned at evening with his face harrowed and pale; and had discovered nothing.

"It will be necessary," said he, "to write to your friends that you have broken the clasp of the necklace and that you will have it repaired. That will give us time to turn around."

She wrote as he dictated.

At the end of a week, they had lost all hope. And Loisel, older by five years, declared:

"We must take measures to replace this jewel."

The next day they took the box which had inclosed it,

to the jeweler whose name was on the inside. He consulted his books:

"It is not I, Madame," said he, "who sold this necklace; I only furnished the casket."

Then they went from jeweler to jeweler seeking a necklace like the other one, consulting their memories, and ill, both of them, with chagrin and anxiety.

In a shop of the Palais-Royal, they found a chaplet of diamonds which seemed to them exactly like the one they had lost. It was valued at forty thousand francs. They could get it for thirty-six thousand.

They begged the jeweler not to sell it for three days. And they made an arrangement by which they might return it for thirty-four thousand francs if they found the other one before the end of February.

Loisel possessed eighteen thousand francs which his father had left him. He borrowed the rest.

He borrowed it, asking for a thousand francs of one, five hundred of another, five louis of this one, and three louis of that one. He gave notes, made ruinous promises, took money of usurers and the whole race of lenders. He compromised his whole existence, in fact, risked his signature, without even knowing whether he could make it good or not, and, harassed by anxiety for the future, by the black misery which surrounded him, and by the prospect of all physical privations and moral torture, he went to get the new necklace, depositing on the merchant's counter thirty-six thousand francs.

When Mrs. Loisel took back the jewels to Mrs. Forestier, the latter said to her in a frigid tone:

"You should have returned them to me sooner, for I might have needed them."

She did open the jewel-box as her friend feared she would. If she should perceive the substitution, what would she think? What should she say? Would she take her for a robber?

Mrs. Loisel now knew the horrible life of necessity. She did her part, however, completely, heroically. It was necessary to pay this frightful debt. She would pay it. They sent away the maid; they changed their lodgings; they rented some rooms under a mansard roof.

She learned the heavy cares of a household, the odious work of a kitchen. She washed the dishes, using her rosy nails upon the greasy pots and the bottoms of the stewpans. She washed the soiled linen, the chemises and dishcloths, which she hung on the line to dry; she took down the refuse to the street each morning and brought up the water, stopping at each landing to breathe. And, clothed like a woman of the people she went to the grocer's, the butcher's, and the fruiterer's, with her basket on her arm, shopping, haggling to the last sou her miserable money.

Every month it was necessary to renew some notes, thus obtaining time, and to pay others.

The husband worked evenings, putting the books of some merchants in order, and nights he often did copying at five sous a page.

And this life lasted for ten years.

At the end of ten years, they had restored all, all, with interest of the usurer, and accumulated interest besides.

Mrs. Loisel seemed old now. She had become a strong, hard woman, the crude woman of the poor household. Her hair badly dressed, her skirts awry, her hands red, she spoke in a loud tone, and washed the floors in large pails of water. But sometimes, when her husband was at the office, she would seat herself before the window and think of that evening party of former times, of that ball where she was so beautiful and so flattered.

How would it have been if she had not lost that necklace? Who knows? Who knows? How singular is life, and how full of changes! How small a thing will ruin or save one!

One Sunday, as she was taking a walk in the Champs-Elysées to rid herself of the cares of the week, she suddenly perceived a woman walking with a child. It was Mrs. Forestier, still young, still pretty, still attractive. Mrs. Loisel was affected. Should she speak to her? Yes, certainly. And now that she had paid, she would tell her all. Why not?

She approached her. "Good morning, Jeanne."

Her friend did not recognize her and was astonished to be so familiarly addressed by this common personage. She stammered:

"But, Madame—I do not know— You must be mistaken—"

"No, I am Matilda Loisel."

Her friend uttered a cry of astonishment: "Oh! my poor Matilda! How you have changed—"

"Yes, I have had some hard days since I saw you; and some miserable ones—and all because of you—"

"Because of me? How is that?"

"You recall the diamond necklace that you loaned me to wear to the Commissioner's ball?"

"Yes, very well."

"Well, I lost it."

"How is that, since you returned it to me?"

"I returned another to you exactly like it. And it has taken us ten years to pay for it. You can understand that it was not easy for us who have nothing. But it is finished and I am decently content."

Madame Forestier stopped short. She said:

"You say that you bought a diamond necklace to replace mine?"

"Yes. You did not perceive it then? They were just alike."

And she smiled with a proud and simple joy. Madame Forestier was touched and took both her hands as she replied:

"Oh! my poor Matilda! Mine were false. They were not worth over five hundred francs!"

A PIECE OF STRING

Along all the roads around Goderville the peasants and their wives were coming toward the burgh because it was market day. The men were proceeding with slow steps, the whole body bent forward at each movement of their long twisted legs, deformed by their hard work, by the weight on the plow which, at the same time, raised the left shoulder and swerved the figure, by the reaping of the wheat which made the knees spread to make a firm "purchase," by all the slow and painful labors of the country. Their blouses, blue, "stiff-starched," shining as if varnished, ornamented with a little design in white at the neck and wrists, puffed about their bony bodies, seemed like balloons ready to carry them off. From each of them a head, two arms, and two feet protruded.

Some led a cow or a calf by a cord, and their wives, walking behind the animal, whipped its haunches with a leafy branch to hasten its progress. They carried large baskets on their arms from which, in some cases, chickens and, in others, ducks thrust out their heads. And they walked with a quicker, livelier step than their husbands. Their spare straight figures were wrapped in a scanty little shawl, pinned over their flat bosoms, and their heads were enveloped in a white cloth glued to the hair and surmounted by a cap.

Then a wagon passed at the jerky trot of a nag, shaking strangely, two men seated side by side and a woman in the bottom of the vehicle, the latter holding on to the sides to lessen the hard jolts.

In the public square of Goderville there was a crowd, a throng of human beings and animals mixed together. The horns of the cattle, the tall hats with long nap of the rich peasant, and the headgear of the peasant women rose above the surface of the assembly. And the clamorous, shrill, screaming voices made a continuous and savage din which sometimes was dominated by the robust lungs of some countryman's laugh, or the long lowing of a cow tied to the wall of a house.

All that smacked of the stable, the dairy and the dirt heap, hay and sweat, giving forth that unpleasant odor, human and animal, peculiar to the people of the field.

Maître Hauchecome, of Breaute, had just arrived at Goderville, and he was directing his steps toward the public square, when he perceived upon the ground a little piece of string. Maître Hauchecome, economical like a true Norman, thought that everything useful ought to be picked up, and he bent painfully, for he suffered from rheumatism. He took the bit of thin cord from the ground and began to roll it carefully when he noticed Maître Malandain, the harness-maker, on the threshold of his door, looking at him. They had heretofore had business together on the subject of a halter, and they were on bad terms, being both good haters. Maître Hauchecome was seized with a sort of shame to be seen thus by his enemy, picking a bit of string out of the dirt. He concealed his "find" quickly under his blouse, then in his trousers' pocket; then he pretended to be still looking on the ground for something which he did not find, and he went toward the market, his head forward, bent double by his pains.

He was soon lost in the noisy and slowly moving crowd, which was busy with interminable bargainings. The peasants milked, went and came, perplexed, always in fear of being cheated, not daring to decide, watching the vendor's eye, ever trying to find the trick in the man and the flaw in the beast.

The women, having placed their great baskets at their feet, had taken out the poultry which lay upon the ground, tied together by the feet, with terrified eyes and scarlet crests.

They heard offers, stated their prices with a dry air and impassive face, or perhaps, suddenly deciding on some proposed reduction, shouted to the customer who was slowly going away: "All right, Maître Authirne, I'll give it to you for that."

Then little by little the square was deserted, and the Angelus ringing at noon, those who had stayed too long, scattered to their shops.

At Jourdain's the great room was full of people eating, as the big court was full of vehicles of all kinds, carts, gigs, wagons, dump carts, yellow with dirt, mended and patched, raising their shafts to the sky like two arms, or perhaps with their shafts in the ground and their backs in the air.

Just opposite the diners seated at the table, the immense fireplace, filled with bright flames, cast a lively heat on the backs of the row on the right. Three spits were turning on which were chickens, pigeons, and legs of mutton; and an appetizing odor of roast beef and gravy dripping over the nicely browned skin rose from the hearth, increased the jovialness, and made everybody's mouth water.

All the aristocracy of the plow ate there, at Maître Jourdain's, tavern keeper and horse dealer, a rascal who had money.

The dishes were passed and emptied, as were the jugs of yellow cider. Everyone told his affairs, his purchases, and sales. They discussed the crops. The weather was favorable for the green things but not for the wheat.

Suddenly the drum beat in the court, before the house. Everybody rose except a few indifferent persons, and ran to the door, or to the windows, their mouths still full and napkins in their hands.

After the public crier had ceased his drum-beating, he called out in a jerky voice, speaking his phrases irregularly:

"It is hereby made known to the inhabitants of Goderville, and in general to all persons present at the market, that there was lost this morning, on the road to Benzeville, between nine and ten o'clock, a black leather pocketbook containing five hundred francs and some business papers. The finder is requested to return same with all haste to the mayor's office or to Maître Fortune Houlbreque of Manneville, there will be twenty francs reward."

Then the man went away. The heavy roll of the drum and the crier's voice were again heard at a distance.

Then they began to talk of this event discussing the chances that Maître Houlbreque had of finding or not finding his pocketbook.

And the meal concluded. They were finishing their coffee when a chief of the gendarmes appeared upon the threshold.

He inquired:

"Is Maître Hauchecome, of Breaute, here?"

Maître Hauchecome, seated at the other end of the table, replied:

"Here I am."

And the officer resumed:

"Maître Hauchecome, will you have the goodness to accompany me to the mayor's office? The mayor would like to talk to you."

The peasant, surprised and disturbed, swallowed at a draught his tiny glass of brandy, rose, and, even more bent than in the morning, for the first steps after each rest were specially difficult, set out, repeating: "Here I am, here I am."

The mayor was awaiting him, seated on an armchair. He was the notary of the vicinity, a stout, serious man, with pompous phrases.

"Maître Hauchecome," said he, "you were seen this morning to pick up, on the road to Benzeville, the pocketbook lost by Maître Houlbreque, of Manneville."

The countryman, astounded, looked at the mayor, already terrified, by this suspicion resting on him without his knowing why.

"Me? Me? Me pick up the pocketbook?"

"Yes, you, yourself."

"Word of honor, I never heard of it."

"But you were seen."

"I was seen, me? Who says he saw me?"

"Monsieur Malandain, the harnessmaker."

The old man remembered, understood, and flushed with anger.

"Ah, he saw me, the clodhopper, he saw me pick up

this string, here, M'sieu, the Mayor." And rummaging in his pocket he drew out the little piece of string.

But the mayor, incredulous, shook his head.

"You will not make me believe, Maître Hauchecome, that Monsieur Malandain, who is a man worthy of credence, mistook this cord for a pocketbook."

The peasant, furious, lifted his hand, spat at one side to attest his honor, repeating:

"It is nevertheless the truth of the good God, the sacred truth, M'sieu' the Mayor. I repeat it on my soul and my salvation."

The mayor resumed:

"After picking up the object, you stood like a stilt, looking a long while in the mud to see if any piece of money had fallen out."

The good, old man choked with indignation and fear.

"How anyone can tell—how anyone can tell—such lies to take away an honest man's reputation! How can anyone—"

There was no use in his protesting, nobody believed him. He was confronted with Monsieur Malandain, who repeated and maintained his affirmation. They abused each other for an hour. At his own request, Maître Hauchecome was searched, nothing was found on him.

Finally the mayor, very much perplexed, discharged him with the warning that he would consult the public prosecutor and ask for further orders.

The news had spread. As he left the mayor's office, the old man was surrounded and questioned with a serious or bantering curiosity, in which there was no indignation. He began to tell the story of the string. No one believed him. They laughed at him.

He went along, stopping his friends, beginning endlessly his statement and his protestations, showing his pockets turned inside out, to prove that he had nothing.

They said:

"Old rascal, get out!"

And he grew angry, becoming exasperated, hot, and distressed at not being believed, not knowing what to do and always repeating himself.

Night came. He must depart. He started on his way with three neighbors to whom he pointed out the place where he had picked up the bit of string; and all along the road he spoke of his adventure.

In the evening he took a turn in the village of Breaute, in order to tell it to everybody. He only met with incredulity.

It made him ill at night.

The next day about one o'clock in the afternoon, Marius Paumelle, a hired man in the employ of Maître Breton, husbandman at Ymanville, returned the pocketbook and its contents to Maître Houlbreque of Manneville.

This man claimed to have found the object in the road; but not knowing how to read, he had carried it to the house and given it to his employer.

The news spread through the neighborhood. Maître Hauchecome was informed of it. He immediately went the circuit and began to recount his story completed by the happy climax. He was in triumph.

"What grieved me so much was not the thing itself, as the lying. There is nothing so shameful as to be placed under a cloud on account of a lie."

He talked of his adventure all day long, he told it on the highway to people who were passing by, in the wineshop to people who were drinking there, and to persons coming out of church the following Sunday. He stopped strangers to tell them about it. He was calm now, and yet something disturbed him without his knowing exactly what it was. People had the air of joking while they listened. They did not seem convinced. He seemed to feel that remarks were being made behind his back.

On Tuesday of the next week he went to the market at Goderville, urged solely by the necessity he felt of discussing the case.

Malandain, standing at his door, began to laugh on seeing him pass. Why?

He approached a farmer from Crequetot, who did not let him finish, and giving him a thump in the stomach said to his face:

"You big rascal."

Then he turned his back on him.

Maître Hauchecome was confused, why was he called a big rascal?

When he was seated at the table, in Jourdain's tavern he commenced to explain "the affair."

A horse dealer from Monvilliers called to him:

"Come, come, old sharper, that's an old trick; I know all about your piece of string!"

Hauchecome stammered:

"But since the pocketbook was found."

But the other man replied:

"Shut up, papa, there is one that finds, and there is one that reports. At any rate you are mixed with it."

The peasant stood choking. He understood. They accused him of having had the pocketbook returned by a confederate, by an accomplice.

He tried to protest. All the table began to laugh.

He could not finish his dinner and went away, in the midst of jeers.

He went home ashamed and indignant, choking with anger and confusion, the more dejected that he was capable with his Norman cunning of doing what they had accused him of, and ever boasting of it as of a good turn. His innocence to him, in a confused way, was impossible to prove, as his sharpness was known. And he was stricken to the heart by the injustice of the suspicion.

Then he began to recount the adventures again, prolonging his history every day, adding each time, new reasons, more energetic protestations, more solemn oaths which he imagined and prepared in his hours of solitude, his whole mind given up to the story of the string. He was believed so much the less as his defense was more complicated and his arguing more subtile.

"Those are lying excuses," they said behind his back.

He felt it, consumed his heart over it, and wore himself out with useless efforts. He wasted away before their very eyes.

The wags now made him tell about the string to amuse them, as they make a soldier who has been on a campaign tell about his battles. His mind, touched to the depth, began to weaken.

Toward the end of December he took to his bed.

He died in the first days of January, and in the delirium of his death struggles he kept claiming his innocence, reiterating:

"A piece of string, a piece of string,—look—here it is, M'sieu' the Mayor."

THE STORY OF A FARM-GIRL

As the weather was very fine, the people on the farm had dined more quickly than usual, and had returned to the fields.

The female servant, Rose, remained alone in the large kitchen, where the fire on the hearth was dying out, under the large boiler of hot water. From time to time she took some water out of it, and slowly washed her plates and dishes, stopping occasionally to look at the two streaks of light which the sun threw on to the long table through the window, and which showed the defects in the glass.

Three venturesome hens were picking up the crumbs under the chairs, while the smell of the poultry yard and the warmth from the cow-stall came in through the half open door, and a cock was heard crowing in the distance.

When she had finished her work, wiped down the table, dusted the mantelpiece, and put the plates on to the high dresser, close to the wooden clock, with its enormous pendulum, she drew a long breath, as she felt rather oppressed, without exactly knowing why. She looked at the black clay walls, the rafters that were blackened with smoke, from which spiders' webs were hanging amid pickled herrings and strings of onions, and then she sat down, rather overcome by the stale emanations from the floor, on which so many things had been spilled. With these was mingled the smell of the pans of milk, which were set out to raise the cream in the adjoining dairy.

She wanted to sew, as usual, but she did not feel strong enough for it, and so she went to get a mouthful of fresh air at the door, which seemed to do her good.

The fowls were lying on the smoking dung-hill; some of them were scratching with one claw in search of worms, while the cock stood up proudly among them. Now and then he selected one of them, and walked round her with a slight cluck of amorous invitation. The hen got up in a careless way as she received his attentions, supported herself on her legs and spread out her wings; then she shook her feathers to shake out the dust, and stretched herself out on the dung-hill again, while he crowed, in sign of triumph, and the cocks in all the neighboring farmyards replied to him, as if they were uttering amorous challenges from farm to farm.

The girl looked at them without thinking; then she raised her eyes and was almost dazzled at the sight of the apple-trees in blossom, which looked almost like powdered heads. Just then, a colt, full of life and friskiness, galloped past her. Twice he jumped over the ditches, and then stopped suddenly, as if surprised at being alone.

She also felt inclined to run; she felt inclined to move and to stretch her limbs, and to repose in the warm, breathless air. She took a few undecided steps, and closed her eyes, for she was seized with a feeling of animal comfort; then she went to look for the eggs in the hen loft. There were thirteen of them, which she took in and put into the storeroom; but the smell from the kitchen disgusted her again and she went out to sit on the grass for a time.

The farmyard, which was surrounded by trees, seemed to be asleep. The tall grass, among which the tall yellow dandelions rose up like streaks of yellow light, was of a vivid green, the fresh spring green. The apple-trees threw their shade all round them, and the thatched houses, on which the blue and yellow iris flowers, with their swordlike leaves, grew, smoked as if the moisture of the stables and barns was coming through the straw.

The girl went to the shed where the carts and traps were kept. Close to it, in a ditch, there was a large patch of violets whose scent was perceptible all round, while beyond it could be seen the open country where the corn was growing, with clumps of trees in the distance, and groups of laborers here and there, who looked as small as dolls, and white horses like toys, who were pulling a child's cart, driven by a man as tall as one's finger.

She took up a bundle of straw, threw it into the ditch and sat down upon it; then, not feeling comfortable, she undid it, spread it out and lay down upon it at full length, on her back, with both arms under her head, and her limbs stretched out.

Gradually her eyes closed, and she was falling into a state of delightful languor. She was, in fact, almost asleep, when she felt two hands on her bosom, and then she sprang up at a bound. It was Jacques, one of the farm laborers, a tall fellow from Picardy, who had been making love to her for a long time. He had been looking after the sheep, and seeing her lying down in the shade, he had come stealthily, and holding his breath, with glistening eyes, and bits of straw in his hair.

He tried to kiss her, but she gave him a smack in the face, for she was as strong as he, and he was shrewd enough to beg her pardon: so they sat down side by side and talked amicably. They spoke about the favorable weather, of their master, who was a good fellow, then of their neighbors, of all the people in the country round, of themselves, of their village, of their youthful days, of their recollections, of their relatives, whom they had not seen for a long time, and might not see again. She grew sad, as she thought of it, while he, with one fixed idea in his head, rubbed against her with a kind of a shiver, overcome by desire.

"I have not seen my mother for a long time," she said. "It is very hard to be separated like that." And she directed her looks into the distance, toward the village in the North, which she had left.

Suddenly, however, he seized her by the neck and kissed her again! but she struck him so violently in the face with her clenched fist, that his nose began to bleed, and he got up and laid his head against the stem of a tree. When she saw that, she was sorry, and going up to him, she said:

"Have I hurt you?"

He, however, only laughed. "No, it was a mere nothing;" though she had hit him right on the middle of the nose. "What a devil!" he said, and he looked at her with admiration, for she had inspired him with a feeling of respect and of a very different kind of admiration, which was the beginning of real love for that tall, strong wench.

When the bleeding had stopped, he proposed a walk, as he was afraid of his neighbor's heavy hand, if they remained side by side like that much longer; but she took his arm of her own accord, in the avenue, as if they had been out for an evening walk, and said: "It is not nice of you to despise me like that, Jacques."

He protested, however. No, he did not despise her. He was in love with her, that was all.

"So you really want to marry me?" she asked.

He hesitated, and then looked at her aside, while she looked straight ahead of her. She had fat, red cheeks, a full, protuberant bust under her muslin dress, thick, red lips, and her neck, which was almost bare, was covered with small beads of perspiration. He felt a fresh access of desire, and putting his lips to her ear, he murmured: "Yes, of course I do."

Then she threw her arms round his neck, and kissed for such a long time, that they both of them lost their breath. From that moment the eternal story of love began between them. They plagued one another in corners; they met in the moonlight under a haystack, and gave each other bruises on the legs, with their heavy nailed boots. By degrees, however, Jacques seemed to grow tired of her: he avoided her; scarcely spoke to her, and did not try any longer to meet her alone, which made her sad and anxious, especially when she found that she was pregnant.

At first, she was in a state of consternation; then she got angry, and her rage increased every day, because she could not meet him, as he avoided her most carefully. At last, one night when everyone in the farmhouse was asleep, she went out noiselessly in her petticoat, with bare feet, crossed the yard and opened the door of the stable where Jacques was lying in a large box of straw, over his horses. He pretended to snore when he heard her coming, but she knelt down by his side and shook him until he sat up.

"What do you want?" he then asked of her. And she with clenched teeth, and trembling with anger, replied:

"I want—I want you to marry me, as you promised."

But he only laughed and replied: "Oh, if a man were to marry all the girls with whom he has made a slip, he would have more than enough to do."

Then she seized him by the throat, threw him on to his back, so that he could not disengage himself from her, and half strangling him, she shouted into his face: "I am *enceinte*, do you hear? I am *enceinte!*"

He gasped for breath, as he was nearly choked, and so they remained, both of them, motionless and without speaking, in the dark silence, which was only broken by the noise that a horse made as he pulled the hay out of the manger, and then slowly chewed it.

When Jacques found that she was the stronger, he stammered out: "Very well, I will marry you, as that is the case."

But she did not believe his promises. "It must be at once," she said. "You must have the banns put up."

"At once," he replied.

"Swear solemnly that you will."

He hesitated for a few moments, and then said: "I swear it, by heaven."

Then she released her grasp, and went away without another word.

She had no chance of speaking to him for several days, and as the stable was now always locked at night, she was afraid to make any noise, for fear of creating a scandal. One day, however, she saw another man come in at dinnertime, and so she said: "Has Jacques left?"

"Yes," the man replied; "I have got his place."

This made her tremble so violently, that she could not take the saucepan off the fire; and later when they were all at work, she went up into her room and cried, burying her head in her bolster, so that she might not be heard. During the day, however, she tried to obtain some information without exciting any suspicions, but she was so overwhelmed by the thoughts of her misfortune, that she fancied that all the people whom she asked, laughed maliciously. All she learned, however, was, that he had left the neighborhood altogether.

II.

Then a cloud of constant misery began for her. She worked mechanically, without thinking of what she was doing, with one fixed idea in her head: "Suppose people were to know."

This continual feeling made her so incapable of reasoning, that she did not even try to think of any means of avoiding the disgrace that she knew must ensue, which was irreparable, and drawing nearer every day, and which was as sure as death itself. She got up every morning long before the others, and persistently tried to look at her figure in a piece of broken looking-glass at which she did her hair, as she was very anxious to know whether anybody would notice a change in her, and during the day she stopped working every few minutes to look at herself from top to toe, to see whether the size of her abdomen did not make her apron look too short.

The months went on. She scarcely spoke now, and when she was asked a question, she did not appear to understand. She had a frightened look, with haggard eyes and trembling hands, which made her master say to her occasionally: "My poor girl, how stupid you have grown lately."

In church, she hid behind a pillar, and no longer ventured to go to confession. She feared to face the priest, to whom she attributed a superhuman power, which enabled him to read people's consciences; and at meal times, the looks of her fellow-servants almost made her faint with mental agony. She was always fancying that she had been found out by the cowherd, a precocious and cunning little lad, whose bright eyes seemed always to be watching her.

One morning the postman brought her a letter, and as she had never received one in her life before, she was so upset by it, that she was obliged to sit down. Perhaps it was from him? But as she could not read, she sat anxious and trembling with that piece of paper covered with ink in her hand; after a time, however, she put it into her pocket, as she did not venture to confide her secret to anyone. She often stopped in her work to look at the lines, written at regular intervals, and terminating in a signature, imagining vaguely that she would suddenly discover their meaning. At last, as she felt half mad with impatience and anxiety, she went to the schoolmaster, who told her to sit down, and read the letter to her, as follows:

"My Dear Daughter:—I write to tell you that I am very ill. Our neighbor, Monsieur Dentu, begs you to come, if you can,

"For your affectionate mother,
"Cesaire Dentu,
"Deputy Mayor."

She did not say a word, and went away, but as soon as she was alone, her legs gave way, and she fell down by the roadside, and remained there till night.

When she got back, she told the farmer her trouble. He allowed her to go home for as long as she wanted, promised to have her work done by a charwoman, and to take her back when she returned.

Her mother died soon after she got there, and the next day Rose gave birth to a seven months' child, a miserable little skeleton, thin enough to make anybody shudder. It seemed to be suffering continually, to judge from the painful manner in which it moved its poor little limbs, which were as thin as a crab's legs, but it lived, for all that. She said that she was married, but that she could not saddle herself with the child, so she left it with some neighbors, who promised to take great care of it, and she went back to the farm.

But then, in her heart, which had been wounded so long, there arose something like brightness, an unknown love for that frail little creature which she had left behind her, but there was fresh suffering in that very love, suffering which she felt every hour and every minute, because she was parted from the child. What pained her most, however, was a mad longing to kiss it, to press it in her arms, to feel the warmth of its little body against her skin. She could not sleep at night; she thought of it the whole day long, and in the evening, when her work was done, she used to sit in

front of the fire and look at it intently, like people do whose
thoughts are far away.

They began to talk about her, and to tease her about her
lover. They asked her whether he was tall, handsome, and
rich. When was the wedding to be, and the christening? And
often she ran away to cry by herself, for these questions
seemed to hurt her, like the prick of a pin, and in order to
forget their jokes, she began to work still more energetically,
and still thinking of her child, she sought for the means of
saving up money for it, and determined to work so that her
master would be obliged to raise her wages.

Then, by degrees, she almost monopolized the work, and
persuaded him to get rid of one servant girl, who had become useless since she had taken to working like two; she
economized in the bread, oil, and candles, in the corn which
they gave to the fowls too extravagantly, and in the fodder
for the horses and cattle, which was rather wasted. She was
as miserly about her master's money as if it had been her
own, and by dint of making good bargains, of getting high
prices for all their produce, and by baffling the peasants'
tricks when they offered anything for sale, he at last intrusted her with buying and selling everything, with the direction of all the laborers, and with the quantity of provisions necessary for the household, so that in a short time
she became indispensable to him. She kept such a strict eye
on everything about her, that under her direction the farm
prospered wonderfully, and for five miles round people
talked of "Master Vallin's servant," and the farmer himself said everywhere: "That girl is worth more than her
weight in gold."

But time passed by, and her wages remained the same.
Her hard work was accepted as something that was due from
every good servant, and as a mere token of her good-will;
and she began to think rather bitterly, that if the farmer
could put fifty or a hundred crowns extra into the bank
every month, thanks to her, she was still only earning her
two hundred francs a year, neither more nor less, and so
she made up her mind to ask for an increase of wages. She
went to see the schoolmaster three times about it, but when
she got there, she spoke about something else. She felt a

kind of modesty in asking for money, as if it were something disgraceful; but at last, one day, when the farmer was having breakfast by himself in the kitchen, she said to him, with some embarrassment, that she wished to speak to him particularly. He raised his head in surprise, with both his hands on the table, holding his knife, with its point in the air, in one, and a piece of bread in the other. He looked fixedly at the girl, who felt uncomfortable under his gaze, but asked for a week's holiday, so that she might get away, as she was not very well. He acceded to her request immediately, and then added, in some embarrassment, himself:

"When you come back, I shall have something to say to you, myself."

III.

The child was nearly eight months old, and she did not know it again. It had grown rosy and chubby all over like a little bundle of living fat. She threw herself on to it as if it had been some prey, and kissed it so violently that it began to scream with terror, and then she began to cry herself, because it did not know her, and stretched out its arms to its nurse, as soon as it saw her. But the next day, it began to get used to her, and laughed when it saw her, and she took it into the fields and ran about excitedly with it, and sat down under the shade of the trees, and then, for the first time in her life, she opened her heart to somebody, and told the infant her troubles, how hard her work was, her anxieties and her hopes, and she quite tired the child with the violence of her caresses.

She took the greatest pleasure in handling it, in washing and dressing it, for it seemed to her that all this was the confirmation of her maternity, and she would look at it, almost feeling surprised that it was hers, and she used to say to herself in a low voice, as she danced it in her arms: "It is my baby, it is my baby."

She cried all the way home as she returned to the farm, and had scarcely got in, before her master called her into his room. She went in, feeling astonished and nervous, without knowing why.

"Sit down there," he said.

She sat down, and for some moments they remained side by side, in some embarrassment, with their arms hanging at their sides, as if they did not know what to do with them, and looking each other in the face, after the manner of peasants.

The farmer, a stout, jovial, obstinate man of forty-five, who had lost two wives, evidently felt embarrassed, which was very unusual with him. But at last he made up his mind, and began to speak vaguely, hesitating a little, and looking out of the window as he talked.

"How is it, Rose," he said, "that you have never thought of settling in life?"

She grew as pale as death, and seeing that she gave him no answer, he went on:

"You are a good, steady, active, and economical girl, and a wife like you would make a man's fortune."

She did not move, but looked frightened; she did not even try to comprehend his meaning, for her thoughts were in a whirl, as if at the approach of some great danger; so after waiting for a few seconds, he went on:

"You see, a farm without a mistress can never succeed, even with a servant like you are."

Then he stopped, for he did not know what else to say, and Rose looked at him with the air of a person who thinks that he is face to face with a murderer, and ready to flee at the slightest movement he may make; but after waiting for about five minutes, he asked her:

"Well, will it suit you?"

"Will what suit me, master?"

And he said, quickly: "Why, to marry me, by Jove!"

She jumped up, but fell back on to her chair as if she had been struck, and there she remained motionless, like a person who is overwhelmed by some great misfortune. But at last the farmer grew impatient, and said: "Come, what more do you want?"

She looked at him almost in terror; then suddenly the tears came into her eyes, and she said twice, in a choking voice: "I cannot, I cannot!"

"Why not?" he asked. "Come, don't be silly; I will give you until to-morrow to think it over."

And he hurried out of the room, very glad to have finished a matter which had troubled him a good deal. He had no doubt that she would the next morning accept a proposal which she could never have expected, and which would be a capital bargain for him, as he thus bound a woman to himself who would certainly bring him more than if she had the best dowry in the district.

Neither could there be any scruples about an unequal match between them, for in the country everyone is very nearly equal. The farmer works just like his laborers do; the latter frequently become masters in their turn, and the female servants constantly become the mistresses of the establishment, without making any change in their life or habits.

Rose did not go to bed that night. She threw herself, dressed as she was, on to her bed, and she had not even strength to cry left in her, she was so thoroughly astonished. She remained quite inert, scarcely knowing that she had a body, and without being at all able to collect her thoughts, though at moments she remembered a part of that which had happened, and then she was frightened at the idea of what might happen. Her terror increased, and every time the great kitchen clock struck the hour, she broke into a perspiration from grief. She lost her head, and had a nightmare; her candle went out, and then she began to imagine that some one had thrown a spell over her, as country people so often fancy, and she felt a mad inclination to run away, to escape and flee before her misfortune, as a ship scuds before the wind.

An owl hooted, and she shivered, sat up, put her hands to her face, into her hair, and all over her body, and then she went downstairs, as if she were walking in her sleep. When she got into the yard, she stooped down, so as not to be seen by any prowling scamp, for the moon, which was setting, shed a bright light over the fields. Instead of opening the gate, she scrambled over the fence, and as soon as she was outside, she started off. She went on straight before her, with a quick, elastic trot, and from time to time, she unconsciously uttered a piercing cry. Her long shadow accompanied her, and now and then some night-bird flew over her head, while the dogs in the farmyards barked, as they heard her pass. One even jumped over the ditch, followed her, and tried to bite her, but she turned round at it, and gave such a terrible yell that the frightened animal ran back, and cowered in silence in its kennel.

The stars grew dim, and the birds began to twitter; day was breaking. The girl was worn out and panting, and when the sun rose in the purple sky, she stopped, for her swollen feet refused to go any further. But she saw a pond in the distance, a large pond whose stagnant water looked like blood under the reflection of this new day, and she limped on with short steps and with her hand on her heart, in order to dip both her feet in it.

She sat down on a tuft of grass, took off her sabots which were full of dust, pulled off her stockings and plunged her legs into the still water, from which bubbles were rising here and there.

A feeling of delicious coolness pervaded her from head to foot, and suddenly, while she was looking fixedly at the deep pool, she was seized with giddiness, and with a mad longing to throw herself into it. All her sufferings would be over in there; over forever. She no longer thought of her child; she only wanted peace, complete rest, and to sleep forever, and she got up with raised arms and took two steps forward. She was in the water up to her thighs, and she was just about to throw herself in, when sharp, pricking pains in her ankles made her jump back. She uttered a cry of despair, for, from her knees to the tips of her feet, long, black leeches were sucking in her life blood, and were swelling, as they adhered to her flesh. She did not dare to touch them, and screamed with horror, so that her cries of despair attracted a peasant, who was driving along at some distance, to the spot. He pulled off the leeches, one by one, applied herbs to the wounds, and drove the girl to her master's farm, in his gig.

She was in bed for a fortnight, and as she was sitting outside the door on the first morning that she got up, the farmer suddenly came and planted himself before her.

"Well," he said, "I suppose the affair is settled, isn't it?"

She did not reply at first, and then, as he remained standing and looking at her intently with his piercing eyes, she said with difficulty: "No, master, I cannot."

But he immediately flew into a rage. "You cannot, girl; you cannot? I should just like to know the reason why?"

She began to cry, and repeated: "I cannot."

He looked at her, and then exclaimed, angrily: "Then I suppose you have a lover?"

"Perhaps that is it," she replied, trembling with shame.

The man got as red as a poppy, and stammered out in a rage: "Ah! So you confess it, you slut! And pray who is the fellow? Some penniless, half-starved ragamuffin, without a roof to his head, I suppose? Who is it, I say?"

And as she gave him no answer, he continued: "Ah! So you will not tell me. Then I will tell you; it is Jean Bauda!"

"No, not he," she exclaimed.

"Then it is Pierre Martin?"

"Oh! no, master."

And he angrily mentioned all the young fellows in the neighborhood, while she denied that he had hit upon the right one, and every moment wiped her eyes with the corner of her blue apron. But he still tried to find it out, with his brutish obstinacy, and, as it were, scratched her heart to discover her secret, as a terrier scratches at a hole to try and get at the animal which he scents in it. Suddenly, however, the man shouted: "By George! It is Jacques, the man who was here last year. They used to say that you were always talking together, and that you thought about getting married."

Rose was choking, and she grew scarlet, while her tears suddenly stopped, and dried up on her cheeks, like drops of water on hot iron, and she exclaimed: "No, it is not he, it is not he!"

"Is that really a fact?" asked the cunning farmer, who partly guessed the truth, and she replied hastily:

"I will swear it; I will swear it to you." She tried to think of something by which to swear, as she did not dare to invoke sacred things.

But he interrupted her: "At any rate, he used to follow you into every corner, and devoured you with his eyes at meal times. Did you ever give him your promise, eh?"

This time she looked her master straight in the face. "No, never, never; I will solemnly swear to you, that if he were to come to-day and ask me to marry him, I would have nothing to do with him."

She spoke with such an air of sincerity, that the farmer hesitated, and then he continued, as if speaking to himself: "What, then? You have not *had a misfortune,* as they call it, or it would have been known, and as it has no consequences, no girl would refuse her master on that account. There must be something at the bottom of it, however."

She could say nothing; she had not the strength to speak, and he asked her again: "You will not?"

"I cannot, master," she said, with a sigh, and he turned on his heel.

She thought she had got rid of him altogether, and spent the rest of the day almost tranquilly, but as worn out as if she, instead of the old white horse, had been turning the threshing machine all day. She went to bed as soon as she could, and fell asleep immediately. In the middle of the night, however, two hands touching the bed woke her. She trembled with fear, but she immediately recognized the farmer's voice, when he said to her: "Don't be frightened. Rose; I have come to speak to you."

She was surprised at first, but when he tried to take liberties with her, she understood what he wanted, and began to tremble violently. She felt quite alone in the darkness, still heavy from sleep, and quite unprotected, by the side of the man who stood near her. She certainly did not consent, but resisted carelessly, herself struggling against that instinct which is always strong in simple natures, and very imperfectly protected, by the undecided will of an exhausted body. She turned her head now to the wall, and now toward the room, in order to avoid the attentions which the farmer tried to press on her, and her body writhed under the coverlet, weakened as she was by the fatigue of the struggle, while he became brutal, intoxicated by desire.

They lived together as man and wife, and one morning

he said to her: "I have put up our banns, and we will get
married next month."

She did not reply, for what could she say? She did not
resist, for what could she do?

IV.

She married him. She felt as if she were in a pit with
inaccessible edges, from which she could never get out, and
all kinds of misfortunes remained hanging over her head,
like huge rocks, which would fall on the first occasion. Her
husband gave her the impression of a man whom she had
stolen, and who would find it out some day or other. And
then she thought of her child, who was the cause of her misfortunes, but was also the cause of all her happiness on
earth. She went to see him twice a year, and she came back
more unhappy each time.

But she gradually grew accustomed to her life, her fears
were allayed, her heart was at rest, and she lived with an
easier mind, although still with some vague fear floating
in her mind. So years went on, and the child was six. She
was almost happy now, when suddenly the farmer's temper
grew very bad.

For two or three years, he seemed to have been nursing
some secret anxiety, to be troubled by some care, some mental disturbance, which was gradually increasing. He remained
at table a long time after dinner, with his head in his hands,
sad and devoured by sorrow. He always spoke hastily, sometimes even brutally, and it even seemed as if he bore a
grudge against his wife, for at times he answered her
roughly, almost angrily.

One day, when a neighbor's boy came for some eggs, and
she spoke rather crossly to him, for she was very busy, her
husband suddenly came in, and said to her in his unpleasant
voice: "If that were your own child, you would not treat
him so."

She was hurt and did not reply, and then she went back
into the house with all her grief awakened afresh. At dinner, the farmer neither spoke to her nor looked at her, and

seemed to hate her, to despise her, to know something about
the affair at last. In consequence, she lost her head and did
not venture to remain alone with him after the meal was
over, but left the room and hastened to the church.

It was getting dusk; the narrow nave was in total darkness, but she heard footsteps in the choir, for the sacristan
was preparing the tabernacle lamp for the night. That spot
of trembling light, which was lost in the darkness of the
arches, looked to Rose like her last hope, and with her eyes
fixed on it, she fell on her knees. The chain rattled as the
little lamps swung up into the air, and almost immediately
the small bell rang out the "Angelus" through the increasing mist. She went up to him, as he was going out.

"Is Monsieur le Curé at home?" she asked.

"Of course he is; this is his dinnertime."

She trembled as she rang the bell of the parsonage. The
priest was just sitting down to dinner, and he made her sit
down also. "Yes, yes, I know all about it; your husband has
mentioned the matter to me that brings you here."

The poor woman nearly fainted, and the priest continued: "What do you want, my child?" And he hastily
swallowed several spoonfuls of soup, some of which dropped
on to his greasy cassock. But Rose did not venture to say
anything more, but got up to go, while the priest said:
"Courage."

So she went out, and returned to the farm, without knowing what she was doing. The farmer was waiting for her, as
the laborers had gone away during her absence, and she
fell heavily at his feet, and shedding a flood of tears, she
said to him: "What have you got against me?"

He began to shout and to swear: "What have I got against
you? That I have no children, by God! When a man takes a
wife, he does not want to be left alone with her until the end
of his days. That is what I have against you. When a cow
has no calves, she is not worth anything, and when a woman
has no children, she is also not worth anything."

She began to cry, and said: "It is not my fault! It is not
my fault!"

He grew rather more gentle when he heard that, and

added: "I do not say that it is, but it is very annoying, all the same."

V.

From that day forward, she had only one thought—to have a child, another child. She confided her wish to everybody, and in consequence of this, a neighbor told her of an infallible method. This was, to make her husband a glass of water with a pinch of ashes in it, every evening. The farmer consented to try it, but without success, so they said to each other: "Perhaps there are some secret ways?" And they tried to find out. They were told of a shepherd who lived ten leagues off, and so Vallin one day drove off to consult him. The shepherd gave him a loaf on which he had made some marks; it was kneaded up with herbs, and both of them were to eat a piece of it before and after their mutual caresses; but they ate the whole loaf without obtaining any results from it.

Next, a schoolmaster unveiled mysteries and processes of love which were unknown in the country, but infallible, so he declared; but none of them had the desired effect. Then the priest advised them to make a pilgrimage to the shrine at Fécamp. Rose went with the crowd and prostrated herself in the abbey, and mingling her prayers with the coarse wishes of the peasants around her, she prayed that she might be fruitful a second time; but it was in vain, and then she thought that she was being punished for her first fault, and she was seized by terrible grief. She was wasting away with sorrow; her husband was growing old prematurely, and was wearing himself out in useless hopes.

Then war broke out between them; he called her names and beat her. They quarreled all day long, and when they were in bed together at night he flung insults and obscenities at her, panting with rage, until one night, not being able to think of any means of making her suffer more, he ordered her to get up and go and stand out of doors in the rain, until daylight. As she did not obey him, he seized her by the neck, and began to strike her in the face with his fists, but she said nothing, and did not move. In his exasperation he knelt on her, and with clenched teeth and mad with rage began to beat her. Then in her despair she rebelled, and flinging him against the wall with a furious gesture, she sat up, and in an altered voice, she hissed: "I have had a child, I have had one! I had it by Jacques; you know Jacques well. He promised to marry me, but he left this neighborhood without keeping his word."

The man was thunderstruck, and could hardly speak, but at last he stammered out: "What are you saying? What are you saying?"

Then she began to sob, and amid her tears she said: "That was the reason why I did not want to marry you. I could not tell you, for you would have left me without any bread for my child. You have never had any children, so you cannot understand, you cannot understand!"

He said again, mechanically, with increasing surprise: "You have a child? You have a child?"

"You won me by force, as I suppose you know. I did not want to marry you," she said, still sobbing.

Then he got up, lighted the candle, and began to walk up and down, with his arms behind him. She was cowering on the bed and crying, and suddenly he stopped in front of her, and said: "Then it is my fault that you have no children?"

She gave him no answer, and he began to walk up and down again, and then, stopping again, he continued: "How old is your child?"

"Just six," she whispered.

"Why did you not tell me about it?" he asked.

"How could I?" she replied, with a sigh.

He remained standing, motionless. "Come, get up," he said.

She got up, with some difficulty, and then when she was standing on the floor, he suddenly began to laugh, with his hearty laugh of his good days, and seeing how surprised she was, he added: "Very well, we will go and fetch the child, as you and I can have none together."

She was so scared that if she had the strength she would assuredly have run away, but the farmer rubbed his hands and said: "I wanted to adopt one, and now we have found one. I asked the Curé about an orphan, some time ago."

Then, still laughing, he kissed his weeping and agitated wife on both cheeks, and shouted out, as if she could not hear him: "Come along, mother, we will go and see whether there is any soup left; I should not mind a plateful."

She put on her petticoat, and they went downstairs; and while she was kneeling in front of the fireplace, and lighting the fire under the saucepan, he continued to walk up and down the kitchen with long strides, and said: "Well, I am really glad at this; I am not saying it for form's sake, but I am glad, I am really very glad."

MME. TELLIER'S EXCURSION

Men went there every evening at about eleven o'clock, just as they went to the *café*. Six or eight of them used to meet there; always the same set, not fast men, but respectable tradesmen, and young men in government or some other employ; and they used to drink their Chartreuse, and tease the girls, or else they would talk seriously with Madame, whom everybody respected, and then would go home at twelve o'clock! The younger men would sometimes stay the night.

It was a small, comfortable house, at the corner of a street behind Saint Etienne's church. From the windows one could see the docks, full of ships which were being unloaded, and on the hill the old, gray chapel, dedicated to the Virgin.

Madame, who came of a respectable family of peasant proprietors in the department of the Eure, had taken up her profession, just as she would have become a milliner or dressmaker. The prejudice against prostitution, which is so violent and deeply rooted in large towns, does not exist in the country places in Normandy. The peasant simply says: "It is a paying business," and sends his daughter to keep a harem of fast girls, just as he would send her to keep a girls' school.

She had inherited the house from an old uncle, to whom it had belonged. Monsieur and Madame who had formerly been innkeepers near Yvetot, had immediately sold their house, as they thought that the business at Fécamp was more profitable. They arrived one fine morning to assume the direction of the enterprise, which was declining on account of the absence of a head. They were good people enough in their way, and soon made themselves liked by their staff and their neighbors.

Monsieur died of apoplexy two years later, for as his new profession kept him in idleness and without exercise, he had grown excessively stout, and his health had suffered. Since Madame had been a widow, all the frequenters of the establishment had wanted her; but people said that personally she was quite virtuous, and even the girls in the house could not discover anything against her. She was tall, stout, and affable, and her complexion, which had become pale in the dimness of her house, the shutters of which were scarcely ever opened, shone as if it had been varnished. She had a fringe of curly, false hair, which gave her a juvenile look, which in turn contrasted strongly with her matronly figure. She was always smiling and cheerful, and was fond of a joke, but there was a shade of reserve about her which her new occupation had not quite made her lose. Coarse words always shocked her, and when any young fellow who had been badly brought up called her establishment by its right name, she was angry and disgusted.

In a word, she had a refined mind, and although she treated her women as friends, yet she very frequently used to say that she and they were not made of the same stuff.

Sometimes during the week she would hire a carriage and take some of her girls into the country, where they used to enjoy themselves on the grass by the side of the little river. They behaved like a lot of girls let out from a school, and used to run races, and play childish games. They would have a cold dinner on the grass, and drink cider, and go home at night with a delicious feeling of fatigue, and in the carriage kiss Madame as a kind mother who was full of goodness and complaisance.

The house had two entrances. At the corner there was a sort of low *café*, which sailors and the lower orders frequented at night, and she had two girls whose special duty it was to attend to that part of the business. With the assistance of the waiter, whose name was Frederic, and who was a short, light-haired, beardless fellow, as strong as a horse, they set the half bottles of wine and the jugs of beer on the shaky marble tables and then, sitting astride on the customers' knees, would urge them to drink.

The three other girls (there were only five in all), formed

a kind of aristocracy, and were reserved for the company on the first floor, unless they were wanted downstairs, and there was nobody on the first floor. The salon of Jupiter, where the tradesmen used to meet, was papered in blue, and embellished with a large drawing representing Leda stretched out under the swan. That room was reached by a winding staircase, which ended at a narrow door opening on to the street, and above it, all night long a little lamp burned, behind wire bars, such as one still sees in some towns, at the foot of the shrine of some saint.

The house, which was old and damp, rather smelled of mildew. At times there was an odor of eau de Cologne in the passages, or a half open door downstairs allowed the noise of the common men sitting and drinking downstairs to reach the first floor, much to the disgust of the gentlemen who were there. Madame, who was quite familiar with those of her customers with whom she was on friendly terms, did not leave the salon. She took much interest in what was going on in the town, and they regularly told her all the news. Her serious conversation was a change from the ceaseless chatter of the three women; it was a rest from the doubtful jokes of those stout individuals who every evening indulged in the commonplace amusement of drinking a glass of liquor in company with girls of easy virtue.

The names of the girls on the first floor were Fernande, Raphaelle, and Rosa "the Jade." As the staff was limited, Madame had endeavored that each member of it should be a pattern, an epitome of each feminine type, so that every customer might find as nearly as possible, the realization of his ideal. Fernande represented the handsome blonde; she was very tall, rather fat, and lazy; a country girl, who could not get rid of her freckles, and whose short, light, almost colorless, tow-like hair, which was like combed-out flax, barely covered her head.

Raphaelle, who came from Marseilles, played the indispensable part of the handsome Jewess. She was thin, with high cheek-bones covered with rouge, and her black hair, which was always covered with pomatum, curled on to her forehead. Her eyes would have been handsome, if the right one had not had had a speck in it. Her Roman nose came down over a square jaw, where two false upper teeth contrasted strangely with the bad color of the rest.

Rosa the Jade was a little roll of fat, nearly all stomach, with very short legs. From morning till night she sang songs, which were alternately indecent or sentimental, in a harsh voice, told silly, interminable tales, and only stopped talking in order to eat, or left off eating in order to talk. She was never still, was as active as a squirrel, in spite of her fat and her short legs; and her laugh, which was a torrent of shrill cries, resounded here and there, ceaselessly, in a bedroom, in the loft, in the *café,* everywhere, and always about nothing.

The two women on the ground floor were Louise, who was nicknamed "la Cocotte," * and Flora, whom they called "Balançière," † because she limped a little. The former always dressed as Liberty, with a tri-colored sash, and the other as a Spanish woman, with a string of copper coins which jingled at every step she took, in her carroty hair. Both looked like cooks dressed up for the carnival, and were like all other women of the lower orders, neither uglier nor better looking than they usually are. In fact they looked just like servants at an inn, and were generally called "the Two Pumps."

A jealous peace, very rarely disturbed, reigned among these five women, thanks to Madame's conciliatory wisdom and to her constant good humor; and the establishment, which was the only one of the kind in the little town, was very much frequented. Madame had succeeded in giving it such a respectable appearance; she was so amiable and obliging to everybody, her good heart was so well known, that she was treated with a certain amount of consideration. The regular customers spent money on her, and were delighted when she was especially friendly toward them. When they met during the day, they would say: "This evening, you know where," just as men say: "At the *café,* after dinner." In a word Madame Tellier's house was somewhere to go to, and her customers very rarely missed their daily meetings there.

---

* Slang for a lady of easy virtue.
† Swing, or seesaw.

One evening, toward the end of May, the first arrival, Monsieur Poulin, who was a timber merchant, and had been mayor, found the door shut. The little lantern behind the grating was not alight; there was not a sound in the house; everything seemed dead. He knocked, gently at first, and then more loudly, but nobody answered the door. Then he went slowly up the street, and when he got to the market place, he met Monsieur Duvert, the gun-maker, who was going to the same place, so they went back together, but did not meet with any better success. But suddenly they heard a loud noise close to them, and on going round the corner of the house, they saw a number of English and French sailors, who were hammering at the closed shutters of the *café* with their fists.

The two tradesmen immediately made their escape, for fear of being compromised, but a low *Pst* stopped them; it was Monsieur Tournevau, the fish-curer, who had recognized them, and was trying to attract their attention. They told him what had happened, and he was all the more vexed at it, as he, a married man, and father of a family, only went there on Saturdays—*securitatis causa,* as he said, alluding to a measure of sanitary policy, which his friend Doctor Borde had advised him to observe. That was his regular evening, and now he would be deprived of it for the whole week.

The three men went as far as the quay together, and on the way they met young Monsieur Philippe, the banker's son, who frequented the place regularly, and Monsieur Pinipesse, the collector. They all returned to the Rue aux Juifs together, to make a last attempt. But the exasperated sailors were besieging the house, throwing stones at the shutters, and shouting, and the five first-floor customers went away as quickly as possible, and walked aimlessly about the streets.

Presently they met Monsieur Dupuis, the insurance agent, and then Monsieur Vassi, the Judge of the Tribunal of Commerce, and they all took a long walk, going to the pier first of all. There they sat down in a row on the granite parapet, and watched the rising tide, and when the promenaders had sat there for some time, Monsieur Tournevau said: "This is not very amusing!"

"Decidedly not," Monsieur Pinipesse replied, and they started off to walk again.

After going through the street on the top of the hill, they returned over the wooden bridge which crosses the Retenue, passed close to the railway, and came out again on to the market place, when suddenly a quarrel arose between Monsieur Pinipesse and Monsieur Tournevau, about an edible fungus which one of them declared he had found in the neighborhood.

As they were out of temper already from annoyance, they would very probably have come to blows, if the others had not interfered. Monsieur Pinipesse went off furious, and soon another altercation arose between the ex-mayor, Monsieur Poulin, and Monsieur Dupuis, the insurance agent, on the subject of the tax-collector's salary, and the profits which he might make. Insulting remarks were freely passing between them, when a torrent of formidable cries were heard, and the body of sailors, who were tired of waiting so long outside a closed house, came into the square. They were walking arm-in-arm, two and two, and formed a long procession, and were shouting furiously. The landsmen went and hid themselves under a gateway, and the yelling crew disappeared in the direction of the abbey. For a long time they still heard the noise, which diminished like a storm in the distance, and then silence was restored. Monsieur Poulin and Monsieur Dupuis, who were enraged with each other, went in different directions, without wishing each other good-bye.

The other four set off again, and instinctively went in the direction of Madame Tellier's establishment, which was still closed, silent, impenetrable. A quiet, but obstinate, drunken man was knocking at the door of the *café;* then he stopped and called Frederic, the waiter, in a low voice, but finding that he got no answer, he sat down on the doorstep, and awaited the course of events.

The others were just going to retire, when the noisy band of sailors reappeared at the end of the street. The French sailors were shouting the "Marseillaise," and the Englishmen, "Rule Britannia." There was a general lurching against the wall, and then the drunken brutes went on their way toward the quay, where a fight broke out between the two nations, in the course of which an Englishman had his arm broken, and a Frenchman his nose split.

The drunken man, who had stopped outside the door, was crying by this time, as drunken men and children cry when they are vexed, and the others went away. By degrees, calm was restored in the noisy town; here and there, at moments, the distant sound of voices could be heard, only to die away in the distance.

One man was still wandering about, Monsieur Tournevau, the fish-curer, who was vexed at having to wait until the next Saturday. He hoped for something to turn up, he did not know what; but he was exasperated at the police for thus allowing an establishment of such public utility, which they had under their control, to be thus closed.

He went back to it, examined the walls, and tried to find out the reason. On the shutter he saw a notice stuck up, so he struck a wax vesta, and read the following, in a large, uneven hand: "Closed on account of the Confirmation."

Then he went away, as he saw it was useless to remain, and left the drunken man lying on the pavement fast asleep, outside the inhospitable door.

The next day, all the regular customers, one after the other, found some reason for going through the Rue aux Juifs with a bundle of papers under their arm, to keep them in countenance, and with a furtive glance they all read that mysterious notice:

> "CLOSED ON ACCOUNT OF THE
> CONFIRMATION."

II.

Madame had a brother, who was a carpenter in their native place, Virville, in the department of Eure. When Madame had still kept the inn at Yvetot, she had stood godmother to that brother's daughter, who had received the name of Constance, Constance Rivet; she herself being a Rivet on her father's side. The carpenter, who knew that his sister was in a good position, did not lose sight of her, although they did not meet often, as they were both kept at home by their occupations, and lived a long way from each other. But when the girl was twelve years old, and about to be confirmed, he seized the opportunity to write to his sister, and ask her to come and be present at the ceremony. Their old parents were dead, and as Madame could not well refuse, she accepted the invitation. Her brother, whose name was Joseph, hoped that by dint of showing his sister attentions, she might be induced to make her will in the girl's favor, as she had no children of her own.

His sister's occupation did not trouble his scruples in the least, and, besides, nobody knew anything about it at Virville. When they spoke of her, they only said: "Madame Tellier is living at Fécamp," which might mean that she was living on her own private income. It was quite twenty leagues from Fécamp to Virville, and for a peasant, twenty leagues on land are more than is crossing the ocean to an educated person. The people at Virville had never been further than Rouen, and nothing attracted the people from Fécamp to a village of five hundred houses, in the middle of a plain, and situated in another department. At any rate, nothing was known about her business.

But the Confirmation was coming on and Madame was in great embarrassment. She had no under-mistress, and did not at all dare to leave her house, even for a day. She feared the rivalries between the girls upstairs and those downstairs would certainly break out; that Frederic would get drunk, for when he was in that state, he would knock anybody down for a mere word. At last, however, she made up her mind to take them all with her, with the exception of the man, to whom she gave a holiday, until the next day but one.

When she asked her brother, he made no objection, but undertook to put them all up for a night. So on Saturday morning the eight o'clock express carried off Madame and her companions in a second-class carriage. As far as Beuzeille they were alone, and chattered like magpies, but at that station a couple got in. The man, an aged peasant dressed in a blue blouse with a folding collar, wide sleeves tight at the wrist, and ornamented with white embroidery, wore an old high hat with long nap. He held an enormous green umbrella in one hand, and a large basket in the other, from which the heads of three frightened ducks protruded. The woman, who sat stiffly in her rustic finery, had a face like a fowl, and with a nose that was as pointed as a bill. She sat down opposite her husband and did not stir, as she was startled at finding herself in such smart company.

There was certainly an array of striking colors in the carriage. Madame was dressed in blue silk from head to foot, and had over her dress a dazzling red shawl of imitation French cashmere. Fernande was panting in a Scottish plaid dress, whose bodice, which her companions had laced as tight as they could, had forced up her falling bosom into a double dome, that was continually heaving up and down, and which seemed liquid beneath the material. Raphaelle, with a bonnet covered with feathers, so that it looked like a nest full of birds, had on a lilac dress with gold spots on it; there was something Oriental about it that suited her Jewish face. Rosa the Jade had on a pink petticoat with large flounces, and looked like a very fat child, an obese dwarf; while the Two Pumps looked as if they had cut their dresses out of old, flowered curtains, dating from the Restoration.

Perceiving that they were no longer alone in the compartment, the ladies put on staid looks, and began to talk of subjects which might give the others a high opinion of them. But at Bolbec a gentleman with light whiskers, with a gold chain, and wearing two or three rings, got in, and put several parcels wrapped in oil cloth into the net over his head. He looked inclined for a joke, and a good-natured fellow.

"Are you ladies changing your quarters?" he asked. The question embarrassed them all considerably. Madame, however, quickly recovered her composure, and said sharply, to avenge the honor of her corps:

"I think you might try and be polite!"

He excused himself, and said: "I beg your pardon, I ought to have said your nunnery."

As Madame could not think of a retort, or perhaps as she thought herself justified sufficiently, she gave him a dignified bow, and pinched in her lips.

Then the gentleman, who was sitting between Rosa the Jade and the old peasant, began to wink knowingly at the ducks, whose heads were sticking out of the basket. When he felt that he had fixed the attention of his public, he began to tickle them under their bills, and spoke funnily to them, to make the company smile.

"We have left our little pond, qu-ack! qu-ack! to make the acquaintance of the little spit, qu-ack! qu-ack!"

The unfortunate creatures turned their necks away to avoid his caresses, and made desperate efforts to get out of their wicker prison, and then, suddenly, all at once, uttered the most lamentable quacks of distress. The women exploded with laughter. They leaned forward and pushed each other, so as to see better; they were very much interested in the ducks, and the gentlemen redoubled his airs, his wit, and his teasing.

Rosa joined in, and leaning over her neighbor's legs, she kissed the three animals on the head. Immediately all the girls wanted to kiss them in turn, and the gentleman took them on to his knees, made them jump up and down and pinched them. The two peasants, who were even in greater consternation than their poultry, rolled their eyes as if they were possessed, without venturing to move, and their old wrinkled faces had not a smile nor a movement.

Then the gentleman, who was a commercial traveler, offered the ladies braces by way of a joke and taking up one of his packages, he opened it. It was a trick, for the parcel contained garters. There were blue silk, pink silk, red silk, violet silk, mauve silk garters, and the buckles were made of two gilt metal Cupids, embracing each other. The girls uttered exclamations of delight, and looked at them with that gravity which is natural to a woman when she is hankering after a bargain. They consulted one another by their looks or in a whisper, and replied in the same manner, and Madame was longingly handling a pair of orange garters that were broader and more imposing than the rest; really fit for the mistress of such an establishment.

"Come, my kittens," he said, "you must try them on."

There was a torrent of exclamations, and they squeezed their petticoats between their legs, as if they thought he was going to ravish them, but he quietly waited his time, and said: "Well, if you will not, I shall pack them up again."

And he added cunningly: "I offer any pair they like, to those who will try them on."

But they would not, and sat up very straight, and looked dignified.

But the Two Pumps looked so distressed that he renewed the offer to them. Flora especially hesitated, and he pressed her:

"Come, my dear, a little courage! Just look at that lilac pair; it will suit your dress admirably."

That decided her, and pulling up her dress she showed a thick leg fit for a milk-maid, in a badly fitting, coarse stocking. The commercial traveler stooped down and fastened the garter below the knee first of all and then above it; and he tickled the girl gently, which made her scream and jump. When he had done, he gave her the lilac pair, and asked: "Who next?"

"I! I!" they all shouted at once, and he began on Rosa the Jade, who uncovered a shapeless, round thing without any ankle, a regular "sausage of a leg," as Raphaelle used to say.

The commercial traveler complimented Fernande, and grew quite enthusiastic over her powerful columns.

The thin tibias of the handsome Jewess met with less flattery, and Louise Cocotte, by way of a joke, put her petticoats over the man's head, so that Madame was obliged to interfere to check such unseemly behavior.

Lastly, Madame herself put out her leg, a handsome, muscular, Norman leg, and in his surprise and pleasure the commercial traveler gallantly took off his hat to salute that master calf, like a true French cavalier.

The two peasants, who were speechless from surprise, looked askance, out of the corners of their eyes. They looked so exactly like fowls, that the man with the light whiskers, when he sat up, said "Co—co—ri—co," under their very noses, and that gave rise to another storm of amusement.

The old people got out at Motteville, with their basket, their ducks, and their umbrella, and they heard the woman say to her husband, as they went away:

"They are sluts, who are off to that cursed place, Paris."

The funny commercial traveler himself got out at Rouen, after behaving so coarsely that Madame was obliged sharply to put him into his right place. She added, as a moral: "This will teach us not to talk to the first comer."

At Oissel they changed trains, and at a little station further on Monsieur Joseph Rivet was waiting for them with a large cart and a number of chairs in it, which was drawn by a white horse.

The carpenter politely kissed all the ladies, and then helped them into his conveyance.

Three of them sat on three chairs at the back, Raphaelle, Madame, and her brother on the three chairs in front, and Rosa, who had no seat, settled herself as comfortably as she could on tall Fernande's knees, and then they set off.

But the horse's jerky trot shook the cart so terribly, that the chairs began to dance, throwing the travelers into the air, to the right and to the left, as if they had been dancing puppets. This made them make horrible grimaces and screams, which, however, were cut short by another jolt of the cart.

They clung to the sides of the vehicle, their bonnets fell on to their backs, their noses on their shoulders, and the white horse trotted on, stretching out his head and holding out his tail quite straight, a little hairless rat's tail, with which he whisked his buttocks from time to time.

Joseph Rivet, with one leg on the shafts and the other bent under him, held the reins with elbows high and kept uttering a kind of chuckling sound, which made the horse prick up its ears and go faster.

The green country extended on either side of the road, and here and there the colza in flower presented a waving expanse of yellow, from which there arose a strong, wholesome, sweet and penetrating smell, which the wind carried to some distance.

The cornflowers showed their little blue heads among the

rye, and the women wanted to pick them, but Monsieur Rivet refused to stop.

Then sometimes a whole field appeared to be covered with blood, so thickly were the poppies growing, and the cart, which looked as if it were filled with flowers of more brilliant hue, drove on through the fields colored with wild flowers, to disappear behind the trees of a farm, then to reappear and go on again through the yellow or green standing crops studded with red or blue.

One o'clock struck as they drove up to the carpenter's door. They were tired out, and very hungry, as they had eaten nothing since they left home. Madame Rivet ran out, and made them alight, one after another, kissing them as soon as they were on the ground. She seemed as if she would never tire of kissing her sister-in-law, whom she apparently wanted to monopolize. They had lunch in the workshop, which had been cleared out for the next day's dinner.

A capital omelette, followed by boiled chitterlings, and washed down by good, sharp cider, made them all feel comfortable.

Rivet had taken a glass so that he might hob-nob with them, and his wife cooked, waited on them, brought in the dishes, took them out, and asked all of them in a whisper whether they had everything they wanted. A number of boards standing against the walls, and heaps of shavings that had been swept into the corners, gave out the smell of planed wood, of carpentering, that resinous odor which penetrates the lungs.

They wanted to see the little girl, but she had gone to church, and would not be back until evening, so they all went out for a stroll in the country.

It was a small village, through which the high road passed. Ten or a dozen houses on either side of the single street had for tenants the butcher, the grocer, the carpenter, the innkeeper, the shoemaker, and the baker, and others.

The church was at the end of the street. It was surrounded by a small churchyard, and four enormous lime-trees, which stood just outside the porch, shaded it completely. It was built of flint, in no particular style, and had a slated steeple. When you got past it, you were in the open country again, which was broken here and there by clumps of trees which hid some homestead.

Rivet had given his arm to his sister out of politeness, although he was in his working clothes, and was walking with her majestically. His wife, who was overwhelmed by Raphaelle's gold-striped dress, was walking between her and Fernande, and rotund Rosa was trotting behind with Louise Cocotte and Flora, the seesaw, who was limping along, quite tired out.

The inhabitants came to their doors, the children left off playing, and a window curtain would be raised, so as to show a muslin cap, while an old woman with a crutch, who was almost blind, crossed herself as if it were a religious procession. They all looked for a long time after those handsome ladies from the town, who had come so far to be present at the confirmation of Joseph Rivet's little girl, and the carpenter rose very much in the public estimation.

As they passed the church, they heard some children singing; little shrill voices were singing a hymn, but Madame would not let them go in, for fear of disturbing the little cherubs.

After a walk, during which Joseph Rivet enumerated the principal landed proprietors, spoke about the yield of the land, and the productiveness of the cows and sheep, he took his flock of women home and installed them in his house, and as it was very small, he had put them into the rooms, two and two.

Just for once, Rivet would sleep in the workshop on the shavings; his wife was going to share her bed with her sister-in-law, and Fernande and Raphaelle were to sleep together in the next room. Louise and Flora were put into the kitchen, where they had a mattress on the floor, and Rosa had a little dark cupboard at the top of the stairs to herself, close to the loft, where the candidate for confirmation was to sleep.

When the girl came in, she was overwhelmed with kisses; all the women wished to caress her, with that need of tender expansion, that habit of professional wheedling which had made them kiss the ducks in the railway carriage.

They took her on to their laps, stroked her soft, light hair, and pressed her in their arms with vehement and spontaneous outbursts of affection, and the child, who was very good-natured and docile, bore it all patiently.

As the day had been a fatiguing one for everybody, they all went to bed soon after dinner. The whole village was wrapped in that perfect stillness of the country, which is almost like a religious silence, and the girls who were accustomed to the noisy evenings of their establishment, felt rather impressed by the perfect repose of the sleeping village. They shivered, not with cold, but with those little shivers of solitude which come over uneasy and troubled hearts.

As soon as they were in bed, two and two together, they clasped each other in their arms, as if to protect themselves against this feeling of the calm and profound slumber of the earth. But Rosa the Jade, who was alone in her little dark cupboard, felt a vague and painful emotion come over her.

She was tossing about in bed, unable to get to sleep, when she heard the faint sobs of a crying child close to her head, through the partition. She was frightened, and called out, and was answered by a weak voice, broken by sobs. It was the little girl who, being used to sleeping in her mother's rooms, was frightened in her small attic.

Rosa was delighted, got up softly so as not to awaken anyone, and went and fetched the child. She took her into her warm bed, kissed her and pressed her to her bosom, caressed her, lavished exaggerated manifestations of tenderness on her, and at last grew calmer herself and went to sleep. And till morning, the candidate for confirmation slept with her head on Rosa's naked bosom.

At five o'clock, the little church bell ringing the "Angelus" woke these women up, who as a rule slept the whole morning long.

The peasants were up already, and the women went busily from house to house, carefully bringing short, starched, muslin dresses in bandboxes, or very long wax tapers, with a bow of silk fringed with gold in the middle, and with dents in the wax for the fingers.

The sun was already high in the blue sky, which still had a rosy tint toward the horizon, like a faint trace of dawn, remaining. Families of fowls were walking about the hen-houses, and here and there a black cock, with a glistening breast, raised his head, crowned by his red comb, flapped his wings, and uttered his shrill crow, which the other cocks repeated. .

Vehicles of all sorts came from neighboring parishes, and discharged tall, Norman women, in dark dresses, with neck-handkerchiefs crossed over the bosom, and fastened with silver brooches, a hundred years old.

The men had put on blouses over their new frock coats, or over their old dress coats of green cloth, the tails 'of which hung down below their blouses. When the horses were in the stable, there was a double line of rustic con-veyances along the road; carts, cabriolets, tilburies, char-à-bancs, traps of every shape and age, resting on their shafts, or pointing them in the air.

The carpenter's house was as busy as a beehive. The ladies, in dressing jackets and petticoats, with their long, thin, light hair, which looked as if it were faded and worn by dyeing, were busy dressing the child, who was standing mo-tionless on a table, while Madame Tellier was directing the movements of her battalion. They washed her, did her hair, dressed her, and with the help of a number of pins, they arranged the folds of her dress, and took in the waist, which was too large.

Then, when she was ready, she was told to sit down and not to move, and the women hurried off to get ready them-selves.

The church bell began to ring again, and its tinkle was lost in the air, like a feeble voice which is soon drowned in space. The candidates came out of the houses, and went to-ward the parochial building which contained the school and the mansion house. This stood quite at one end of the village, while the church was situated at the other.

The parents, in their very best clothes, followed their

children with awkward looks, and with the clumsy movements of bodies that are always bent at work.

The little girls disappeared in a cloud of muslin, which looked like whipped cream, while the lads, who looked like embryo waiters in a *café,* and whose heads shone with pomatum, walked with their legs apart, so as not to get any dust or dirt on to their black trousers.

It was something for the family to be proud of; a large number of relatives from distant parts surrounded the child, and, consequently, the carpenter's triumph was complete.

Madame Tellier's regiment, with its mistress at its head, followed Constance; her father gave his arm to his sister, her mother walked by the side of Raphaelle, Fernande with Rosa, and the Two Pumps together. Thus they walked majestically through the village, like a general's staff in full uniform, while the effect on the village was startling.

At the school, the girls arranged themselves under the Sister of Mercy, and the boys under the schoolmaster, and they started off, singing a hymn as they went. The boys led the way, in two files, between the two rows of vehicles, from which the horses had been taken out, and the girls followed in the same order. As all the people in the village had given the town ladies the precedence out of politeness, they came immediately behind the girls, and lengthened the double line of the procession still more, three on the right and three on the left, while their dresses were as striking as a bouquet of fireworks.

When they went into the church, the congregation grew quite excited. They pressed against each other, they turned round, they jostled one another in order to see. Some of the devout ones almost spoke aloud, so astonished were they at the sight of these ladies, whose dresses were trimmed more elaborately than the priest's chasuble.

The Mayor offered them his pew, the first one on the right, close to the choir, and Madame Tellier sat there with her sister-in-law; Fernande and Raphaelle, Rosa the Jade, and the Two Pumps occupied the second seat, in company with the carpenter.

The choir was full of kneeling children, the girls on one side, and the boys on the other, and the long wax tapers which they held, looked like lances, pointing in all directions. Three men were standing in front of the lectern, singing as loud as they could.

They prolonged the syllables of the sonorous Latin indefinitely, holding on to the Amens with interminable *a—a's,* which the serpent of the organ kept up in the monotonous, long-drawn-out notes, emitted by the deep-throated pipes.

A child's shrill voice took up the reply, and from time to time a priest sitting in a stall and wearing a biretta, got up, muttered something, and sat down again. The three singers continued, with their eyes fixed on the big book of plain-song lying open before them on the outstretched wings of an eagle, mounted on a pivot.

Then silence ensued. The service went on, and toward the end of it, Rosa, with her head in both her hands, suddenly thought of her mother, and her village church on a similar occasion. She almost fancied that that day had returned, when she was so small, and almost hidden in her white dress, and she began to cry.

First of all she wept silently, the tears dropped slowly from her eyes, but her emotion increased with her recollections, and she began to sob. She took out her pocket-handkerchief, wiped her eyes, and held it to her mouth, so as not to scream, but it was useless.

A sort of rattle escaped her throat, and she was answered by two other profound, heart-breaking sobs; for her two neighbors, Louise and Flora, who were kneeling near her, overcome by similar recollections, were sobbing by her side. There was a flood of tears, and as weeping is contagious. Madame soon found that her eyes were wet, and on turning to her sister-in-law, she saw that all the occupants of the pew were crying.

Soon, throughout the church, here and there, a wife, a mother, a sister, seized by the strange sympathy of poignant emotion, and agitated by the grief of those handsome ladies on their knees, who were shaken by their sobs, was moistening her cambric pocket-handkerchief, and pressing her beating heart with her left hand.

Just as the sparks from an engine will set fire to dry grass, so the tears of Rosa and of her companions infected the whole congregation in a moment. Men, women, old men, and lads in new blouses were soon sobbing; something superhuman seemed to be hovering over their heads—a spirit, the powerful breath of an invisible and all-powerful being.

Suddenly a species of madness seemed to pervade the church, the noise of a crowd in a state of frenzy, a tempest of sobs and of stifled cries. It passed over the people like gusts of wind which bow the trees in a forest, and the priest, overcome by emotion, stammered out incoherent prayers, those inarticulate prayers of the soul, when it soars toward heaven.

The people behind him gradually grew calmer. The cantors, in all the dignity of their white surplices, went on in somewhat uncertain voices, and the organ itself seemed hoarse, as if the instrument had been weeping. The priest, however, raised his hand, as a sign for them to be still, and went to the chancel steps. All were silent, immediately.

After a few remarks on what had just take place, which he attributed to a miracle, he continued, turning to the seats where the carpenter's guests were sitting:

"I especially thank you, my dear sisters, who have come from such a distance, and whose presence among us, whose evident faith and ardent piety have set such a salutary example to all. You have edified my parish; your emotion has warmed all hearts; without you, this day would not, perhaps, have had this really divine character. It is sufficient, at times, that there should be one chosen to keep in the flock, to make the whole flock blessed."

His voice failed him again, from emotion, and he said no more, but concluded the service.

They all left the church as quickly as possible; the children themselves were restless, tired with such a prolonged tension of the mind. Besides, the elders were hungry, and one after another left the churchyard, to see about dinner.

There was a crowd outside, a noisy crowd, a babel of loud voices, in which the shrill Norman accent was discernible. The villagers formed two ranks, and when the children appeared, each family seized their own.

The whole houseful of women caught hold of Constance, surrounded her and kissed her, and Rosa was especially demonstrative. At last she took hold of one hand, while Madame Tellier held the other, and Raphaelle and Fernande held up her long muslin petticoat, so that it might not drag in the dust. Louise and Flora brought up the rear with Madame Rivet, and the child, who was very silent and thoughtful, set off home, in the midst of this guard of honor.

The dinner was served in the workshop, on long boards supported by trestles, and through the open door they could see all the enjoyment that was going on. Everywhere people were feasting; through every window could be seen tables surrounded by people in their Sunday clothes. There was merriment in every house—men sitting in their shirt sleeves, drinking cider, glass after glass.

In the carpenter's house the gaiety took on somewhat of an air of reserve, the consequence of the emotion of the girls in the morning. Rivet was the only one who was in good cue, and he was drinking to excess. Madame Tellier was looking at the clock every moment, for, in order not to lose two days following, they ought to take the 3.55 train, which would bring them to Fécamp by dark.

The carpenter tried very hard to distract her attention, so as to keep his guests until the next day. But he did not succeed, for she never joked when there was business to be done, and as soon as they had had their coffee she ordered her girls to make haste and get ready. Then, turning to her brother, she said:

"You must have the horse put in immediately," and she herself went to complete her preparations.

When she came down again, her sister-in-law was waiting to speak to her about the child, and a long conversation took place, in which, however, nothing was settled. The carpenter's wife finessed, and pretended to be very much moved, and Madame Tellier, who was holding the girl on her knees, would not pledge herself to anything definite, but merely gave vague promises: she would not forget her, there was plenty of time, and then, they were sure to meet again.

But the conveyance did not come to the door, and the women did not come downstairs. Upstairs, they even heard

loud laughter, falls, little screams, and much clapping of
hands, and so, while the carpenter's wife went to the stable
to see whether the cart was ready, Madame went upstairs.

Rivet, who was very drunk and half undressed, was
vainly trying to kiss Rosa, who was choking with laughter.
The Two Pumps were holding him by the arms and trying
to calm him, as they were shocked at such a scene after that
morning's ceremony; but Raphaelle and Fernande were urg-
ing him on, writhing and holding their sides with laughter,
and they uttered shrill cries at every useless attempt that
the drunken fellow made.

The man was furious, his face was red, his dress dis-
ordered, and he was trying to shake off the two women who
were clinging to him, while he was pulling Rosa's bodice,
with all his might, and ejaculating: "Won't you, you slut?"

But Madame, who was very indignant, went up to her
brother, seized him by the shoulders, and threw him out of
the room with such violence that he fell against a wall in
the passage, and a minute afterward, they heard him pump-
ing water on to his head in the yard. When he came back
with the cart, he was already quite calmed down.

They seated themselves in the same way as they had
done the day before, and the little white horse started off
with his quick, dancing trot. Under the hot sun, their fun,
which had been checked during dinner, broke out again.
The girls now were amused at the jolts which the wagon gave,
pushed their neighbors' chairs, and burst out laughing
every moment, for they were in the vein for it, after Rivet's
vain attempt.

There was a haze over the country, the roads were glar-
ing, and dazzled their eyes. The wheels raised up two trails
of dust, which followed the cart for a long time along the
highroad, and presently Fernande, who was fond of music,
asked Rosa to sing something. She boldly struck up the "Gros
Curé de Meudon," but Madame made her stop immediately
as she thought it a song which was very unsuitable for such
a day, and added:

"Sing us something of Béranger's."

After a moment's hesitation, Rosa began Béranger's song,

"The Grandmother," in her worn-out voice, and all the girls, and even Madame herself, joined in the chorus:

> "How I regret
> My dimpled arms,
> My well-made legs,
> And my vanished charms!"

"That is first-rate," Rivet declared, carried away by the rhythm. They shouted the refrain to every verse, while Rivet beat time on the shafts with his foot, and on the horse's back with the reins. The animal, himself, carried away by the rhythm, broke into a wild gallop, and threw all the women in a heap, one on top of the other, in the bottom of the conveyance.

They got up, laughing as if they were crazy, and the song went on, shouted at the top of their voices, beneath the burning sky and among the ripening grain, to the rapid gallop of the little horse, who set off every time the refrain was sung, and galloped a hundred yards, to their great delight. Occasionally a stone breaker by the roadside sat up, and looked at the wild and shouting female load, through his wire spectacles.

When they got out at the station, the carpenter said:

"I am sorry you are going; we might have had some fun together."

But Madame replied very sensibly: "Everything has its right time, and we cannot always be enjoying ourselves."

And then he had a sudden inspiration: "Look here, I will come and see you at Fécamp next month." And he gave a knowing look, with his bright and roguish eyes.

"Come," Madame said, "you must be sensible; you may come if you like, but you are not to be up to any of your tricks."

He did not reply, and as they heard the whistle of the train he immediately began to kiss them all. When it came to Rosa's turn, he tried to get to her mouth, which she, however, smiling with her lips closed, turned away from him each time by a rapid movement of her head to one side. He held her in his arms, but he could not attain his object, as his large whip, which he was holding in his hand and waving behind the girl's back in desperation, interfered with his efforts.

"Passengers for Rouen, take your seats, please!" a guard cried, and they got in. There was a slight whistle followed by a loud one from the engine, which noisily puffed out its first jet of steam, while the wheels began to turn a little, with visible effort. Rivet left the station and went to the gate by the side of the line to get another look at Rosa, and as the carriage full of human merchandise passed him, he began to crack his whip and to jump, singing at the top of his voice:

> "How I regret
> My dimpled arms,
> My well-made legs,
> And my vanished charms!"

And then he watched a white pocket-handkerchief, which somebody was waving, as it disappeared in the distance.

III.

They slept the peaceful sleep of quiet consciences, until they got to Rouen. When they returned to the house, refreshed and rested, Madame could not help saying:

"It was all very well, but I was already longing to get home."

They hurried over their supper, and then, when they had put on their usual light evening costumes, waited for their usual customers. The little colored lamp outside the door told the passers-by that the flock had returned to the fold, and in a moment the news spread, nobody knew how, or by whom.

Monsieur Philippe, the banker's son, even carried his audacity so far as to send a special messenger to Monsieur Tournevau who was in the bosom of his family.

The fish-curer used every Sunday to have several cousins to dinner, and they were having coffee, when a man came in with a letter in his hand. Monsieur Tournevau was much excited; he opened the envelope and grew pale; it only contained these words in pencil:

"The cargo of fish has been found; the ship has come into port; good business for you. Come immediately."

He felt in his pocket, gave the messenger two-pence, and suddenly blushing to his ears, he said: "I must go out." He handed his wife the laconic and mysterious note, rang the bell, and when the servant came in, he asked her to bring him his hat and overcoat immediately. As soon as he was in the street, he began to run, and the way seemed to him to be twice as long as usual, in consequence of his impatience.

Madame Tellier's establishment had put on quite a holiday look. On the ground floor, a number of sailors were making a deafening noise, and Louise and Flora drank with one and the other, so as to merit their name of the Two Pumps more than ever. They were being called for everywhere at once; already they were not quite sober enough for their business, and the night bid fair to be a very jolly one.

The upstairs room was full by nine o'clock. Monsieur Vassi, the Judge of the Tribunal of Commerce, Madame's usual Platonic wooer, was talking to her in a corner, in a low voice, and they were both smiling, as if they were about to come to an understanding.

Monsieur Poulin, the ex-mayor, was holding Rosa on his knees; and she, with her nose close to his, was running her hands through the old gentleman's white whiskers.

Tall Fernande, who was lying on the sofa, had both her feet on Monsieur Pinipesse the tax-collector's stomach, and her back on young Monsieur Philippe's waistcoat; her right arm was round his neck, and she held a cigarette in her left.

Raphaelle appeared to be discussing matters with Monsieur Dupuis, the insurance agent, and she finished by saying "Yes, my dear, I will."

Just then, the door opened suddenly, and Monsieur Tournevau came in. He was greeted with enthusiastic cries of: "Long live Tournevau!" and Raphaelle, who was twirling round, went and threw herself into his arms. He seized her in a vigorous embrace, and without saying a word, lifting her up as if she had been a feather, he carried her through the room.

Rosa was chatting to the ex-mayor, kissing him every moment, and pulling both his whiskers at the same time in order to keep his head straight.

Fernande and Madame remained with the four men, and Monsieur Philippe exclaimed: "I will pay for some champagne; get three bottles, Madame Tellier." And Fernande gave him a hug, and whispered to him: "Play us a waltz, will you?" So he rose and sat down at the old piano in the corner, and managed to get a hoarse waltz out of the entrails of the instrument.

The tall girl put her arms round the tax-collector, Madame asked Monsieur Vassi to take her in his arms, and the two couples turned round, kissing as they danced. Monsieur Vassi, who had formerly danced in good society, waltzed with such elegance that Madame was quite captivated.

Frederic brought the champagne; the first cork popped, and Monsieur Philippe played the introduction to a quadrille, through which the four dancers walked in society fashion, decorously, with propriety of deportment, with bows, and curtsies, and then they began to drink.

Monsieur Philippe next struck up a lively polka, and Monsieur Tournevau started off with the handsome Jewess, whom he held up in the air, without letting her feet touch the ground. Monsieur Pinipesse and Monsieur Vassi had started off with renewed vigor and from time to time one or other couple would stop to toss off a long glass of sparkling wine. The dance was threatening to become never-ending, when Rosa opened the door.

"I want to dance," she exclaimed. And she caught hold of Monsieur Dupuis, who was sitting idle on the couch, and the dance began again.

But the bottles were empty. "I will pay for one," Monsieur Tournevau said.

"So will I," Monsieur Vassi declared.

"And I will do the same," Monsieur Dupuis remarked.

They all began to clap their hands, and it soon became a regular ball. From time to time, Louise and Flora ran upstairs quickly, had a few turns while their customers down-stairs grew impatient, and then they returned regretfully to the *café*. At midnight they were still dancing.

Madame shut her eyes to what was going on, and she had long private talks in corners with Monsieur Vassi, as if to settle the last details of something that had already been agreed upon.

At last, at one o'clock, the two married men, Monsieur Tournevau and Monsieur Pinippesse, declared that they were going home, and wanted to pay. Nothing was charged for except the champagne, and that only cost six francs a bottle, instead of ten, which was the usual price, and when they expressed their surprise at such generosity, Madame, who was beaming, said to them:

"We don't have a holiday every day."

MADEMOISELLE FIFI

The Major Graf* von Farlsberg, the Prussian commandant, was reading his newspaper, lying back in a great armchair, with his booted feet on the beautiful marble fireplace, where his spurs had made two holes, which grew deeper every day, during the three months that he had been in the château of Urville.

A cup of coffee was smoking on a small, inlaid table, which was stained with liquors, burnt by cigars, notched by the penknife of the victorious officer, who occasionally would stop while sharpening a pencil, to jot down figures, or to make a drawing on it, just as it took his fancy.

When he had read his letters and the German newspapers, which his baggage-master had brought him, he got up, and after throwing three or four enormous pieces of green wood on to the fire—for these gentlemen were gradually cutting down the park in order to keep themselves warm—he went to the window. The rain was descending in torrents, a regular Normandy rain, which looked as if it were being poured out by some furious hand, a slanting rain, which was as thick as a curtain, and which formed a kind of wall with oblique stripes, and which deluged everything, a regular rain, such as one frequently experiences in the neighborhood of Rouen, which is the watering-pot of France.

For a long time the officer looked at the sodden turf, and at the swollen Andelle beyond it, which was overflowing its banks, and he was drumming a waltz from the Rhine on the windowpanes, with his fingers, when a noise made him turn round; it was his second in command, Captain Baron von Kelweinstein.

The major was a giant, with broad shoulders, and a long,

* Count.

fair beard, which hung like a cloth on to his chest. His whole, solemn person suggested the idea of a military peacock, a peacock who was carrying his tail spread out on to his breast. He had cold, gentle, blue eyes, and the scar from a sword-cut, which he received in the war with Austria; he was said to be an honorable man, as well as a brave officer.

The captain, a short, red-faced man, who was tightly girthed in at the waist, had his red hair cropped quite close to his head, and in certain lights almost looked as if he had been rubbed over with phosphorus. He had lost two front teeth one night, though he could not quite remember how. This defect made him speak so that he could not always be understood, and he had a bald patch on the top of his head, which made him look rather like a monk, with a fringe of curly, bright, golden hair round the circle of bare skin.

The commandant shook hands with him, and drank his cup of coffee (the sixth that morning) at a draught, while he listened to his subordinate's report of what had occurred; and then they both went to the window, and declared that it was a very unpleasant outlook. The major, who was a quiet man, with a wife at home, could accommodate himself to everything; but the captain, who was rather fast, being in the habit of frequenting low resorts, and much given to women, was mad at having been shut up for three months in the compulsory chastity of that wretched hole.

There was a knock at the door, and when the commandant said, "Come in," one of their automatic soldiers appeared, and by his mere presence announced that breakfast was ready. In the dining-room, they met three other officers of lower rank: a lieutenant, Otto von Grossling, and two sub-lieutenants, Fritz Scheunebarg, and Count von Eyrick, a very short, fair-haired man, who was proud and brutal toward men, harsh toward prisoners, and very violent.

Since he had been in France, his comrades had called him nothing but "Mademoiselle Fifi." They had given him that nickname on account of his dandified style and small waist, which looked as if he wore stays, from his pale face, on which his budding mustache scarcely showed, and on account of the habit he had acquired of employing the French expression, *fi, fi donc,* which he pronounced with a slight whistle, when he wished to express his sovereign contempt for persons or things.

The dining-room of the château was a magnificent long room, whose fine old mirrors, now cracked by pistol bullets, and Flemish tapestry, now cut to ribbons and hanging in rags in places, from sword-cuts, told too well what Mademoiselle Fifi's occupation was during his spare time.

There were three family portraits on the walls; a steel-clad knight, a cardinal, and a judge, who were all smoking long porcelain pipes, which had been inserted into holes in the canvas, while a lady in a long, pointed waist proudly exhibited an enormous pair of mustaches, drawn with a piece of charcoal.

The officers ate their breakfast almost in silence in that mutilated room, which looked dull in the rain, and melancholy under its vanquished appearance, although its old, oak floor had become as solid as the stone floor of a public-house.

When they had finished eating, and were smoking and drinking, they began, as usual, to talk about the dull life they were leading. The bottle of brandy and of liquors passed from hand to hand, and all sat back in their chairs, taking repeated sips from their glasses, and scarcely removing the long, bent stems, which terminated in china bowls painted in a manner to delight a Hottentot, from their mouths.

As soon as their glasses were empty, they filled them again, with a gesture of resigned weariness, but Mademoiselle Fifi emptied his every minute, and a soldier immediately gave him another. They were enveloped in a cloud of strong tobacco smoke; they seemed to be sunk in a state of drowsy, stupid intoxication, in that dull state of drunkenness of men who have nothing to do, when suddenly, the baron sat up, and said: "By Heavens! This cannot go on; we must think of something to do." And on hearing this, Lieutenant Otto and Sub-lieutenant Fritz, who preeminently possessed the grave, heavy German countenance, said: "What, Captain?"

He thought for a few moments, and then replied: "What?

Well, we must get up some entertainment, if the commandant will allow us."

"What sort of an entertainment, captain?" the major asked, taking his pipe out of his mouth.

"I will arrange all that, commandant," the baron said: "I will send *Le Devoir* to Rouen, who will bring us some ladies. I know where they can be found. We will have supper here, as all the materials are at hand, and, at least, we shall have a jolly evening."

Graf von Farlsberg shrugged his shoulders with a smile: "You must surely be mad, my friend."

But all the other officers got up, surrounded their chief, and said: "Let captain have his own way, commandant; it is terribly dull here."

And the major ended by yielding. "Very well," he replied, and the baron immediately sent for *Le Devoir*.

The latter was an old corporal who had never been seen to smile, but who carried out all orders of his superiors to the letter, no matter what they might be. He stood there, with an impassive face, while he received the baron's instructions, and then went out; five minutes later a large wagon belonging to the military train, covered with a miller's tilt, galloped off as fast as four horses could take it, under the pouring rain, and the officers all seemed to awaken from their lethargy, their looks brightened, and they began to talk.

Although it was raining as hard as ever, the major declared that it was not so dull, and Lieutenant von Grossling said with conviction, that the sky was clearing up, while Mademoiselle Fifi did not seem to be able to keep in his place. He got up, and sat down again, and his bright eyes seemed to be looking for something to destroy. Suddenly, looking at the lady with the mustaches, the young fellow pulled out his revolver, and said: "You shall not see it." And without leaving his seat he aimed, and with two successive bullets cut out both the eyes of the portrait.

"Let us make a mine!" he then exclaimed, and the conversation was suddenly interrupted, as if they had found some fresh and powerful subject of interest. The mine was his invention, his method of destruction, and his favorite amusement.

When he left the château, the lawful owner, Count Fernand d'Amoys d'Urville, had not had time to carry away or to hide anything, except the plate, which had been stowed away in a hole made in one of the walls, so that, as he was very rich and had good taste, the large drawing-room, which opened into the dining-room, had looked like the gallery in a museum, before his precipitate flight.

Expensive oil-paintings, water-colors, and drawings hung upon the walls, while on the tables, on the hanging shelves, and in elegant glass cupboards, there were a thousand knick-knacks: small vases, statuettes, groups in Dresden china, grotesque Chinese figures, old ivory, and Venetian glass, which filled the large room with their precious and fantastical array.

Scarcely anything was left now; not that the things had been stolen, for the major would not have allowed that, but Mademoiselle Fifi *would have a mine*, and on that occasion all the officers thoroughly enjoyed themselves for five minutes. The little marquis went into the drawing-room to get what he wanted, and he brought back a small, delicate china teapot, which he filled with gunpowder, and carefully introduced a piece of German tinder into it, through the spout. Then he lighted it, and took this infernal machine into the next room; but he came back immediately, and shut the door. The Germans all stood expectantly, their faces full of childish, smiling curiosity, and as soon as the explosion had shaken the château, they all rushed in at once.

Mademoiselle Fifi, who got in first, clapped his hands in delight at the sight of a terra-cotta Venus, whose head had been blown off, and each picked up pieces of porcelain, and wondered at the strange shape of the fragments, while the major was looking with a paternal eye at the large drawing-room which had been wrecked in such a Neronic fashion, and which was strewn with the fragments of works of art. He went out first, and said, with a smile: "He managed that very well!"

But there was such a cloud of smoke in the dining-room

mingled with the tobacco smoke, that they could not
breathe, so the commandant opened the window, and all the
officers, who had gone into the room for a glass of cognac
went up to it.

The moist air blew into the room, and brought a sort of
spray with it, which powdered their beards. They looked at
the tall trees which were dripping with the rain, at the
broad valley which was covered with mist, and at the church
spire in the distance, which rose up like a gray point in the
beating rain.

The bells had not rung since their arrival. That was the
only resistance which the invaders had met with in the
neighborhood. The parish priest had not refused to take
in and to feed the Prussian soldiers; he had several times
even drunk a bottle of beer or claret with the hostile commandant, who often employed him as a benevolent inter-
mediary; but it was no use to ask him for a single stroke
of the bells; he would sooner have allowed himself to be
shot. That was his way of protesting against the invasion,
peaceful and silent protest, the only one, he said, which
was suitable to a priest, who was a man of mildness, and
not of blood; and everyone, for twenty-five miles round,
praised Abbé Chantavoine's firmness and heroism, in venturing to proclaim the public mourning by the obstinate silence of his church bells.

The whole village grew enthusiastic over his resistance,
and was ready to back up their pastor and to risk anything, as they looked upon that silent protest as the safe-
guard of the national honor. It seemed to the peasants that
thus they had deserved better of their country than Belfort
and Strassburg, that they had set an equally valuable
example, and that the name of their little village would become immortalized by that; but with that exception, they
refused their Prussian conquerors nothing.

The commandant and his officers laughed among themselves at that inoffensive courage, and as the people in the
whole country round showed themselves obliging and com-
pliant toward them, they willingly tolerated their silent
patriotism. Only little Count Wilhelm would have liked to
have forced them to ring the bells. He was very angry at

his superior's politic compliance with the priest's scruples, and every day he begged the commandant to allow him to sound "ding-dong, ding-dong," just once, only just once, just by way of a joke. And he asked it like a wheedling woman, in the tender voice of some mistress who wishes to obtain something, but the commandant would not yield, and to console *herself*, Mademoiselle Fifi made a *mine* in the chateau.

The five men stood there together for some minutes, inhaling the moist air, and at last, Lieutenant Fritz said, with a laugh: "The ladies will certainly not have fine weather for their drive." Then they separated, each to his own duties, while the captain had plenty to do in seeing about the dinner.

When they met again, as it was growing dark, they began to laugh at seeing each other as dandified and smart as on the day of a grand review. The commandant's hair did not look as gray as it did in the morning, and the captain had shaved—had only kept his mustache on, which made him look as if he had a streak of fire under his nose.

In spite of the rain, they left the window open, and one of them went to listen from time to time. At a quarter past six the baron said he heard a rumbling in the distance. They all rushed down, and soon the wagon drove up at a gallop with its four horses, splashed up to their backs, steaming and panting. Five women got out at the bottom of the steps, five handsome girls whom a comrade of the captain, to whom *Le Devoir* had taken his card, had selected with care.

They had not required much pressing, as they were sure of being well treated, for they had got to know the Prussians in the three months during which they had had to do with them. So they resigned themselves to the men as they did to the state of affairs. "It is part of our business, so it must be done," they said as they drove along; no doubt to allay some slight, secret scruples of conscience.

They went into the dining-room immediately, which looked still more dismal in its dilapidated state, when it was lighted up; while the table covered with choice dishes, the beautiful china and glass, and the plate, which had

been found in the hole in the wall where its owner had hid-
dent it, gave to the place the look of a bandits' resort, where
they were supping after committing a robbery. The captain was radiant; he took hold of the women as if he were
familiar with them; appraising them, kissing them, valuing
them for what they were worth as *ladies of pleasure;* and
when the three young men wanted to appropriate one each,
he opposed them authoritatively, reserving to himself the
right to apportion them justly, according to their several
ranks, so as not to wound the hierarchy. Therefore, so as to
avoid all discussion, jarring, and suspicion of partiality, he
placed them all in a line according to height, and address-
ing the tallest, he said in a voice of command:

"What is your name?"

"Pamela," she replied, raising her voice.

Then he said: "Number One, called Pamela, is adjudged
to the commandant."

Then, having kissed Blondina, the second, as a sign of
proprietorship, he proffered stout Amanda to Lieutenant
Otto, Eva, "the Tomato," to Sublieutenant Fritz, and Rachel,
the shortest of them all, a very young, dark girl, with eyes
as black as ink, a Jewess, whose snub nose confirmed by
exception the rule which allots hooked noses to all her
race, to the youngest officer, frail Count Wilhelm von Eyrick.

They were all pretty and plump, without any distinctive
features, and all were very much alike in look and person,
from their daily dissipation, and the life common to houses
of public accommodation.

The three younger men wished to carry off their women
immediately, under the pretext of finding them brushes
and soap; but the captain wisely opposed this, for he said
they were quite fit to sit down to dinner, and that those
who went up would wish for a change when they came
down, and so would disturb the other couples, and his expe-
rience in such matters carried the day. There were only
many kisses; expectant kisses.

Suddenly Rachel choked, and began to cough until the
tears came into her eyes, while smoke came through her
nostrils. Under pretense of kissing her, the count had blown

a whiff of tobacco into her mouth. She did not fly into a rage, and did not say a word, but she looked at her possessor with latent hatred in her dark eyes.

They sat down to dinner. The commandant seemed delighted; he made Pamela sit on his right, and Blondina on his left, and said, as he unfolded his table napkin: "That was a delightful idea of yours, captain."

Lieutenants Otto and Fritz, who were as polite as if they had been with fashionable ladies, rather intimidated their neighbors, but Baron von Kelweinstein gave the reins to all his vicious propensities, beamed, made doubtful remarks, and seemed on fire with his crown of red hair. He paid them compliments in French from the other side of the Rhine, and sputtered out gallant remarks, only fit for a low pothouse, from between his two broken teeth.

They did not understand him, however, and their intelligence did not seem to be awakened until he uttered nasty words and broad expressions, which were mangled by his accent. Then all began to laugh at once, like mad women, and fell against each other, repeating the words, which the baron then began to say all wrong, in order that he might have the pleasure of hearing them say doubtful things. They gave him as much of that stuff as he wanted, for they. were drunk after the first bottle of wine, and, becoming themselves once more, and opening the door to their usual habits, they kissed the mustaches on the right and left of them, pinched their arms, uttered furious cries, drank out of every glass, and sang French couplets, and bits of German songs, which they had picked up in their daily intercourse with the enemy.

Soon the men themselves, intoxicated by that which was displayed to their sight and touch, grew very amorous, shouted and broke the plates and dishes, while the soldiers behind them waited on them stolidly. The commandant was the only one who put any restraint upon himself.

Mademoiselle Fifi had taken Rachel on to his knees, and, getting excited, at one moment kissed the little black curls on her neck, inhaling the pleasant warmth of her body, and all the savor of her person, through the slight space there was between her dress and her skin, and at another pinched her furiously through the material, and made her scream, for he was seized with a species of ferocity, and tormented by his desire to hurt her. He often held her close to him, as if to make her part of himself, and put his lips in a long kiss on the Jewess's rosy mouth, until she lost her breath; and at last he bit her until a stream of blood ran down her chin and on to her bodice.

For the second time, she looked him full in the face, and as she bathed the wound, she said: "You will have to pay for that!"

But he merely laughed a hard laugh, and said: "I will pay."

At dessert, champagne was served, and the commandant rose, and in the same voice in which he would have drunk to the health of the Empress Augusta, he drank: "To our ladies!" Then a series of toasts began, toasts worthy of the lowest soldiers and of drunkards, mingled with filthy jokes, which were made still more brutal by their ignorance of the language. They got up, one after the other, trying to say something witty, forcing themselves to be funny, and the women, who were so drunk that they almost fell off their chairs, with vacant looks and clammy tongues, applauded madly each time.

The captain, who no doubt wished to impart an appearance of gallantry to the orgy, raised his glass again, and said: "To our victories over hearts!" Thereupon Lieutenant Otto, who was a species of bear from the Black Forest, jumped up, inflamed and saturated with drink, and seized by an access of alcoholic patriotism, cried: "To our victories over France!"

Drunk as they were, the women were silent, and Rachel turned round with a shudder, and said: "Look here, I know some Frenchmen, in whose presence you would not dare to say that." But the little count, still holding her on his knees, began to laugh, for the wine had made him very merry, and said: "Ha! ha! ha! I have never met any of them, myself. As soon as we show ourselves, they run away!"

The girl, who was in a terrible rage, shouted into his face: "You are lying, you dirty scoundrel!"

For a moment, he looked at her steadily, with his bright eyes upon her, as he had looked at the portrait before he destroyed it with revolver bullets, and then he began to laugh: "Ah! yes, talk about them, my dear! Should we be here now, if they were brave?" Then getting excited, he exclaimed: "We are the masters! France belongs to us!" She jumped off his knees with a bound, and threw herself into her chair, while he rose, held out his glass over the table, and repeated: "France and the French, the woods, the fields, and the houses of France belong to us!"

The others, who were quite drunk, and who were suddenly seized by military enthusiasm, the enthusiasm of brutes, seized their glasses, and shouting, "Long live Prussia!" emptied them at a draught.

The girls did not protest, for they were reduced to silence, and were afraid. Even Rachel did not say a word, as she had no reply to make, and then the little count put his champagne glass, which had just been refilled, on to the head of the Jewess, and exclaimed: "All the women in France belong to us, also!"

At that she got up so quickly that the glass upset, spilling the amber colored wine on to her black hair as if to baptize her, and broke into a hundred fragments as it fell on to the floor. With trembling lips, she defied the looks of the officer, who was still laughing, and she stammered out, in a voice choked with rage: "That—that—that—is not true,—for you shall certainly not have any French women."

He sat down again, so as to laugh at his ease, and trying effectually to speak in the Parisian accent, he said: "That is good, very good! Then what did you come here, for, my dear?"

She was thunderstruck, and made no reply for a moment, for in her agitation she did not understand him at first; but as soon as she grasped his meaning, she said to him indignantly and vehemently: "I! I! am not a woman; I am only a strumpet, and that is all that Prussians want."

Almost before she had finished, he slapped her full in her face; but as he was raising his hand again, as if he would strike her, she, almost mad with passion, took up a small dessert knife from the table, and stabbed him right in the neck, just above the breastbone. Something that he was going to say, was cut short in his throat, and he sat there, with his mouth half open, and a terrible look in his eyes.

All the officers shouted in horror, and leaped up tumultuously; but throwing her chair between Lieutenant Otto's legs, who fell down at full length, she ran to the window, opened it before they could seize her, and jumped out into the night and pouring rain.

In two minutes, Mademoiselle Fifi was dead. Fritz and Otto drew their swords and wanted to kill the women, who threw themselves at their feet and clung to their knees. With some difficulty the major stopped the slaughter, and had the four terrified girls locked up in a room under the care of two soldiers. Then he organized the pursuit of the fugitive, as carefully as if he were about to engage in a skirmish, feeling quite sure that she would be caught.

The table, which had been cleared immediately, now served as a bed on which to lay Fifi out, and the four officers made for the window, rigid and sobered, with the stern faces of soldiers on duty, and tried to pierce through the darkness of the night, amid the steady torrent of rain. Suddenly, a shot was heard, and then another, a long way off; and for four hours they heard, from time to time, near or distant reports and rallying cries, strange words uttered as a call, in guttural voices.

In the morning they all returned. Two soldiers had been killed and three others wounded by their comrades in the ardor of that chase, and in the confusion of such a nocturnal pursuit, but they had not caught Rachel.

Then the inhabitants of the district were terrorized, the houses were turned topsy-turvy, the country was scoured and beaten up, over and over again, but the Jewess did not seem to have left a single trace of her passage behind her.

When the general was told of it, he gave orders to hush up the affair, so as not to set a bad example to the army, but he severely censured the commandant, who in turn punished his inferiors. The general had said: "One does not go to war in order to amuse oneself, and to caress prostitutes." And Graf von Farlsberg, in his exasperation, made up his mind to have his revenge on the district, but as he required a pretext for showing severity, he sent for the priest, and ordered him to have the bell tolled at the funeral of Count von Eyrick.

Contrary to all expectation, the priest showed himself humble and most respectful, and when Mademoiselle Fifi's body left the Château d'Urville on its way to the cemetery, carried by soldiers, preceded, surrounded, and followed by soldiers, who marched with loaded rifles, for the first time the bell sounded its funereal knell in a lively manner, as if a friendly hand were caressing it. At night it sounded again, and the next day, and every day; it rang as much as anyone could desire. Sometimes even, it would start at night, and sound gently through the darkness, seized by strange joy, awakened, one could not tell why. All the peasants in the neighborhood declared that it was bewitched, and nobody, except the priest and the sacristan would now go near the church tower, and they went because a poor girl was living there in grief and solitude, secretly nourished by those two men.

She remained there until the German troops departed, and then one evening the priest borrowed the baker's cart, and himself drove his prisoner to Rouen. When they got there, he embraced her, and she quickly went back on foot to the establishment from which she had come, where the proprietress, who thought that she was dead, was very glad to see her.

A short time afterward, a patriot who had no prejudices, who liked her because of her bold deed, and who afterward loved her for herself, married her, and made a lady of her.

USELESS BEAUTY

A very elegant victoria, with two beautiful black horses, was drawn up in front of the mansion. It was a day in the latter end of June, about half past five in the afternoon, and the sun shone warm and bright into the large court-yard.

The Countess de Mascaret came down just as her husband, who was coming home, appeared in the carriage entrance. He stopped for a few moments to look at his wife and grew rather pale. She was very beautiful, graceful, and distinguished looking, with her long oval face, her complexion like gilt ivory, her large gray eyes, and her black hair; and she got into her carriage without looking at him, without even seeming to have noticed him, with such a particularly high-bred air, that the furious jealousy by which he had been devoured for so long again gnawed at his heart. He went up to her and said: "You are going for a drive?"

She merely replied disdainfully: "You see I am!"

"In the Bois de Boulogne?"

"Most probably."

"May I come with you?"

"The carriage belongs to you."

Without being surprised at the tone of voice in which she answered him, he got in and sat down by his wife's side, and said: "Bois de Boulogne." The footman jumped up by the coachman's side, and the horses as usual pawed the ground and shook their heads until they were in the street. Husband and wife sat side by side, without speaking. He was thinking how to begin a conversation, but she maintained such an obstinately hard look, that he did not venture to make the attempt. At last, however, he cunningly, accidentally as it were, touched the Countess's gloved hand with his own, but she drew her arm away, with a movement which was so expressive of disgust, that he remained thoughtful, in spite of his usual authoritative and despotic character. "Gabrielle!" said he at last.

"What do you want?"

"I think you are looking adorable."

She did not reply, but remained lying back in the carriage, looking like an irritated queen. By that time they were driving up the Champs-Elysées, toward the Arc de Triomphe. That immense monument, at the end of the long avenue, raised its colossal arch against the red sky, and the sun seemed to be sinking on to it, showering fiery dust on it from the sky.

The stream of carriages, with the sun reflecting from the bright, plated harness and the shining lamps, were like a double current flowing, one toward the town and one toward the wood, and the Count de Mascaret continued: "My dear Gabrielle!"

Then, unable to bear it any longer, she replied in an exasperated voice: "Oh! do leave me in peace, pray! I am not even at liberty to have my carriage to myself, now." He, however, pretended not to hear her, and continued: "You have never looked so pretty as you do to-day."

Her patience was decidedly at an end, and she replied with irrepressible anger: "You are wrong to notice it, for I swear to you that I will never have anything to do with you in that way again." He was stupefied and agitated, and his violent nature gaining the upper hand, he exclaimed: "What do you mean by that?" in such a manner as revealed rather the brutal master than the amorous man. But she replied in a low voice, so that the servants might not hear, amid the deafening noise of the wheels:

"Ah! What do I mean by that? What do I mean by that? Now I recognize you again! Do you want me to tell everything?"

"Yes."

"Everything that has been on my heart, since I have been the victim of your terrible selfishness?"

He had grown red with surprise and anger, and he growled between his closed teeth: "Yes, tell me everything."

He was a tall, broad-shouldered man, with a big, red beard, a handsome man, a nobleman, a man of the world, who passed as a perfect husband and an excellent father, and now for the first time since they had started she turned toward him, and looked him full in the face: "Ah! You will hear some disagreeable things, but you must know that I am prepared for everything, that I fear nothing, and you less than anyone, to-day."

He also was looking into her eyes, and already was shaking with passion; then he said in a low voice: "You are mad."

"No, but I will no longer be the victim of the hateful penalty of maternity, which you have inflicted on me for eleven years! I wish to live like a woman of the world, as I have the right to do, as all women have the right to do."

He suddenly grew pale again, and stammered: "I do not understand you."

"Oh! yes; you understand me well enough. It is now three months since I had my last child, and as I am still very beautiful, and as, in spite of all your efforts you cannot spoil my figure, as you just now perceived, when you saw me on the outside flight of steps, you think it is time that I should become *enceinte* again."

"But you are talking nonsense!"

"No, I am not; I am thirty, and I have had seven children, and we have been married eleven years, and you hope that this will go on for ten years longer, after which you will leave off being jealous."

He seized her arm and squeezed it, saying: "I will not allow you to talk to me like that, for long."

"And I shall talk to you till the end, until I have finished all I have to say to you, and if you try to prevent me, I shall raise my voice so that the two servants, who are on the box, may hear. I only allowed you to come with me for that object, for I have these witnesses, who will oblige you to listen to me, and to contain yourself; so now, pay attention to what I say. I have always felt an antipathy for you, and I have always let you see it, for I have never lied, Monsieur. You married me in spite of myself; you forced my parents, who were in embarrassed circumstances, to give

me to you, because you were rich, and they obliged me
to marry you, in spite of my tears.

"So you bought me, and as soon as I was in your power,
as soon as I had become your companion, ready to attach
myself to you, to forget your coercive and threatening
proceedings, in order that I might only remember that I
ought to be a devoted wife and to love you as much as it
might be possible for me to love you, you became jealous—
you—as no man has ever been before, with the base, ignoble jealousy of a spy, which was as degrading for you as
it was for me. I had not been married eight months, when
you suspected me of every perfidiousness, and you even
told me so. What a disgrace! And as you could not prevent
me from being beautiful, and from pleasing people, from
being called in drawing-rooms, and also in the newspapers,
one of the most beautiful women in Paris, you tried everything you could think of to keep admirers from me, and
you hit upon the abominable idea of making me spend
my life in a constant state of motherhood, until the time
when I should disgust every man. Oh! do not deny it! I did
not understand it for some time, but then I guessed it. You
even boasted about it to your sister, who told me of it, for
she is fond of me and was disgusted at your boorish coarse-
ness.

"Ah! Remember our struggles, doors smashed in, and
locks forced! For eleven years you have condemned me
to the existence of a brood mare. Then as soon as I was pregnant, you grew disgusted with me, and I saw nothing of
you for months, and I was sent into the country, to the family mansion, among fields and meadows, to bring forth
my child. And when I reappeared, fresh, pretty, and inde-
structible, still seductive and constantly surrounded by
admirers, hoping that at last I should live a little like a
young rich woman who belongs to society, you were seized
by jealousy again, and you recommenced to persecute me
with that infamous and hateful desire from which you
are suffering at this moment, by my side. And it is not the
desire of possessing me—for I should never have refused
myself to you—but it is the wish to make me unsightly.

"Beside this, that abominable and mysterious circum-

stance took place, which I was a long time in penetrating
(but I grew acute by dint of watching your thoughts and
actions). You attached yourself to your children with all
the security which they gave you while I bore them in my
womb. You felt affection for them, with all your aversion
for me, and in spite of your ignoble fears, which were
momentarily allayed by your pleasure in seeing me a mother.

"Oh! how often have I noticed that joy in you! I have
seen it in your eyes and guessed it. You loved your children as victories, and not because they were of your own
blood. They were victories over me, over my youth, over
my beauty, over my charms, over the compliments which
were paid me, and over those who whispered round me,
without paying them to me. And you are proud of them,
you make a parade of them, you take them out for drives
in your coach in the Bois de Boulogne, and you give them
donkey rides at Montmorency. You take them to theatrical
matinées so that you may be seen in the midst of them, and
that people may say: 'What a kind father!' and that it may
be repeated."

He had seized her wrist with savage brutality, and
squeezed it so violently that she was quiet, though she
nearly cried out with the pain. Then he said to her in a
whisper:

"I love my children, do you hear? What you have just
told me is disgraceful in a mother. But you belong to me;
I am master—your master. I can exact from you what I
like and when I like—and I have the law on my side."

He was trying to crush her fingers in the strong grip of
his large, muscular hand, and she, livid with pain, tried in
vain to free them from that vise which was crushing them;
the agony made her pant, and the tears came into her eyes.
"You see that I am the master, and the stronger," he said.
And when he somewhat loosened his grip, she asked him:
"Do you think that I am a religious woman?"

He was surprised and stammered: "Yes."

"Do you think that I could lie, if I swore to the truth of
anything to you, before an altar on which Christ's body is?"

"No."

"Will you go with me to some church?"

"What for?"

"You shall see. Will you?"

"If you absolutely wish it, yes."

She raised her voice and said: "Philip!" And the coachman, bending down a little, without taking his eyes from his horses, seemed to turn his ear alone toward his mistress, who said: "Drive to St. Philip-du-Roule's." And the victoria, which had reached the entrance of the Bois de Boulogne, returned to Paris.

Husband and wife did not exchange a word during the drive. When the carriage stopped before the church, Madame de Mascaret jumped out, and entered it, followed by the Count, a few yards behind her. She went, without stopping, as far as the choir-screen, and falling on her knees at a chair, she buried her face in her hands. She prayed for a long time, and he, standing behind her, could see that she was crying. She wept noiselessly, like women do weep when they are in great and poignant grief. There was a kind of undulation in her body, which ended in a little sob, hidden and stifled by her fingers.

But Count de Mascaret thought that the situation was long drawn out, and he touched her on the shoulder. That contact recalled her to herself, as if she had been burned, and getting up, she looked straight into his eyes.

"This is what I have to say to you. I am afraid of nothing, whatever you may do to me. You may kill me if you like. One of your children is not yours, and one only; that I swear to you before God, who hears me here. That is the only revenge which was possible for me, in return for all your abominable male tyrannies, in return for the penal servitude of childbearing to which you have condemned me. Who was my lover? That you will never know! You may suspect everyone, but you will never find out. I gave myself up to him, without love and without pleasure, only for the sake of betraying you, and he made me a mother. Which is his child? That also you will never know. I have seven: try and find out! I intended to tell you this later, for one cannot completely avenge oneself on a man by deceiving him, unless he knows it. You have driven me to confess it to-day; now I have finished."

She hurried through the church, toward the open door, expecting to hear behind her the quick steps of her husband whom she had defied, and to be knocked to the ground by a blow of his fist, but she heard nothing, and reached her carriage. She jumped into it at a bound, overwhelmed with anguish, and breathless with fear; she called out to the coachman, "Home!" and the horses set off at a quick trot.

II.

The Countess de Mascaret was waiting in her room for dinner time, like a criminal sentenced to death awaits the hour of his execution. What was he going to do? Had he come home? Despotic, passionate, ready for any violence as he was, what was he meditating, what had he made up his mind to do? There was no sound in the house, and every moment she looked at the clock. Her maid had come and dressed her for the evening, and had then left the room again. Eight o'clock struck; almost at the same moment there were two knocks at the door, and the butler came in and told her that dinner was ready.

"Has the Count come in?"

"Yes, Madame la Comtesse; he is in the dining-room."

For a moment she felt inclined to arm herself with a small revolver, which she had bought some weeks before, foreseeing the tragedy which was being rehearsed in her heart. But she remembered that all the children would be there, and she took nothing except a smelling-bottle. He rose somewhat ceremoniously from his chair. They exchanged a slight bow, and sat down. The three boys, with their tutor, Abbé Martin, were on her right, and the three girls, with Miss Smith, their English governess, were on her left. The youngest child, who was only three months old, remained upstairs with his nurse.

The Abbé said grace, as was usual when there was no company, for the children did not come down to dinner when there were guests present; then they began dinner. The Countess, suffering from emotion which she had not at all calculated upon, remained with her eyes cast down, while the Count scrutinized, now the three boys, and now the three girls with uncertain, unhappy looks, which traveled from one to the other. Suddenly, pushing his wineglass from him, it broke, and the wine was spilt on the tablecloth, and at the slight noise caused by this little accident, the Countess started up from her chair, and for the first time they looked at each other. Then, almost every moment, in spite of themselves, in spite of the irritation of their nerves caused by every glance, they did not cease to exchange looks, rapid as pistol shots.

The Abbé, who felt that there was some cause for embarrassment which he could not divine, tried to get up a conversation, and started various subjects, but his useless efforts gave rise to no ideas and did not bring out a word. The Countess, with feminine tact and obeying the instincts of a woman of the world, tried to answer him two or three times, but in vain. She could not find words, in the perplexity of her mind, and her own voice almost frightened her in the silence of the large room, where nothing else was heard except the slight sound of plates and knives and forks.

Suddenly, her husband said to her, bending forward: "Here, amid your children, will you swear to me that what you told me just now is true?"

The hatred which was fermenting in her veins suddenly roused her, and replying to that question with the same firmness with which she had replied to his looks, she raised both her hands, the right pointing toward the boys and the left toward the girls, and said in a firm, resolute voice, and without any hesitation: "On the heads of my children, I swear that I have told you the truth."

He got up and throwing his table napkin on to the table with an exasperated movement, turned round and flung his chair against the wall. Then he went out without another word, while she, uttering a deep sigh, as if after a first victory, went on in a calm voice: "You must not pay any attention to what your father has just said, my darlings; he was very much upset a short time ago, but he will be all right again, in a few days."

Then she talked with the Abbé and with Miss Smith, and had tender, pretty words for all her children; those sweet spoiling mother's ways which unlock little hearts.

When dinner was over, she went into the drawing-room with all her little following. She made the elder ones chatter, and when their bedtime came she kissed them for a long time, and then went alone into her room.

She waited, for she had no doubt that he would come, and she made up her mind then, as her children were not with her, to defend her human flesh, as she defended her life as a woman of the world; and in the pocket of her dress she put the little loaded revolver which she had bought a few weeks before. The hours went by, the hours struck, and every sound was hushed in the house. Only cabs continued to rumble through the streets, but their noise was only heard vaguely through the shuttered and curtained windows.

She waited, energetic, and nervous, without any fear of him now, ready for anything, and almost triumphant, for she had found means of torturing him continually, during every moment of his life.

But the first gleams of dawn came in through the fringe at the bottom of her curtains, without his having come into her room, and then she awoke to the fact, much to her surprise, that he was not coming. Having locked and bolted her door, for greater security, she went to bed at last, and remained there, with her eyes open, thinking, and barely understanding it all, without being able to guess what he was going to do.

When her maid brought her tea, she at the same time gave her a letter from her husband. He told her that he was going to undertake a longish journey, and in a postscript he added that his lawyer would provide her with such money as she might require for her expenses.

III.

It was at the opera, between two of the acts in "Robert the Devil." In the stalls, the men were standing up, with their hats on, their waistcoats cut very low so as to show a large amount of white shirt front, in which the gold and precious stones of their studs glistened. They were looking at the boxes crowded with ladies in low dresses, covered with diamonds and pearls, women who seemed to expand like flowers in that illuminated hothouse, where the beauty of their faces and the whiteness of their shoulders seemed to bloom for inspection, in the midst of the music and of human voices.

Two friends, with their backs to the orchestra, were scanning those parterres of elegance, that exhibition of real or false charms, of jewels, of luxury, and of pretension which showed itself off all round the Grand Theater. One of them, Roger de Salnis, said to his companion, Bernard Grandin: "Just look how beautiful Countess de Mascaret still is."

Then the elder, in turn, looked through his opera glasses at a tall lady in a box opposite, who appeared to be still very young, and whose striking beauty seemed to appeal to men's eyes in every corner of the house. Her pale complexion, of an ivory tint, gave her the appearance of a statue, while a small, diamond coronet glistened on her black hair like a cluster of stars.

When he had looked at her for some time, Bernard Grandin replied with a jocular accent of sincere conviction: "You may well call her beautiful!"

"How old do you think she is?"

"Wait a moment. I can tell you exactly, for I have known her since she was a child, and I saw her make her *début* into society when she was quite a girl. She is—she is—thirty—thirty-six."

"Impossible!"

"I am sure of it."

"She looks twenty-five."

"She has had seven children."

"It is incredible."

"And what is more, they are all seven alive, as she is a very good mother. I go to the house, which is a very quiet and pleasant one, occasionally, and she presents the phenomenon of the family in the midst of the world."

"How very strange! And have there never been any reports about her?"

"Never."

"But what about her husband? He is peculiar, is he not?"

"Yes and no. Very likely there has been a little drama between them, one of those little domestic dramas which one suspects, which one never finds out exactly, but which one guesses pretty nearly."

"What is it?"

"I do not know anything about it. Mascaret leads a very fast life now, after having been a model husband. As long as he remained a good spouse, he had a shocking temper and was crabbed and easily took offense, but since he has been leading his present, rackety life, he has become quite indifferent; but one would guess that he has some trouble, a worm gnawing somewhere, for he has aged very much."

Thereupon the two friends talked philosophically for some minutes about the seecret, unknowable troubles, which differences of character or perhaps physical antipathies, which were not perceived at first, give rise to in families. Then Roger de Salnis, who was still looking at Madame de Mascaret through his opera-glasses, said:

"It is almost incredible that that woman has had seven children!"

"Yes, in eleven years; after which, when she was thirty, she put a stop to her period of production in order to enter into the brilliant period of entertaining, which does not seem near coming to an end."

"Poor women!"

"Why do you pity them?"

"Why? Ah! my dear fellow, just consider! Eleven years of maternity, for such a woman! What a hell! All her youth, all her beauty, every hope of success, every poetical ideal of a bright life, sacrificed to that abominable law of reproduction which turns the normal woman into a mere machine for maternity."

"What would you have? It is only Nature!"

"Yes, but I say that Nature is our enemy, that we must always fight against Nature, for she is continually bringing us back to an animal state. You may be sure that God has not put anything on this earth that is clean, pretty, elegant, or accessory to our ideal, but the human brain has done it. It is we who have introduced a little grace, beauty, unknown charm, and mystery into creation by singing about it, interpreting it, by admiring it as poets, idealizing it as artists, and by explaining it as learned men who make mistakes, who find ingenious reasons, some grace and beauty, some unknown charm and mystery in the various phenomena of Nature.

"God only created coarse beings, full of the germs of disease, and who, after a few years of bestial enjoyment, grow old and infirm, with all the ugliness and all the want of power of human decrepitude. He only seems to have made them in order that they may reproduce their species in a repulsive manner, and then die like ephemeral insects. I said, *reproduce their species in a repulsive manner,* and I adhere to that expression. What is there as a matter of fact, more ignoble and more repugnant than that ridiculous act of the reproduction of living beings, against which all delicate minds always have revolted, and always will revolt? Since all the organs which have been invented by this economical and malicious Creator serve two purposes, why did he not choose those that were unsullied, in order to intrust them with that sacred mission, which is the noblest and the most exalted of all human functions? The mouth which nourishes the body by means of material food, also diffuses abroad speech and thought. Our flesh revives itself by means of itself, and at the same time, ideas are communicated by it. The sense of smell, which gives the vital air to the lungs, imparts all the perfumes of the world to the brain: the smell of flowers, of woods, of trees, of the sea. The ear, which enables us to communicate with our fellowmen, has also allowed us to invent music, to create dreams, happiness, the infinite, and even physical pleasure, by means of sounds!

"But one might say that the Creator wished to prohibit man from ever ennobling and idealizing his commerce with women. Nevertheless, man has found love, which is not a bad reply to that sly Deity, and he has ornamented it so much with literary poetry, that woman often forgets the contact she is obliged to submit to. Those among us who are powerless to deceive themselves have invented vice and

refined debauchery, which is another way of laughing at
God, and of paying homage, immodest homage, to beauty.

"But the normal man makes children; just a beast that
is coupled with another by law.

"Look at that woman! Is it not abominable to think that
such a jewel, such a pearl, born to be beautiful, admired,
fêted, and adored, has spent eleven years of her life in pro-
viding heirs for the Count de Mascaret?"

Bernard Grandin replied with a laugh: "There is a great
deal of truth in all that, but very few people would understand you."

Salnis got more and more animated. "Do you know how
I picture God myself?" he said. "As an enormous, creative
organ unknown to us, who scatters millions of worlds into
space, just as one single fish would deposit its spawn in the
sea. He creates, because it is His function as God to do so,
but He does not know what He is doing, and is stupidly
prolific in His work, and is ignorant of the combinations of
all kinds which are produced by His scattered germs. Human thought is a lucky little local, passing accident, which
was totally unforeseen, and is condemned to disappear
with this earth, and to recommence perhaps here or else-
where, the same or different, with fresh combinations of
eternally new beginnings. We owe it to this slight accident
which has happened to His intellect, that we are very uncomfortable in this world which was not made for us, which
had not been prepared to recieve us, to lodge and feed us,
or to satisfy reflecting beings, and we owe it to Him also
that we have to struggle without ceasing against what are
still called the designs of Providence, when we are really
refined and civilized beings."

Grandin, who was listening to him attentively, as he had
long known the surprising outbursts of his fancy, asked
him: "Then you believe that human thought is the spontaneous product of blind, divine parturition?"

"Naturally. A fortuitous function of the nerve-centers of
our brain, like some unforeseen chemical action which is
due to new mixtures, and which also resembles a product of
electricity, caused by friction or the unexpected proximity
of some substance, and which, lastly, resembles the phe-

nomena caused by the infinite and fruitful fermentations
of living matter.

"But, my dear fellow, the truth of this must be evident
to anyone who looks about him. If human thought, ordained
by an omniscient Creator, had been intended to be what it
has become, altogether different from mechanical thoughts
and resignation, so exacting, inquiring, agitated, tormented,
would the world which was created to receive the beings
which we now are have been this unpleasant little dwelling
place for poor fools, this salad plot, this rocky, wooded, and
spherical kitchen garden where your improvident Providence
has destined us to live naked, in caves or under trees, nourished on the flesh of slaughtered animals, our brethren, or
on raw vegetables nourished by the sun and the rain?

"But it is sufficient to reflect for a moment, in order to
understand that this world was not made for such creatures
as we are. Thought, which is developed by a miracle in
the nerves of the cells and our brain, powerless, ignorant,
and confused as it is, and as it will always remain, makes
all of us who are intellectual beings eternal and wretched
exiles on earth.

"Look at this earth, as God has given it to those who in-
habit it. Is it not visibly and solely made, planted and covered with forests, for the sake of animals? What is there for
us? Nothing. And for them? Everything. They have nothing
to do but to eat, or go hunting and eat each other, according to their instincts, for God never foresaw gentleness and
peaceable manners; He only foresaw the death of creatures which were bent on destroying and devouring each
other. Are not the quail, the pigeon, and the partridge the
natural prey of the hawk? the sheep, the stag, and the ox
that of the great flesh-eating animals, rather than meat that
has been fattened to be served up to us with truffles, which
have been unearthed by pigs, for our special benefit?

"As to ourselves, the more civilized, intellectual, and refined we are, the more we ought to conquer and subdue
that animal instinct, which represents the will of God in us.
And so, in order to mitigate our lot as brutes, we have discovered and made everything, beginning with houses, then
exquisite food, sauces, sweetmeats, pastry, drink, stuffs,

clothes, ornaments, beds, mattresses, carriages, railways, and innumerable machines, besides arts and sciences, writing and poetry. Every ideal comes from us as well as the amenities of life, in order to make our existence as simple reproducers, for which divine Providence solely intended us, less monotonous and less hard.

"Look at this theater. Is there not here a human world created by us, unforeseen and unknown by Eternal destinies, comprehensible by our minds alone, a sensual and intellectual distraction, which has been invented solely by and for that discontented and restless little animal that we are.

"Look at that woman, Madame de Mascaret. God intended her to live in a cave naked, or wrapped up in the skins of wild animals, but is she not better as she is? But, speaking of her, does anyone know why and how her brute of a husband, having such a companion by his side, and especially after having been boorish enough to make her a mother seven times, has suddenly left her, to run after bad women?"

Grandin replied: "Oh! my dear fellow, this is probably the only reason. He found that always living with her was becoming too expensive in the end, and from reasons of domestic economy, he has arrived at the same principles which you lay down as a philosopher."

Just then the curtain rose for the third act, and they turned round, took off their hats, and sat down.

IV.

The Count and Countess Mascaret were sitting side by side in the carriage which was taking them home from the opera, without speaking. But suddenly the husband said to his wife: "Gabrielle!"

"What do you want?"

"Don't you think that this has lasted long enough?"

"What?"

"The horrible punishment to which you have condemned me for the last six years."

"What do you want? I cannot help it."

"Then tell me which of them it is?"

"Never."

"Think that I can no longer see my children or feel them round me, without having my heart burdened with this doubt. Tell me which of them it is, and I swear that I will forgive you, and treat it like the others."

"I have not the right to."

"You do not see that I can no longer endure this life, this thought which is wearing me out, or this question which I am constantly asking myself, this question which tortures me each time I look at them. It is driving me mad."

"Then you have suffered a great deal?" she said.

"Terribly. Should I, without that, have accepted the horror of living by your side, and the still greater horror of feeling and knowing that there is one among them whom I cannot recognize, and who prevents me from loving the others?"

She repeated: "Then you have really suffered very much?" And he replied in a constrained and sorrowful voice:

"Yes, for do I not tell you every day that it is intolerable torture to me? Should I have remained in that house, near you and them, if I did not love them. Oh! You have behaved abominably toward me. All the affection of my heart I have bestowed upon my children, and that you know. I am for them a father of the olden time, as I was for you a husband of one of the families of old, for by instinct I have remained a natural man, a man of former days. Yes, I will confess it, you have made me terribly jealous, because you are a woman of another race, of another soul, with other requirements. Oh! I shall never forget the things that you told me, but from that day, I troubled myself no more about you. I did not kill you, because then I should have had no means on earth of ever discovering which of our—of your children is not mine. I have waited, but I have suffered more than you would believe, for I can no longer venture to love them, except, perhaps, the two eldest; I no longer venture to look at them, to call them to me, to kiss them; I cannot take them on to my knee without asking myself: 'Can it be this one?' I have been correct in my behavior toward you for six years, and even kind and complaisant; tell me the truth, and I swear that I will do nothing unkind."

He thought, in spite of the darkness of the carriage, that he could perceive that she was moved, and feeling certain that she was going to speak at last, he said: "I beg you, I beseech you to tell me."

"I have been more guilty than you think perhaps," she replied; "but I could no longer endure that life of continual pregnancy, and I had only one means of driving you from my bed. I lied before God, and I lied, with my hand raised to my children's heads, for I have never wronged you."

He seized her arm in the darkness, and squeezing it as he had done on that terrible day of their drive in the Bois de Boulogne, he stammered: "Is that true?"

"It is true."

But he in terrible grief said with a groan: "I shall have fresh doubts that will never end! When did you lie, the last time or now? How am I to believe you at present? How can one believe a woman after that? I shall never again know what I am to think. I would rather you had said to me: 'It is Jacques, or, it is Jeanne.'"

The carriage drove them into the courtyard of their mansion, and when it had drawn up in front of the steps, the Count got down first as usual, and offered his wife his arm, to help her up. And then, as soon as they had reached the first floor he said: "May I speak to you for a few moments longer?"

And she replied: "I am quite willing."

They went into a small drawing-room, while a footman in some surprise, lit the wax candles. As soon as he had left the room and they were alone, he continued: "How am I to know the truth? I have begged you a thousand times to speak, but you have remained dumb, impenetrable, inflexible, inexorable, and now to-day, you tell me that you have been lying. For six years you have actually allowed me to believe such a thing! No, you are lying now, I do not know why, but out of pity for me, perhaps?"

She replied in a sincere and convincing manner: "If I

had not done so, I should have had four more children in the last six years!"

And he exclaimed: "Can a mother speak like that?"

"Oh!" she replied, "I do not at all feel that I am the mother of children who have never been born, it is enough for me to be the mother of those that I have, and to love them with all my heart. I am—we are—women who belong to the civilized world, Monsieur, and we are no longer, and we refuse to be, mere females who restock the earth."

She got up, but he seized her hands. "Only one word, Gabrielle. Tell me the truth!"

"I have just told you. I have never dishonored you."

He looked her full in the face, and how beautiful she was, with her gray eyes, like the cold sky. In her dark hair dress, on that opaque night of black hair, there shone the diamond coronet, like a cluster of stars. Then he suddenly felt, felt by a kind of intuition, that this grand creature was not merely a being destined to perpetuate his race, but the strange and mysterious product of all the complicated desires which have been accumulating in us for centuries but which have been turned aside from their primitive and divine object, and which have wandered after a mystic, imperfectly seen, and intangible beauty. There are some women like that, women who blossom only for our dreams, adorned with every poetical attribute of civilization, with that ideal luxury, coquetry, and æsthetic charm which should surround the living statue who brightens our life.

Her husband remained standing before her, stupefied at the tardy and obscure discovery, confusedly hitting on the cause of his former jealousy, and understanding it all very imperfectly. At last he said: "I believe you, for I feel at this moment that you are not lying, and formerly, I really thought that you were."

She put out her hand to him: "We are friends then?"

He took her hand and kissed it, and replied: "We are friends. Thank you, Gabrielle."

Then he went out, still looking at her, and surprised that she was still so beautiful, and feeling a strange emotion arising in him, which was, perhaps, more formidable than antique and simple love.

THAT PIG OF A MORIN

"There, my friend," I said to Labarbe, "you have just repeated those five words, 'That pig of a Morin.' Why on earth do I never hear Morin's name mentioned without his being called a *pig?*"

Labarbe, who is a Deputy, looked at me with eyes like an owl's, and said: "Do you mean to say that you do not know Morin's story, and yet come from La Rochelle?" I was obliged to declare that I did not know Morin's story, and then Labarbe rubbed his hands, and began his recital.

"You knew Morin, did you not, and you remember his large linen-draper's shop on the Quai de la Rochelle?"

"Yes, perfectly."

"All right, then. You must know that in 1862 or '63 Morin went to spend a fortnight in Paris for pleasure, or for his pleasures, but under the pretext of renewing his stock, and you also know what a fortnight in Paris means for a country shopkeeper; it makes his blood grow hot. The theater every evening, women's dresses rustling up against you, and continual excitement; one goes almost mad with it. One sees nothing but dancers in tights, actresses in very low dresses, round legs, fat shoulders, all nearly within reach of one's hands, without daring or being able to touch, and one scarcely ever tastes an inferior dish. And one leaves it, with heart still all in a flutter, and a mind still exhilarated by a sort of longing for kisses which tickle one's lips.

"Morin was in that state when he took his ticket for La Rochelle by the 8:40 night express. And he was walking up and down the waiting-room at the station, when he stopped suddenly in front of a young lady who was kissing an old one. She had her veil up, and Morin murmured with delight: 'By Jove, what a pretty woman!'

144

"When she had said 'Good-bye' to the old lady, she went into the waiting-room, and Morin followed her; then she went on to the platform and Morin still followed her; then she got into an empty carriage, and he again followed her. There were very few travelers by the express, the engine whistled, and the train started. They were alone. Morin devoured her with his eyes. She appeared to be about nineteen or twenty, and was fair, tall, and with demure looks. She wrapped a railway rug round her legs and stretched herself on the seat to sleep.

"Morin asked himself: 'I wonder who she is?' And a thousand conjectures, a thousand projects went through his head. He said to himself: 'So many adventures are told as happening on railway journeys, that this may be one that is going to present itself to me. Who knows? A piece of good luck like that happens very quickly, and perhaps I need only be a little venturesome. Was it not Danton who said: "Audacity, more audacity, and always audacity." If it was not Danton it was Mirabeau, but that does not matter. But then, I have no audacity, and that is the difficulty. Oh! If one only knew, if one could only read people's minds! I will bet that every day one passes by magnificent opportunities without knowing it, though a gesture would be enough to let me know that she did not ask for anything better.

"Then he imagined to himself combinations which led him to triumph. He pictured some chivalrous deed, or merely some slight service which he rendered her, a lively, gallant conversation which ended in a declaration, which ended in—in what you think.

"But he could find no opening; had no pretext, and he waited for some fortunate circumstance, with his heart ravaged, and his mind topsy-turvy. The night passed, and the pretty girl still slept, while Morin was meditating his own fall. The day broke and soon the first ray of sunlight appeared in the sky, a long, clear ray which shone on the face of the sleeping girl, and woke her, so she sat up, looked at the country, then at Morin and smiled. She smiled like a happy woman, with an engaging and bright look, and Morin trembled. Certainly that smile was intended for him, it was a discreet invitation, the signal which he was waiting for. That smile meant to say: 'How stupid, what a ninny, what a dolt, what a donkey you are, to have sat there on your seat like a post all night.

" 'Just look at me, am I not charming? And you have sat like that for the whole night, when you have been alone with a pretty woman, you great simpleton!'

"She was still smiling as she looked at him, she even began to laugh; and he lost his head trying to find something suitable to say, no matter what. But he could think of nothing, nothing, and then, seized with a coward's courage, he said to himself: 'So much the worse, I will risk everything,' and suddenly, without the slightest warning, he went toward her, his arms extended, his lips protruding and seizing her in his arms kissed her.

"She sprang up with a bound, crying out: 'Help! help!' and screaming with terror; then she opened the carriage door, and waved her arm outside; then mad with terror she was trying to jump out, while Morin, who was almost distracted, and feeling sure that she would throw herself out, held her by her skirt and stammered: 'Oh! Madame! Oh! Madame!'

"The train slackened speed, and then stopped. Two guards rushed up at the young woman's frantic signals, and she threw herself into their arms, stammering: 'That man wanted—wanted—to—to—' And then she fainted.

"They were at Mauzé station, and the gendarme on duty arrested Morin. When the victim of his brutality had regained her consciousness, she made her charge against him, and the police drew it up. The poor linen-draper did not reach home till night, with a prosecution hanging over him for an outrage on morals in a public place.

II.

"At that time I was editor of the 'Fanal des Charentes,' and I used to meet Morin every day at the Café du Commerce. The day after his adventure he came to see me, as he did not know what to do. I did not hide my opinion from him, but said to him: 'You are no better than a pig. No decent man behaves like that.'

"He cried. His wife had given him a beating, and he foresaw his trade ruined, his name dragged through the mire and dishonored, his friends outraged and taking no more notice of him. In the end he excited my pity, and I sent for my colleague Rivet, a bantering, but very sensible little man, to give us his advice.

"He advised me to see the Public Prosecutor, who was a friend of mine, and so I sent Morin home, and went to call on the magistrate. He told me that the woman who had been insulted was a young lady, Mademoiselle Henriette Bonnel, who had just received her certificate as governess in Paris, and·spent her holidays with her uncle and aunt, who were very respectable tradespeople in Mauzé, and what made Morin's case all the more serious was, that the uncle had lodged a complaint. But the public official had consented to let the matter drop if this complaint were withdrawn, so that we must try and get him to do this.

"I went back to Morin's and found him in bed, ill with excitement and distress. His wife, a tall, rawboned woman with a beard, was abusing him continually, and she showed me into the room, shouting at me: 'So you have come to see that pig of a Morin. Well, there he is, the darling!' And she planted herself in front of the bed, with her hands on her hips. I told him how matters stood, and he begged me to go and see her uncle and aunt. It was a delicate mission, but I undertook it, and the poor devil never ceased repeating: 'I assure you I did not even kiss her, no, not even that. I will take my oath to it!'

"I replied: 'It is all the same; you are nothing but a pig.' And I took a thousand francs which he gave me, to employ them as I thought best, but as I did not care venturning to her uncle's house alone, I begged Rivet to go with me, which he agreed to do, on the condition that we went immediately, for he had some urgent business at La Rochelle that afternoon. So two hours later we rang at the door of a nice country house. A pretty girl came and opened the door to us, who was assuredly the young lady in question, and I said to Rivet in a low voice: 'Confound it! I begin to understand Morin!'

"The uncle, Monsieur Tonnelet, subscribed to the 'Fanal,' and was a fervent political co-religionist of ours. He received us with open arms, and congratulated us and wished us joy; he was delighted at having the two editors in his house, and Rivet whispered to me: 'I think we shall be able to arrange the matter of that pig of a Morin for him.'

"The niece had left the room, and I introduced the delicate subject. I waved the specter of scandal before his eyes; I accentuated the inevitable depreciation which the young lady would suffer if such an affair got known, for nobody would believe in a simple kiss. The good man seemed undecided, but could not make up his mind about anything without his wife, who would not be in until late that evening. But suddenly he uttered an exclamation of triumph: 'Look here, I have an excellent idea. I will keep you here to dine and sleep, and when my wife comes home, I hope we shall be able to arrange matters.'

"Rivet resisted at first, but the wish to extricate that pig of a Morin decided him, and we accepted the invitation. So the uncle got up radiant, called his niece, and proposed that we should take a stroll in his grounds, saying: 'We will leave serious matters until the morning.' Rivet and he began to talk politics, while I soon found myself lagging a little behind with the girl, who was really charming! charming! and with the greatest precaution I began to speak to her about her adventure, and try to make her my ally. She did not, however, appear the least confused, and listened to me like a person who was enjoying the whole thing very much.

"I said to her: 'Just think, Mademoiselle, how unpleasant it will be for you. You will have to appear in court, to encounter malicious looks, to speak before everybody, and to recount that unfortunate occurrence in the railway-carriage, in public. Do you not think, between ourselves, that it would have been much better for you to have put that dirty scoundrel back into his place without calling for assistance, and merely to have changed your carriage?' She began to laugh, and replied: 'What you say is quite true!

but what could I do? I was frightened, and when one is frightened, one does not stop to reason with oneself. As soon as I realized the situation, I was very sorry that I had called out, but then it was too late. You must also remember that the idiot threw himself upon me like a madman, without saying a word and looking like a lunatic. I did not even know what he wanted of me.'

"She looked me full in the face, without being nervous or intimidated, and I said to myself: 'She is a funny sort of girl, that: I can quite see how that pig Morin came to make a mistake,' and I went on, jokingly: 'Come, Mademoiselle, confess that he was excusable, for after all, a man cannot find himself opposite such a pretty girl as you are, without feeling a legitimate desire to kiss her.'

"She laughed more than ever, and showed her teeth, and said: 'Between the desire and the act, Monsieur, there is room for respect.' It was a funny expression to use, although it was not very clear, and I asked abruptly: 'Well now, supposing I were to kiss you now, what would you do?' She stopped to look at me from head to foot, and then said calmly: 'Oh! you? That is quite another matter.'

"I knew perfectly well, by Jove, that it was not the same thing at all, as everybody in the neighborhood called me 'Handsome Labarbe.' I was thirty years old in those days, but I asked her: 'And why, pray?'

"She shrugged her shoulders, and replied: 'Well, because you are not so stupid as he is.' And then she added, looking at me slyly: 'Nor so ugly, either.'

"Before she could make a movement to avoid me, I had implanted a hearty kiss on her cheek. She sprang aside, but it was too late, and then she said: 'Well, you are not very bashful, either! But don't do that sort of thing again.'

"I put on a humble look and said in a low voice: 'Oh! Mademoiselle, as for me, if I long for one thing more than another, it is to be summoned before a magistrate on the same charge as Morin.'

" 'Why?' she asked.

"Looking steadily at her, I replied: 'Because you are one of the most beautiful creatures living; because it would be an honor and a glory for me to have offered you violence, and because people would have said, after seeing you: "Well, Labarbe has richly deserved what he has got, but he is a lucky fellow, all the same." '

"She began to laugh heartily again, and said: 'How funny you are!' And she had not finished the word *funny*, before I had her in my arms and was kissing her ardently wherever I could find a place, on her forehead, on her eyes, on her lips occasionally, on her cheeks, in fact, all over her head, some part of which she was obliged to leave exposed, in spite of herself, in order to defend the others. At last she managed to release herself, blushing and angry. 'You are very unmannerly, Monsieur,' she said, 'and I am sorry I listened to you.'

"I took her hand in some confusion, and stammered out: 'I beg your pardon, Mademoiselle. I have offended you; I have acted like a brute! Do not be angry with me for what I have done. If you knew—'

"I vainly sought for some excuse, and in a few moments she said: 'There is nothing for me to know, Monsieur.' But I had found something to say, and I cried: 'Mademoiselle, I love you!'

"She was really surprised, and raised her eyes to look at me, and I went on: 'Yes, Mademoiselle, and pray listen to me. I do not know Morin, and I do not care anything about him. It does not matter to me the least if he is committed for trial and locked up meanwhile. I saw you here last year, and I was so taken with you, that the thought of you has never left me since, and it does not matter to me whether you believe me or not. I thought you adorable, and the remembrance of you took such a hold on me that I longed to see you again, and so I made use of that fool Morin as a pretext, and here I am. Circumstances have made me exceed the due limits of respect, and I can only beg you to pardon me.'

"She read the truth in my looks, and was ready to smile again; then she murmured: 'You humbug!' But I raised my hand, and said in a sincere voice (and I really believe that I was sincere): 'I swear to you that I am speaking the truth.' She replied quite simply: 'Really?'

"We were alone, quite alone, as Rivet and her uncle

had disappeared in a side walk, and I made her a real declaration of love, while I squeezed and kissed her hands, and
she listened to it as to something new and agreeable, without exactly knowing how much of it she was to believe,
while in the end I felt agitated, and at last really myself believed what I said. I was pale, anxious, and trembling, and
I gently put my arm round her waist, and spoke to her
softly, whispering into the little curls over her ears. She
seemed dead, so absorbed in thought was she.

"Then her hand touched mine, and she pressed it, and I
gently circled her waist with a trembling, and gradually a
firmer grasp. She did not move now, and I touched her
cheeks with my lips, and suddenly, without seeking them
mine met hers. It was a long, long kiss, and it would have
lasted longer still, if I had not heard a *Hum! Hum!* just behind me. She made her escape through the bushes, and I
turning round saw Rivet coming toward me, and walking in
the middle of the path. He said without even smiling: 'So
that is the way in which you settle the affair of that pig
Morin.'

"I replied, conceitedly: 'One does what one can, my dear
fellow. But what about the uncle? How have you got on
with him? I will answer for the niece.'

" 'I have not been so fortunate with him,' he replied.
Whereupon I took his arm, and we went indoors.

III.

"Dinner made me lose my head altogether. I sat beside
her, and my hand continually met hers under the tablecloth, my foot touched hers, and our looks encountered
each other.

"After dinner we took a walk by moonlight, and I whispered all the tender things I could think of to her. I held
her close to me, kissed her every moment, moistening my
lips against hers, while her uncle and Rivet were disputing
as they walked in front of us. We went in, and soon a messenger brought a telegram from her aunt, saying that she
would return by the first train the next morning, at seven
o'clock.

"'Very well, Henriette,' her uncle said, 'go and show the gentlemen their rooms.' She showed Rivet his first, and he whispered to me: 'There was no danger of her taking us into yours first.' Then she took me to my room, and as soon as she was alone with me, I took her in my arms again and tried to excite her senses and overcome her resistance, but when she felt that she was near succumbing, she escaped out of the room, and I got between the sheets, very much put out and excited and feeling rather foolish, for I knew that I should not sleep much. I was wondering how I could have committed such a mistake, when there was a gnetle knock at my door, and on my asking who was there, a low voice replied: 'I.'

"I dressed myself quickly and opened the door, and she came in: 'I forgot to ask you what you take in the morning,' she said, 'chocolate, tea, or coffee?' I put my arms around her impetuously and said, devouring her with kisses: 'I will take—I will take—' But she freed herself from my arms, blew out my candle, and disappeared, and left me alone in the dark, furious, trying to find some matches and not able to do so. At last I got some and I went into the passage, feeling half mad, with my candlestick in my hand.

"What was I going to do? I did not stop to reason, I only wanted to find her, and I would. I went a few steps without reflecting, but then I suddenly thought to myself: 'Suppose I should go into the uncle's room, what should I say?' And I stood still, with my head a void, and my heart beating.

"But in a few moments, I thought of an answer: 'Of course, I shall say that I was looking for Rivet's room, to speak to him about an important matter,' and I began to inspect all the doors, trying to find hers, and at last I took hold of a handle at a venture, turned it and went in. There was Henriette, sitting on her bed and looking at me in tears. So I gently turned the key, and going up to her on tiptoe, I said: 'I forgot to ask you for something to read, Mademoiselle.' I will not tell you the book I read, but it is the most wonderful of romances, the most divine of poems. And when once I had turned the first page, she let me turn over as many leaves as I liked, and I got through so many chapters that our candles were quite burned out.

"Then, after thanking her, I was stealthily returning to my room, when a rough hand seized me, and a voice—it was Rivet's—whispered in my ear: 'So you have not yet quite settled that affair of Morin's?'

"At seven o'clock the next morning, she herself brought me a cup of chocolate. I have never drunk anything like it, soft, velvety, perfumed, delicious. I could scarcely take away my lips from the cup, and she had hardly left the room when Rivet came in. He seemed nervous and irritable like a man who had not slept, and he said to me crossly: 'If you go on like this, you will end by spoiling the affair of that pig of a Morin!'

"At eight o'clock the aunt arrived. Our discussion was very short, for they withdrew their complaint, and I left five hundred francs for the poor of the town. They wanted to keep us for the day, and they arranged an excursion to go and see some ruins. Henriette made signs to me to stay, behind her uncle's back, and I accepted, but Rivet was determined to go, and though I took him aside, and begged and prayed him to do this for me he appeared quite exasperated and kept saying to me: 'I have had enough of that pig of a Morin's affair, do you hear?'

"Of course I was obliged to go also, and it was one of the hardest moments of my life. I could have gone on arranging that business as long as I lived, and when we were in the railway carriage, after shaking hands with her in silence, I said to Rivet: 'You are a mere brute!' And he replied: 'My dear fellow, you were beginning to excite me confoundedly.'

"On getting to the 'Fanal' office, I saw a crowd waiting for us, and as soon as they saw us, they all exclaimed: 'Well, have you settled the affair of that pig of a Morin?' All La Rochelle was excited about it, and Rivet, who had got over his ill humor on the journey, had great difficulty in keeping himself from laughing as he said: 'Yes, we have managed it, thanks to Labarbe.' And we went to Morin's.

"He was sitting in an easy-chair, with mustard plasters on his legs, and cold bandages on his head, nearly dead with misery. He was coughing with the short cough of a dying man, without anyone knowing how he had caught it, and his wife seemed like a tigress ready to eat him. As soon as he saw us he trembled violently as to make his hands and knees shake, so I said to him immediately: 'It is all settled, you dirty scamp, but don't do such a thing again.'

"He got up choking, took my hands and kissed them as if they had belonged to a prince, cried, nearly fainted, embraced Rivet, and even kissed Madame Morin, who gave him such a push as to send him staggering back into his chair. But he never got over the blow; his mind had been too much upset. In all the country round, moreover, he was called nothing but that pig of a Morin, and the epithet went through him like a sword-thrust every time he heard it. When a street-boy called after him: 'Pig!' he turned his head instinctively. His friends also overwhelmed him with horrible jokes and used to chaff him, whenever they were eating ham, by saying: 'It's a bit of you!' He died two years later.

"As for myself, when I was a candidate for the Chamber of Deputies in 1875, I called on the new notary at Foncerre, Monsieur Belloncle, to solicit his vote, and a tall, handsome, and evidently wealthy lady received me. 'You do not know me again?' she said.

"I stammered out: 'But—no, Madame.'

" 'Henriette Bonnel?'

" 'Ah!' And I felt myself turning pale, while she seemed perfectly at her ease, and looked at me with a smile.

"As soon as she had left me alone with her husband, he took both my hands, and squeezing them as if he meant to crush them, he said: 'I have been intending to go and see you for a long time, my dear sir, for my wife has very often talked to me about you. I know under what painful circumstances you made her acquaintance, and I know also how perfectly you behaved, how full of delicacy, tact, and devotion you showed yourself in the affair—' He hesitated, and then said in a lower tone, as if he had been saying something low and coarse: 'In the affair of that pig of a Morin.' "

THE SIGNAL

The little Marchioness de Rennedon was still asleep in her dark and perfumed bedroom.

In her soft, low bed, between sheets of delicate cambric, fine as lace and caressing as a kiss, she was sleeping alone and tranquil, the happy and profound sleep of divorced women.

She was awakened by loud voices in the little blue drawing-room, and she recognized her dear friend, the little Baroness de Grangerie, who was disputing with the lady's maid, because the latter would not allow her to go into the Marchioness's room. So the little Marchioness got up, opened the door, drew back the door-hangings and showed her head, nothing but her fair head, hidden under a cloud of hair.

"What is the matter with you, that you have come so early?" she asked. "It is not nine o'clock yet."

The little Baroness, who was very pale, nervous, and feverish, replied: "I must speak to you. Something horrible has happened to me."

"Come in, my dear."

She went in, they kissed each other and the little Marchioness got back into her bed, while the lady's maid opened the windows to let in light and air. Then when she had left the room, Madame de Rennedon went on: "Well, tell me what it is."

Madame de Grangerie began to cry, shedding those pretty bright tears which make women more charming. She sobbed out, without wiping her eyes, so as not to make them red: "Oh, my dear, what has happened to me is abominable, abominable. I have not slept all night, not a minute; do you hear, not a minute. Here, just feel my heart, how it is beating."

And taking her friend's hand, she put it on her breast, on that firm, round covering of women's hearts which often suffices men, and prevents them from seeking beneath. But her heart was really beating violently.

She continued: "It happened to me yesterday during the day, at about four o'clock—or half past four; I cannot say exactly. You know my apartments, and you know that my little drawing-room, where I always sit, looks on to the Rue Saint-Lazare, and that I have a mania for sitting at the window to look at the people passing. The neighborhood of the railway station is very gay; so full of motion and lively—just what I like! So, yesterday, I was sitting in the low chair which I have placed in my window recess; the window was open and I was not thinking of anything, simply breathing the fresh air. You remember how fine it was yesterday!

"Suddenly, I remarked a woman sitting at the window opposite—a woman in red. I was in mauve, you know, my pretty mauve costume. I did not know the woman, a new lodger, who had been there a month, and as it has been raining for a month, I had not yet seen her, but I saw immediately that she was a bad girl. At first I was very much shocked and disgusted that she should be at the window just as I was; and then by degrees, it amused me to watch her. She was resting her elbows on the window ledge, and looking at the men, and the men looked at her also, all or nearly all. One might have said that they knew of her presence by some means as they got near the house, that they scented her, as dogs scent game, for they suddenly raised their heads, and exchanged a swift look with her, a sort of freemason's look. Hers said: 'Will you?' Theirs replied: 'I have no time,' or else: 'Another day'; or else: 'I have not got a sou'; or else: 'Hide yourself, you wretch!'

"You cannot imagine how funny it was to see her carrying on such a piece of work, though after all it is her regular business.

"Occasionally she shut the window suddenly, and I saw a gentleman go in. She had caught him like a fisherman hooks a gudgeon. Then I looked at my watch, and I found that they never stopped longer than from twelve to twenty minutes. In the end she really infatuated me, the spider! And then the creature is so ugly.

"I asked myself: 'How does she manage to make herself understood so quickly, so well and so completely? Does she add a sign of the head or a motion of the hands to her looks?' And I took my opera-glasses to watch her proceedings. Oh! they were very simple: first of all a glance, then a smile, then a slight sign with the head which meant: 'Are you coming up?' But it was so slight, so vague, so discreet, that it required a great deal of knack to succeed as she did. And I asked myself: 'I wonder if I could do that little movement, from below upward, which was at the same time bold and pretty, as well as she does,' for her gesture was very pretty.

"I went and tried it before the looking-glass, and my dear, I did it better than she, a great deal better! I was enchanted, and resumed my place at the window.

"She caught nobody more then, poor girl, nobody. She certainly had no luck. It must really be very terrible to earn one's bread in that way, terrible and amusing occasionally, for really some of these men one meets in the street are rather nice.

"After that they all came on my side of the road and none on hers; the sun had turned. They came one after the other, young, old, dark, fair, gray, white. I saw some who looked very nice, really very nice, my dear, far better than my husband or than yours—I mean than your late husband, as you have got a divorce. Now you can choose.

"I said to myself: 'If I give them the sign, will they understand me, who am a respectable woman?' And I was seized with a mad longing to make that sign to them. I had a longing, a terrible longing; you know, one of those longings which one cannot resist! I have some like that occasionally. How silly such things are, don't you think so? I believe that we women have the souls of monkeys. I have been told (and it was a physician who told me) that the brain of a monkey is very like ours. Of course we must imitate some one or other. We imitate our husbands when we love them, during the first months after our marriage, and then our lovers, our female friends, our confessors when they are nice. We assume their ways of thought, their manners of speech, their words, their gestures, everything. It is very foolish.

"However, as for me, when I am much tempted to do a thing I always do it, and so I said to myself: 'I will try it once, on one man only, just to see. What can happen to me? Nothing whatever! We shall exchange a smile and that will be all and I shall deny it, most certainly.'

"So I began to make my choice, I wanted some one nice, very nice, and suddenly I saw a tall, fair, very good-looking fellow coming along. I like fair men, as you know. I looked at him, he looked at me; I smiled, he smiled, I made the movement, oh! so faintly; he replied *yes* with his head, and there he was, my dear! He came in at the large door of the house.

"You cannot imagine what passed through my mind then! I thought I should go mad. Oh! how frightened I was. Just think, he will speak to the servants! To Joseph, who is devoted to my husband! Joseph would certainly think that I had known that gentleman for a long time.

"What could I do, just tell me? And he would ring in a moment. What could I do, tell me? I thought I would go and meet him, and tell him he had made a mistake, and beg him to go away. He would have pity on a woman, on a poor woman: So I rushed to the door and opened it, just at the moment when he was going to ring the bell, and I stammered out, quite stupidly: 'Go away, Monsieur, go away; you have made a mistake, a terrible mistake; I took you for one of my friends whom you are very like. Have pity on me, Monsieur.'

"But he only began to laugh, my dear, and replied: 'Good morning, my dear, I know all about your little story, you may be sure. You are married, and so you want forty francs instead of twenty, and you shall have them, so just show the way.'

"And he pushed me in, closed the door, and as I remained standing before him, horror-struck, he kissed me, put his arm round my waist and made me go back into the drawing-room, the door of which had remained open. Then he began to look at everything like an auctioneer, and continued: 'By Jove, it is very nice in your rooms, very nice. You must be very down on your luck just now, to do the window business!'

"Then I began to beg him again: 'Oh! Monsieur, go away, please go away! My husband will be coming in soon, it is just his time. I swear that you have made a mistake!' But he answered quite coolly: 'Come, my beauty, I have had enough of this nonsense, and if your husband comes in, I will give him five francs to go and have a drink at the *café* opposite.' And then seeing Raoul's photograph on the chimneypiece, he asked me: 'Is that your—your husband?'

" 'Yes, that is he.'

" 'He looks like a nice, disagreeable sort of fellow. And who is this? One of your friends?'

"It was your photograph, my dear, you know, the one in ball dress. I did not know any longer what I was saying and I stammered: 'Yes, it is one of my friends.'

" 'She is very nice; you shall introduce me to her.'

"Just then the clock struck five, and Raoul comes home every day at half past! Suppose he were to come home before the other had gone, just fancy what would have happened! Then—then—I completely lost my head—altogether—I thought—I thought—that—that—the best thing would be—to get rid—of—of this man—as quickly as possible— The sooner it was over—you understand."

The little Marchioness de Rennedon had begun to laugh, to laugh madly, with her head buried in her pillow, so that the whole bed shook, and when she was a little calmer she asked:

"And—and—was he good-looking?"

"Yes."

"And yet you complain?"

"But—but—don't you see, my dear, he said—he said— he should come again to-morrow—at the same time—and I—I am terribly frightened— You have no idea how tenacious he is and obstinate— What can I do—tell me—what can I do?"

The little Marchioness sat up in bed to reflect, and then she suddenly said: "Have him arrested!"

The little Baroness looked stupefied, and stammered out: "What do you say? What are you thinking of? Have him arrested? Under what pretext?"

"That is very simple. Go to the Commissary of Police and say that a gentleman has been following you about for three months; that he had the insolence to go up to your apartments yesterday; that he has threatened you with another visit to-morrow, and that you demand the protection of the law, and they will give you two police officers who will arrest him."

"But, my dear, suppose he tells——"

"They will not believe him, you silly thing, if you have told your tale cleverly to the commissary, but they will believe you, who are an irreproachable woman, and in society."

"Oh! I shall never dare to do it."

"You must dare, my dear, or you are lost."

"But think that he will—he will insult me if he is arrested."

"Very well, you will have witnesses, and he will be sentenced."

"Sentenced to what?"

"To pay damages. In such cases, one must be pitiless!"

"Ah! speaking of damages—there is one thing that worries me very much—very much indeed. He left me two twenty-franc pieces on the mantelpiece."

"Two twenty-francs pieces?"

"Yes."

"No more?"

"No."

"That is very little. It would have humiliated me. Well?"

"Well! What am I to do with that money?"

The little Marchioness hesitated for a few seconds, and then she replied in a serious voice:

"My dear—you must make—you must make your husband a little present with it. That will be only fair!"

THE DEVIL

The peasant was standing opposite the doctor, by the bedside of the dying old woman, and she, calmly resigned and quite lucid, looked at them and listened to their talking. She was going to die, and she did not rebel at it, for her life was over—she was ninety-two.

The July sun streamed in at the window and through the open door and cast its hot flames on to the uneven brown clay floor, which had been stamped down by four generations of clodhoppers. The smell of the fields came in also, driven by the brisk wind, and parched by the noontide heat. The grasshoppers chirped themselves hoarse, filling the air with their shrill noise, like that of the wooden crickets which are sold to children at fair time.

The doctor raised his voice and said: "Honoré, you cannot leave your mother in this state; she may die at any moment." And the peasant, in great distress, replied: "But I must get in my wheat, for it has been lying on the ground a long time, and the weather is just right for it; what do you say about it, Mother?" And the dying woman, still possessed by her Norman avariciousness, replies *yes* with her eyes and her forehead, and so urged her son to get in his wheat, and to leave her to die alone. But the doctor got angry, and stamping his foot he said: "You are no better than a brute, do you hear, and I will not allow you to do it. Do you understand? And if you must get in your wheat today, go and fetch Rapet's wife and make her look after your mother. I *will* have it. And if you do not obey me, I will let you die like a dog, when you are ill in your turn; do you hear me?"

The peasant, a tall, thin fellow with slow movements, who was tormented by indecision, by his fear of the doctor and his keen love for saving, hesitated, calculated, and stammered out: "How much does La Rapet charge for attending sick people?"

"How should I know?" the doctor cried. "That depends upon how long she is wanted for. Settle it with her, by Jove! But I want her to be here within an hour, do you hear."

So the man made up his mind. "I will go for her," he replied; "don't get angry, doctor." And the latter left, calling out as he went: "Take care, you know, for I do not joke when I am angry!" And as soon as they were alone, the peasant turned to his mother, and said in a resigned voice: "I will go and fetch La Rapet, as the man will have it. Don't go off while I am away."

And he went out in his turn.

La Rapet, who was an old washerwoman, watched the dead and the dying of the neighborhood, and then, as soon as she had sewn her customers into that linen cloth from which they would emerge no more, she went and took up her irons to smooth the linen of the living. Wrinkled like a last year's apple, spiteful, envious, avaricious with a phenomenal avarice, bent double, as if she had been broken in half across the loins, by the constant movement of the iron over the linen, one might have said that she had a kind of monstrous and cynical affection for a death struggle. She never spoke of anything but of the people she had seen die, of the various kinds of deaths at which she had been present, and she related, with the greatest minuteness, details which were always the same, just like a sportsman talks of his shots.

When Honoré Bontemps entered her cottage, he found her preparing the starch for the collars of the village women, and he said: "Good evening; I hope you are pretty well, Mother Rapet."

She turned her head round to look at him and said: "Fairly well, fairly well, and you?"

"Oh! as for me, I am as well as I could wish, but my mother is very sick."

"Your mother?"

"Yes, my mother!"

"What's the matter with her?"

"She is going to turn up her toes, that's what's the matter with her!"

The old woman took her hands out of the water and asked with sudden sympathy: "Is she as bad as all that?"

"The doctor says she will not last till morning."

"Then she certainly is very bad!" Honoré hesitated, for he wanted to make a few preliminary remarks before coming to his proposal, but as he could hit upon nothing, he made up his mind suddenly.

"How much are you going to ask to stop with her till the end? You know that I am not rich, and I cannot even afford to keep a servant-girl. It is just that which has brought my poor mother to this state, too much work and fatigue! She used to work for ten, in spite of her ninety-two years. You don't find any made of that stuff nowadays!"

La Rapet answered gravely: "There are two prices: Forty sous by day and three francs by night for the rich, and twenty sous by day, and forty by night for the others. You shall pay me the twenty and forty." But the peasant reflected, for he knew his mother well. He knew how tenacious of life, how vigorous and unyielding she was. He knew, too, that she might last another week, in spite of the doctor's opinion, and so he said resolutely: "No, I would rather you would fix a price until the end. I will take my chance, one way or the other. The doctor says she will die very soon. If that happens, so much the better for you, and so much the worse for me, but if she holds out till to-morrow or longer, so much the better for me and so much the worse for you!"

The nurse looked at the man in astonishment, for she had never treated a death as a speculative job, and she hesitated, tempted by the idea of the possible gain. But almost immediately she suspected that he wanted to juggle her. "I can say nothing until I have seen your mother," she replied.

"Then come with me and see her."

She washed her hands, and went with him immediately. They did not speak on the road; she walked with short, hasty steps, while he strode on with his long legs, as if he were crossing a brook at every step. The cows lying down in the fields, overcome by the heat, raised their heads heavily and lowed feebly át the two passers-by, as if to ask them for some green grass.

When they got near the house, Honoré Bontemps murmured: "Suppose it is all over?" And the unconscious wish that it might be so showed itself in the sound of his voice.

But the old woman was not dead. She was lying on her back, on her wretched bed, her hands covered with a pink cotton counterpane, horribly thin, knotty paws, like some strange animal's, or like crabs' claws, hands closed by rheumatism, fatigue, and the work of nearly a century which she had accomplished.

La Rapet went up to the bed and looked at the dying woman, felt her pulse, tapped her on the chest, listened to her breathing, and asked her questions, so as to hear her speak: then, having looked at her for some time longer, she went out of the room, followed by Honoré. His decided opinion was, that the old woman would not last out the night, and he asked: "Well?" And the sick-nurse replied: "Well, she may last two days, perhaps three. You will have to give me six francs, everything included."

"Six francs! six francs!" he shouted. "Are you out of your mind? I tell you that she cannot last more than five or six hours!" And they disputed angrily for some time, but as the nurse said she would go home, as the time was slipping away, and as his wheat would not come to the farmyard of its own accord, he agreed to her terms at last:

"Very well, then, that is settled; six francs including everything, until the corpse is taken out."

"That is settled, six francs."

And he went away, with long strides, to the wheat, which was lying on the ground under the hot sun which ripens the grain, while the sick-nurse returned to the house.

She had brought some work with her, for she worked without stopping by the side of the dead and dying, sometimes for herself, sometimes for the family, who employed her as seamstress also, paying her rather more in that capacity. Suddenly she asked:

"Have you received the last sacrament, Mother Bontemps?"

The old peasant woman said "No" with her head, and La Rapet, who was very devout, got up quickly: "Good heavens, is it possible? I will go and fetch the curé"; and she rushed off to the parsonage so quickly, that the urchins in the street thought some accident had happened, when they saw her trotting off like that.

The priest came immediately in his surplice, preceded by a choir-boy, who rang a bell to announce the passage of the Host through the parched and quiet country. Some men, working at a distance, took off their large hats and remained motionless until the white vestment had disappeared behind some farm buildings; the women who were making up the sheaves stood up to make the sign of the cross; the frightened black hens ran away along the ditch until they reached a well-known hole through which they suddenly disappeared, while a foal, which was tied up in a meadow, took fright at the sight of the surplice and began to gallop round at the length of its rope, kicking violently. The choirboy, in his red cassock, walked quickly, and the priest, the square biretta on his bowed head, followed him, muttering some prayers. Last of all came La Rapet, bent almost double, as if she wished to prostrate herself; she walked with folded hands, as if she were in church.

Honoré saw them pass in the distance, and he asked: "Where is our priest going to?" And his man, who was more acute, replied: "He is taking the sacrament to your mother, of course!"

The peasant was not surprised and said: "That is quite possible," and went on with his work.

Mother Bontemps confessed, received absolution and extreme unction, and the priest took his departure, leaving the two women alone in the suffocating cottage. La Rapet began to look at the dying woman, and to ask herself whether it could last much longer.

The day was on the wane, and a cooler air came in stronger puffs, making a view of Epinal, which was fastened to the wall by two pins, flap up and down. The scanty

window curtains, which had formerly been white, but were
now yellow and covered with fly-specks, looked as if they
were going to fly off, and seemed to struggle to get away, like
the old woman's soul.

Lying motionless, with her eyes open, the old mother
seemed to await the death which was so near, and which
yet delayed its coming, with perfect indifference. Her short
breath whistled in her throat. It would stop altogether soon,
and there would be one woman less in the world, one whom
nobody would regret.

At nightfall Honoré returned, and when he went up to
the bed and saw that his mother was still alive he asked:
"How is she?" just as he had done formerly, when she had
been sick. Then he sent La Rapet away, saying to her:
"To-morrow morning at five o'clock, without fail." And
she replied: "To-morrow at five o'clock."

She came at daybreak, and found Honoré eating his soup,
which he had made himself, before going to work.

"Well, is your mother dead?" asked the nurse.

"She is rather better, on the contrary," he replied, with
a malignant look out of the corner of his eyes. Then he
went out.

La Rapet was seized with anxiety, and went up to the
dying woman, who was in the same state, lethargic and impassive, her eyes open and her hands clutching the counterpane. The nurse perceived that this might go on thus for
two days, four days, eight days, even, and her avaricious
mind was seized with fear. She was excited to fury against
the cunning fellow who had tricked her, and against the
woman who would not die.

Nevertheless she began to sew and waited with her eyes
fixed on the wrinkled face of Mother Bontemps. When
Honoré returned to breakfast he seemed quite satisfied,
and even in a bantering humor, for he was carrying in his
wheat under very favorable circumstances.

La Rapet was getting exasperated; every passing minute
now seemed to her so much time and money stolen from
her. She felt a mad inclination to choke this old ass, this
headstrong old fool, this obstinate old wretch—to stop that

short, rapid breath, which was robbing her of her time and money, by squeezing her throat a little. But then she reflected on the danger of doing so, and other thoughts came into her head, so she went up to the bed and said to her: "Have you ever seen the Devil?"

Mother Bontemps whispered: "No."

Then the sick-nurse began to talk and to tell her tales likely to terrify her weak and dying mind. "Some minutes before one dies the Devil appears," she said, "to all. He has a broom in his hand, a saucepan on his head and he utters loud cries. When anybody had seen him, all was over, and that person had only a few moments longer to live"; and she enumerated all those to whom the Devil had appeared that year: Josephine Loisel, Eulalie Ratier, Sophie Padagnau, Séraphine Grospied.

Mother Bontemps, who was at last most disturbed in mind, moved about, wrung her hands, and tried to turn her head to look at the other end of the room. Suddenly La Rapet disappeared at the foot of the bed. She took a sheet out of the cupboard and wrapped herself up in it; then she put the iron pot on to her head, so that its three short bent feet rose up like horns, took a broom in her right hand and a tin pail in her left, which she threw up suddenly, so that it might fall to the ground noisily.

Certainly when it came down, it made a terrible noise. Then, climbing on to a chair, the nurse showed herself, gesticulating and uttering shrill cries into the pot which covered her face, while she menaced the old peasant woman, who was nearly dead, with her broom.

Terrified, with a mad look on her face, the dying woman made a superhuman effort to get up and escape; she even got her shoulders and chest out of bed; then she fell back with a deep sigh. All was over, and La Papet calmly put everything back into its place; the broom into the corner by the cupboard, the sheet inside it, the pot on to the hearth, the pail on to the floor, and the chair against the wall. Then with a professional air, she closed the dead woman's enormous eyes, put a plate on the bed and poured some holy water into it, dipped the twig of boxwood into it, and kneeling down, she fervently repeated the prayers for the dead, which she knew by heart, as a matter of business.

When Honoré returned in the evening, he found her praying. He calculated immediately that she had made twenty sous out of him, for she had only spent three days and one night there, which made five francs altogether, instead of the six which he owed her.

THE MAD WOMAN

"I can tell you a terrible story about the Franco-Prussian war," Monsieur d'Endolin said to some friends assembled in the smoking-room of Baron de Ravot's château. "You know my house in the Faubourg de Cormeil. I was living there when the Prussians came, and I had for a neighbor a kind of mad woman, who had lost her senses in consequence of a series of misfortunes. At the age of seven and twenty she had lost her father, her husband, and her newly born child, all in the space of a month.

"When death has once entered into a house, it almost invariably returns immediately, as if it knew the way, and the young woman, overwhelmed with grief, took to her bed and was delirious for six weeks. Then a species of calm lassitude succeeded that violent crisis, and she remained motionless, eating next to nothing, and only moving her eyes. Every time they tried to make her get up, she screamed as if they were about to kill her, and so they ended by leaving her continually in bed, and only taking her out to wash her, to change her linen, and to turn her mattress.

"An old servant remained with her, to give her something to drink, or a little cold meat, from time to time. What passed in that despairing mind? No one ever knew, for she did not speak at all now. Was she thinking of the dead? Was she dreaming sadly, without any precise recollection of anything that had happened? Or was her memory as stagnant as water without any current? But however this may have been, for fifteen years she remained thus inert and secluded.

"The war broke out, and in the beginning of December the Germans came to Cormeil. I can remember it as if it were but yesterday. It was freezing hard enough to split the stones, and I myself was lying back in an armchair, being unable to move on account of the gout, when I heard their heavy and regular tread, and could see them pass from my window.

"They defiled past interminably, with that peculiar motion of a puppet on wires, which belongs to them. Then the officers billeted their men on the inhabitants, and I had seventeen of them. My neighbor, the crazy woman, had a dozen, one of whom was the Commandant, a regular violent, surly swashbuckler.

"During the first few days, everything went on as usual. The officers next door had been told that the lady was ill, and they did not trouble themselves about that in the least, but soon that woman whom they never saw irritated them. They asked what her illness was, and were told that she had been in bed for fifteen years, in consequence of terrible grief. No doubt they did not believe it, and thought that the poor mad creature would not leave her bed out of pride, so that she might not come near the Prussians, or speak to them or even see them.

"The Commandant insisted upon her receiving him. He was shown into the room and said to her roughly: 'I must beg you to get up, Madame, and come downstairs so that we may all see you.' But she merely turned her vague eyes on him, without replying, and so he continued: 'I do not intend to tolerate any insolence, and if you do not get up of your own accord, I can easily find means to make you walk without any assistance.'

"But she did not give any signs of having heard him, and remained quite motionless. Then he got furious, taking that calm silence for a mark of supreme contempt; so he added: 'If you do not come downstairs to-morrow—' And then he left the room.

"The next day the terrified old servant wished to dress her, but the mad woman began to scream violently, and resisted with all her might. The officer ran upstairs quickly, and the servant threw herself at his feet and cried: 'She will not come down, Monsieur, she will not. Forgive her, for she is so unhappy."

"The soldier was embarrassed, as in spite of his anger, he did not venture to order his soldiers to drag her out. But suddenly he began to laugh, and gave some orders in German, and soon a party of soldiers was seen coming out supporting a mattress as if they were carrying a wounded man. On that bed, which had been unmade, the mad woman, who was still silent, was lying quite quietly, for she was quite indifferent to anything that went on, as long as they let her lie. Behind her, a soldier was carrying a parcel of feminine attire, and the officer said, rubbing his hands: 'We will just see whether you cannot dress yourself alone, and take a little walk.'

"And then the procession went off in the direction of the forest of Imauville; in two hours the soldiers came back alone, and nothing more was seen of the mad woman. What had they done with her? Where had they taken her to? No one knew.

"The snow was falling day and night, and enveloped the plain and the woods in a shroud of frozen foam, and the wolves came and howled at our very doors.

"The thought of that poor lost woman haunted me, and I made several applications to the Prussian authorities in order to obtain some information, and was nearly shot for doing so. When spring returned, the army of occupation withdrew, but my neighbor's house remained closed, and the grass grew thick in the garden walks. The old servant had died during the winter, and nobody troubled any longer about the occurrence; I alone thought about it constantly. What had they done with the woman? Had she escaped through the forest? Had somebody found her, and taken her to a hospital, without being able to obtain any information from her? Nothing happened to relieve my doubts; but by degrees, time assuaged my fears.

"Well, in the following autumn the woodcock were very plentiful, and as my gout had left me for a time, I dragged myself as far as the forest. I had already killed four or five of the long-billed birds, when I knocked over one which fell into a ditch full of branches, and I was obliged to get into it, in order to pick it up, and I found that it had fallen close to

a dead, human body. Immediately the recollection of the
mad woman struck me like a blow in the chest. Many other
people had perhaps died in the wood during that disastrous
year, but though I do not know why, I was sure, sure, I tell
you, that I should see the head of that wretched maniac.

"And suddenly I understood, I guessed everything. They
had abandoned her on that mattress in the cold, deserted
wood; and, faithful to her fixed idea, she had allowed herself to perish under that thick and light counterpane of
snow, without moving either arms or legs.

"Then the wolves had devoured her, and the birds had
built their nests with the wool from her torn bed, and I
took charge of her bones. I only pray that our sons may
never see any wars again."

LOVE'S AWAKENING

No one was surprised at the marriage of Mr. Simon Lebrument and Miss Jean Cordier. Mr. Lebrument came to buy out the office of Mr. Papillon; he needed, it was understood, money with which to pay for it; and Miss Jean Cordier had three hundred thousand francs clear, in stocks and bonds.

Mr. Lebrument was a handsome bachelor, who had style, the style of a notary, a provincial style, but, after all, some style, which was a rare thing at Boutigny-le-Rebours.

Miss Cordier had grace and freshness, grace a little awkward and freshness a little fixed up; but she was nevertheless, a pretty girl, desirable and entertaining.

The wedding ceremonies turned Boutigny topsy-turvy. The married couple was much admired when they returned to the conjugal domicile to conceal their happiness, having resolved to make a little, simple journey to Paris, after they had spent a few days together.

It was charming, these few days together, as Mr. Lebrument knew how to manage his early relations with his wife with a delicacy, a directness, and sense of fitness that was remarkable. He took for his motto: "Everything comes to him who waits." He knew how to be patient and energetic at the same time. His success was rapid and complete.

At the end of four days Mrs. Lebrument adored her husband. She could not bear to be a moment away from him. He must be near her all day long, that she might caress his hands, his beard, his nose, etc. She would sit upon his knees and, taking him by the ears, would say: "Open your mouth and shut your eyes." He opened his mouth with confidence, shut his eyes halfway, and then would receive a very long, sweet kiss that made great shivers in his back. And in his turn, he never had enough caresses, enough lips,

173

enough hands, enough of anything with which to enjoy his wife from morning until evening, and from evening until morning.

As soon as the first week had slipped away he said to his young companion:

"If you wish, we might leave for Paris Tuesday of next week. We shall be like lovers who are not married; go about to the theaters, the restaurants, the concert *cafés*, and everywhere, everywhere."

She jumped for joy. "Oh! yes, yes," she replied, "let us go as soon as possible."

"And as we must not forget anything, you might ask your father to have your dowry ready; I will take it with me, and at the same time pay Mr. Papillon."

She answered: "I will speak to him about it to-morrow morning."

Then he seized her in his arms and began again the little tendernesses she loved so much, and had reveled in now for eight days.

The Tuesday following, the father-in-law and the mother-in-law accompanied their daughter and son-in-law to the station, whence they set out for the capital. The father-in-law remarked:

"I tell you it is imprudent to carry so much money in your pocketbook." And the young notary smiled.

"Do not be disturbed, father-in-law," he answered, "I am accustomed to these things. You know that in my profession it often happens that I have nearly a million about me. By carrying it with me, we escape a lot of formalities and delays, to say the least. Do not give yourself any uneasiness."

Then the trainman cried out, "All aboard!" and they hurried into a compartment where they found themselves with two old ladies.

Lebrument murmured in his wife's ear: "How annoying! Now I cannot smoke."

She answered in a low tone: "I am sorry too, but not on account of your cigar."

The engine puffed and started. The journey lasted an

hour, during which they could not say anything of importance, because the two old ladies did not go to sleep.

When they were in the Saint-Lazare station, in Paris, Mr. Lebrument said to his wife:

"If you wish, my dear, we will first go and breakfast on the Boulevard, then return at our leisure to find our trunk and give it to the porter of some hotel."

She consented immediately: "Oh! yes," said she, "let us breakfast in some restaurant. Is it far from here?"

"Yes, rather far, but we will take an omnibus."

She was astonished: "Why not a cab?" she asked.

He groaned as he said smilingly: "And you are economical! A cab for five minutes' ride, at six sous per minute! You do not deprive yourself of anything!"

"That is true," said she, a little confused.

A large omnibus was passing, with three horses at a trot. Lebrument hailed it: "Conductor! eh, conductor!"

The heavy carriage stopped. The young notary pushed his wife inside, saying hurriedly, in a low voice:

"You get in while I climb up on the outside to smoke at least a cigarette before breakfast."

She had not time for any answer. The conductor, who had seized her by the arm to aid her in mounting the steps, pushed her into the 'bus, where she landed, half-frightened, upon a seat, and in a sort of stupor watched the feet of her husband through the windows at the back, as he climbed to the top of the imperial.

There she remained immovable between a large gentleman who smelled of a pipe and an old woman who smelled of a dog. All the other travelers, in two mute lines,—a grocer's boy, a workman, a sergeant of infantry, a gentleman with gold-rimmed spectacles and a silk cap with enormous visors, like gutters, and two ladies with an important, mincing air, which seemed to say: We are here, although we should be in a better place. Then there were two good sisters, a little girl in long hair, and an undertaker. The assemblage had the appearance of a collection of caricatures in a freak museum, a series of expressions of the human countenance, like a row of grotesque puppets which one knocks down at a fair.

The jolts of the carriage made them toss their heads a little, and as they shook, the flesh of their cheeks trembled; and the disturbance of the rolling wheels gave them an idiotic or sleepy look.

The young woman remained inert: "Why did he not come with me?" she asked herself. A vague sadness oppressed her. He might, indeed, have deprived himself of his cigar!

The good sisters gave the signal to stop. They alighted, one after the other, leaving an odor of old and faded skirts.

Soon after they were gone another stopped the 'bus. A cook came in, red and out of breath. She sat down and placed her basket of provisions upon her knees. A strong odor of dishwater pervaded the omnibus.

"It is further than I thought," said the young woman to herself.

The undertaker got out and was replaced by a coachman who smelled of a stable. The girl in long hair was succeeded by an errand-boy who exhaled the perfume of his walks.

The notary's wife perceived all these things, ill at ease and so disheartened that she was ready to weep without knowing why.

Some others got out, still others came in. The omnibus went on through the interminable streets, stopped at the station, and began its route again.

"How far it is!" said Jean. "Especially when one has nothing for diversion and cannot sleep!" She had not been so much fatigued for many days.

Little by little all the travelers got out. She remained alone, all alone. The conductor shouted:

"Vaugirard!"

As she blushed he again repeated: "Vaugirard!"

She looked at him not understanding that this must be addressed to her as all her neighbors had gone. For the third time the man said: "Vaugirard!"

Then she asked: "Where are we?"

He answered in a gruff voice: "We are at Vaugirard Miss; I've told you twenty times already."

"Is it far from the Boulevard?" she asked.

"What Boulevard?"

"The Italian Boulevard."

"We passed that a long time ago."

"Ah! Will you be kind enough to tell my husband?"

"Your husband? Where is he?"

"On the outside."

"On the outside! It has been a long time since there was anybody there."

She made a terrified gesture. Then she said:

"How can it be? It is not possible. He got up there when I entered the omnibus. Look again; he must be there."

The conductor became rude: "Come, little one, this is talk enough. If there is one man lost, there are ten to be found. Scamper out now! You will find another in the street."

The tears sprang to her eyes. She insisted: "But, sir, you are mistaken, I assure you that you are mistaken. He had a large pocketbook in his hand."

The employee began to laugh: "A large pocketbook? I remember. Yes, he got out at the Madeleine. That's right! He's left you behind! Ha! ha!"

The carriage was standing still. She got down and looked up, in spite of herself, to the roof, with an instinctive movement of the eye. It was totally deserted.

Then she began to weep aloud, without thinking that anyone was looking at or listening to her. Finally she said:

"What is going to become of me?"

The inspector came up and inquired: "What's the matter?"

The conductor answered in a jocose fashion:

"This lady's husband has left her on the way."

The other replied: "Now, now, that is nothing. I am at your service." And he turned on his heels.

Then she began to walk ahead, too much frightened, too much excited to think even where she was going. Where was she going? What should she do? How could such an error have occurred? Such an act of carelessness, of disregard, of unheard of distraction!

She had two francs in her pocket. To whom could she

apply? Suddenly she remembered her cousin Barral, who was a clerk in the office of Naval Affairs.

She had just enough to hire a cab; she would go to him. And she met him just as he was starting for his office. Like Lebrument, he carried a large pocketbook under his arm.

She leaned out of the carriage and called: "Henry!"

He stopped, much surprised.

"Jean," said he, "here?—and alone? Where do you come from? What are you doing?"

She stammered, with her eyes full of tears: "My husband is lost somewhere—"

"Lost? where?"

"On the omnibus."

"On the omnibus! Oh!"

And she related to him the whole story, weeping much over the adventure.

He listened reflectively, and then asked:

"This morning? And was his head perfectly clear?"

"Oh! yes! And he had my dowry."

"Your dowry? The whole of it?"

"Yes, the whole of it—in order to pay for his office."

"Well, my dear cousin, your husband, whoever he is, is probably watching the wheel—this minute."

She did not yet comprehend. She stammered: "My husband—you say—"

"I say that he has run off with your—your capital—and that's all about it."

She remained standing there, suffocated with grief, murmuring:

"Then he is—he is—a wretch!"

Then, overcome with emotion, she fell on her cousin's shoulder, sobbing violently.

As people were stopping to look at them, he guided her gently into the entrance of his house, supporting her body. They mounted the steps, and as the maid came to open the door he ordered her:

"Sophie, run to the restaurant and bring breakfast for two persons. I shall not go to the office this morning."

ONE PHASE OF LOVE

The walls of the cell were bare and whitewashed. A narrow, barred window, so high that it could not easily be reached, lighted this little room; the crazy man, seated on a straw chair, looked at us with a fixed eye, vague and haunting. He was thin, with wrinkled cheeks and almost white hair that one would think had grown white in a few months. His clothes seemed too large for his dried-up limbs, his shrunken chest, and hollow body. One felt that this man had been ravaged by his thoughts, by a thought, as fruit is by a worm. His madness, his idea, was there in his head, obstinate, harassing, devouring. It was eating his body, little by little. It, the Invisible, the Impalpable, the Unseizable, the Immaterial Idea gnawed his flesh, drank his blood, and extinguished his life.

What a mystery, that this man should be killed by a Thought! He is an object of fear and pity, this madman! What strange dream, frightful and deadly, can dwell in his forehead, to fold such profound and ever-changing wrinkles in it?

The doctor said to me: "He has terrible paroxysms of rage, and is one of the most singularly demented people I have ever seen. His madness is of an amorous, erotic kind. He is a sort of necrophile. He has written a journal which shows as plainly as daylight the malady of his mind. His madness is visible, so to speak. If you are interested, you may run through this document."

I followed the doctor into his office and he gave me the journal of this miserable man.

"Read it," said he, "and give me your opinion about it."

Here is what the little book contained:

"Up to the age of thirty-two years I lived tranquilly with-

179

out love. Life appeared to me very simple, very good, and very easy. I was rich. I had a taste for some things, but had never felt a passion for anything. It was good to live! I awoke happy each day, to do things which it pleased me to do, and I went to bed satisfied with calm hope for the next day and a future without care.

"I had had some mistresses without ever having my heart torn by desire or my soul bruised by love after the possession. It is good so to live. It is better to love, but terrible. Still those who love like everybody else should find happiness, less than mine, perhaps, for love has come to me in an unbelievable manner.

"Being rich, I collected ancient furniture and antiques. Often I thought of the unknown hands which had touched these things, of the eyes that had admired them, and the hearts that had loved them—for one does love such things! I often remained for hours and hours looking at a little watch of the last century. It was so dainty, so pretty with its enamel and gold embossing. And it still went, as on the day when some woman had bought it, delighted in the possession of so fine a jewel. It had not ceased to palpitate, to live its mechanical life, but had ever continued its regular ticktack, although a century had passed. Who then had first carried it upon her breast, in the warmth of the dress—the heart of the watch beating against the heart of the woman? What hand had held it at the ends of its warm fingers, then wiped the enameled shepherds, tarnished a little by the moisture of the skin? What eyes had looked upon this flowered dial awaiting the hour, the dear hour, the divine hour?

"How I wished to see her, to know her, the woman who had chosen this rare and exquisite object. But she is dead! I am possessed by a desire for women of former times; I love all those who have loved long ago. The story of past tenderness fills my heart with regrets. Oh! beauty, the smiles, the caresses of youth, the hopes! These things should be eternal!

"How I have wept, during whole nights, over the women of old, so beautiful, so tender, so sweet, whose lips have opened to the ·kiss, and who are now dead! The kiss is immortal! It goes from lip to lip, from century to century, from age to age! Men take it and give it and die.

"The past attracts me, the present frightens me, because the future is death. I regret all that which is gone, I weep for those who have lived; I wish to stop the hour, to arrest time. But it goes, it goes, it passes away, and it takes me, from second to second, a little of me for the annihilation of tomorrow. And I shall never live again.

"Adieu, women of yesterday, I love you.

"And yet I have nothing to complain of. I have found her whom I awaited, and I have tasted through her of inconceivable pleasure.

"I was roaming around Paris on a sunny morning, with joyous foot and happy soul, looking in the shops with the vague interest of a stroller. All at once I saw in a shop of antiquities, an Italian piece of furniture of the XVIIth century. It was very beautiful, very rare. I attributed it to a Venetian artist, named Vitelli, who belonged to that epoch. Then I passed along.

"Why did the remembrance of this piece of furniture follow me with so much force that I went back over my steps? I stopped again before the shop to look at it, and felt that it tempted me.

"What a singular thing is temptation! One looks at an object, and, little by little, it seduces you, troubles you, takes possession of you like the face of a woman. Its charm enters into you, a strange charm which comes from its form, its color, and its physiognomy. Already one loves it, wishes it, desires it. A need of possession takes you, a pleasant need at first, because timid, but increasing, becoming violent and irresistible. And the merchants seem to suspect, from the look in the eye, this secret, increasing desire. I bought that piece of furniture and had it carried to my house immediately. I placed it in my room.

"Oh! I pity those who do not know this sweet hobby of the collector with the trinket which he finally buys. He caresses it with his eye and hand as if it were flesh; he returns every moment to it, thinks of it continually, wherever he goes and whatever he may be doing. The thought of it follows him into the street, into the world, everywhere. And

when he re-enters his house, before even removing his
gloves or his hat, he goes to look at it with the tenderness
of a lover.

"Truly, for eight days I adored that piece of furniture.
I kept opening its doors and drawers; I handled it with delight and tasted all the intimate joys of possession.

"One evening in feeling the thickness of a panel, I perceived that there might be a hiding-place there. My heart
began to beat and I passed the night in searching out the
secret, without being able to discover it.

"I came upon it the next day by forcing a piece of metal
into a crevice in the paneling. A shelf slipped, and I saw,
exposed upon a lining of black velvet, a marvelous head of
hair that had belonged to some woman.

"Yes, a head of hair, an enormous twist of blonde hair,
also red, which had been cut off near the skin and tied together with a golden cord.

"I stood there stupefied, trembling and disturbed! An
almost insensible perfume, so old that it seemed like the
soul of an odor, arose from this mysterious drawer and this
most surprising relic.

"I took it gently, almost religiously, and lifted it from its
resting-place. Immediately it unwound, spreading out its
golden billows upon the floor, where it fell, thick and light,
supple and brilliant, like the fiery tail of a comet.

"A strange emotion seized me. To whom had this belonged? When? Under what circumstances? Why had it
been shut up in this piece of furniture? What adventure,
what drama was connected with this souvenir? Who had
cut it off? Some lover, on a day of parting? Some husband,
on a day of vengeance? Or, perhaps, some woman herself,
who bore on her brow the look of despair? Was it at the
hour of entering the cloister that she had thrown there this
fortune of love, as a token left to the world of the living?
Was it the hour closing the tomb upon the young and beautiful dead, that he who adored her took this diadem of her
head, the only thing he could preserve of her, the only living part of her body that would not perish, the only thing
that he could still love and caress and kiss, in the transport
of his grief?

"Was it not strange, that this hair should remain there thus, when there was no longer any vestige of the body with which she was born?

"It curled about my fingers and touched my skin with a singular caress, the caress of death. I felt myself affected, as if I were going to weep.

"I kept it a long time in my hands, then it seemed to me that it had some effect upon me, as if something of the soul still remained in it. And I laid it upon the velvet again, the velvet blemished by time, then pushed in the drawer, shut the doors of the closet, and betook myself to the street to dream.

"I walked straight ahead, full of sadness, and full of trouble, of the kind of trouble that remains in the heart after the kiss of love. It seemed to me I had lived in former times, and that I had known this woman.

"And Villon's lines came to my lips, bringing with them a sob:

" 'Tell me in what far-off land
  The Roman beauty, Flora, lives;
Hipparchia, Thais' cousin, and
  All the beauty nature gives;
Echo speak, thy voice awake
Over river, stream, and lake,
Where are beauty's smiles and tears?
And where the snows of other years?

" 'Blanche, as fair as lily's chalice,
  Singing sweet, with voice serene,
Bertha Broadfoot, Beatrice, Alice,
  Ermengarde, Le Mayne's dear queen?
Where is Joan, the good Lorraine,
Whom th' English brought to death and fame?
Where are all, O wisest seers,
And where the snows of other years?'

"When I returned to my house I had a strange desire to see my strange treasure again. I took it up and felt it, and in touching it a long shiver ran through my body.

"For some days, however, I remained in my ordinary state, although the thought of this hair never left me. Whenever I came in, it was my first desire to look at it and handle it. I would turn the key of the secretary with the same trembling that one has in opening the door of his well-beloved, for I had in two hands and in my heart a confused, singular, continued, sensual need of burying my fingers in this charming rivulet of dead hair.

"Then, when I had finished caressing it, when I had returned it to its resting-place, I always felt that it was there, as if it were something alive, concealed, imprisoned; I felt it and I still desired it; again I had the imperious need of touching it, of feeling it, of enervating myself to the point of weariness from contact with this cold, glistening, irritating, exciting, delicious hair.

"I lived thus a month or two, I know not how long, with this thing possessing me, haunting me. I was happy and tortured, as in the expectation of love, as one is after the avowal which precedes the embrace.

"I would shut myself up alone with it in order to feel it upon my skin, to bury my lips in it, to kill it, and bite it. I would roll it around my face, drink it in, drown my eyes in its golden waves, and finally see the blond life beyond it.

"I loved it! Yes, I loved it. I could no longer live away from it, nor be contented an hour without seeing it. I expected—I expected—what? I know not—her!

"One night I was suddenly awakened with a feeling that I was not alone in my room. I was alone, however. But I could not go to sleep again; and, as I was tossing in the fever of insomnia, I rose and went to look at the twist of hair. It appeared to me sweeter than usual, and more animated.

"Could the dead return? The kisses with which I had warmed it failed to give me happiness, and I carried it to my bed and lay down with it, pressing it to my lips, as one does a mistress he hopes to enjoy.

"The dead returned! She came! Yes, I saw her, touched her, possessed her as she was when alive in former times, large, blonde, plump, with cool breasts, and with hips in form of a lyre. And I followed that divine, undulating line from the throat to the feet, in all the curves of the flesh with my caresses.

"Yes, I possessed her, every day and every night. She had returned, Death, Death the Beautiful, the Adorable, the Mysterious, the Unknown, and returned every night.

"My happiness was so great that. I could not conceal it. I found near her a superhuman delight, and in possessing this Unseizable, Invisible Death, knew a profound, inexplicable joy. No lover ever tasted joys more ardent or more terrible.

"I knew not how to conceal my happiness. I loved this possession so much that I could not bear to leave it. I carried it with me always, everywhere. I walked with it through the city, as if it were my wife, conducting it to the theater and to restaurants as one would a mistress. But they saw it,—and guessed—they took me, and threw me into prison, like a malefactor. They took it away—oh! misery!—"

The manuscript stopped there. And suddenly, as I raised my wondering eyes to the doctor, a frightful cry, a howl of fury and exasperated desire filled the asylum.

"Listen," said the doctor, "it is necessary to douse that obscene maniac with water five times a day. It is only Sergeant Bertrand, the man who fell in love with the dead."

I stammered, moved with astonishment, horror, and pity: "But that hair—did it really exist?"

The doctor got up, opened a closet full of vials and instruments, and threw toward me, across his office, a long thick rope of blond hair, which flew toward me like a bird of gold.

I trembled at feeling upon my hands its caressing, light touch. And I stood there, my heart beating with disgust and desire, the disgust we have in coming in contact with objects connected with crimes, and the desire like that which comes with the temptation to test some infamous and mysterious thing.

Shrugging his shoulders, the doctor added: "The mind of man is capable of anything."

THE WILL

I knew that tall young fellow, René de Bourneval. He was an agreeable man, though of a rather melancholy turn of mind, and prejudiced against everything, very skeptical, and fond of tearing worldly hypocrisies to pieces. He often used to say:

"There are no honorable men, or, at any rate, they only appear so when compared to low people."

He had two brothers, whom he shunned, the Messieurs de Courcils. I thought they were by another father, on account of the difference in the name. I had frequently heard that something strange had happened in the family, but I did not know the details.

As I took a great liking to him, we soon became intimate, and one evening, when I had been dining with him alone, I asked him, by chance: "Are you by your mother's first or second marriage?" He grew rather pale; then he flushed, and did not speak for a few moments, he was visibly embarrassed. Then he smiled in that melancholy and gentle manner peculiar to him, and said:

"My dear friend, if it will not weary you, I can give you some very strange particulars about my life. I know you to be a sensible man, so I do not fear that our friendship will suffer by my revelations, and should it suffer, I should not care about having you for my friend any longer.

"My mother, Madame de Courcils, was a poor, little, timid woman, whom her husband had married for the sake of her fortune. Her whole life was a continual martyrdom. Of a loving, delicate mind, she was constantly ill-treated by the man who ought to have been my father, one of those boors called country gentlemen. A month after their marriage he was living with a servant, and besides that, the wives and daughters of his tenants were his mistresses,

186

which did not prevent him from having three children by his wife, that is, if you count me in. My mother said nothing, and lived in that noisy house like a little mouse. Set aside, disparaged, nervous, she looked at people with bright, uneasy, restless eyes, the eyes of some terrified creature which can never shake off its fear. And yet she was pretty, very pretty and fair, a gray blonde, as if her hair had lost its color through her constant fears.

"Among Monsieur de Courcils's friends who constantly came to the château there was an ex-cavalry officer, a widower, a man to be feared, a man at the same time tender and violent, and capable of the most energetic resolution, Monsieur de Bourneval, whose name I bear. He was a tall, thin man, with a heavy black mustache, and I am very like him. He was a man who had read a great deal, and whose ideas were not like those of most of his class. His great-grandmother had been a friend of J. J. Rousseau, and you might have said that he had inherited something of this ancestral connection. He knew the "Contrat Social" and the "Nouvelle Héloïse" by heart, and, indeed, all those philosophical books which led the way to the overthrow of our old usages, prejudices, superannuated laws, and imbecile morality.

"It seems that he loved my mother, and she loved him, but their intrigue was carried on so secretly that no one guessed it. The poor, neglected, unhappy woman must have clung to him in a despairing manner, and in her intimacy with him must have imbibed all his ways of thinking, theories of free thought, audacious ideas of independent love. But as she was so timid that she never ventured to speak aloud, it was all driven back, condensed, and expressed in her heart, which never opened itself.

"My two brothers were very cruel to her, like their father, and never gave her a caress. Used to seeing her count for nothing in the house, they treated her rather like a servant, and so I was the only one of her sons who really loved her, and whom she loved.

"When she died I was seventeen, and I must add, in order that you may understand what follows, that there had been a lawsuit between my father and my mother. Their property had been separated, to my mother's advantage, as, thanks to the workings of the law and the intelligent devotion of a lawyer to her interests, she had preserved the right to make her will in favor of anyone she pleased.

"We were told that there was a will lying at the lawyer's, and were invited to be present at the reading of it. I can remember it, as if it were yesterday. It was a grand, dramatic, yet burlesque and surprising scene, brought about by the posthumous revolt of a dead woman, by a cry for liberty from the depths of her tomb, on the part of a martyred woman who had been crushed by a man's habits during her life, and, who, from her grave, uttered a despairing appeal for independence.

"The man who thought that he was my father, a stout, ruddy-faced man, who gave you the idea of a butcher, and my brothers, two great fellows of twenty and twenty-two, were waiting quietly in their chairs. Monsieur de Bourneval, who had been invited to be present, came in and stood behind me. He was very pale, and bit his mustache, which was turning gray. No doubt he was prepared for what was going to happen. The lawyer, after opening the envelope in our presence, double-locked the door and began to read the will, which was sealed with red wax, and the contents of which he knew not."

My friend stopped suddenly and got up, and from his writing-table took an old paper, unfolded it, kissed it and then continued:

"This is the will of my beloved mother:

"I, the undersigned, Anne-Catherine-Geneviève-Mathilde de Croixluce, the legitimate wife of Léopold-Joseph Gontran de Courcils, sound in body and mind, here express my last wishes:

"I first of all ask God, and then my dear son René, to pardon me for the act I am about to commit. I believe that my child's heart is great enough to understand me, and to forgive me. I have suffered my whole life long. I was married out of calculation, then despised, misunderstood, oppressed, and constantly deceived by my husband.

"I forgive him, but I owe him nothing.

"My eldest sons never loved me, never caressed me, scarcely treated me as a mother, but during my whole life I was everything that I ought to have been, and I owe them nothing more after my death. The ties of blood cannot exist without daily and constant affection. An ungrateful son is less than a stranger; he is a culprit, for he has no right to be indifferent toward his mother.

"I have always trembled before men, before their unjust laws, their inhuman customs, their shameful prejudices. Before God, I have no longer any fear. Dead, I fling aside disgraceful hypocrisy; I dare to speak my thoughts, and to avow and to sign the secret of my heart.

"I therefore leave that part of my fortune of which the law allows me to dispose, as a deposit with my dear lover Pierre-Gennes-Simon de Bourneval, to revert afterward to our dear son René.

"(This wish is, moreover, formulated more precisely in a notarial deed.)

"And I declare before the Supreme Judge who hears me, that I should have cursed Heaven and my own existence, if I had not met my lover's deep, devoted, tender, unshaken affection, if I had not felt in his arms that the Creator made His creatures to love, sustain, and console each other, and to weep together in the hours of sadness.

"Monsieur de Courcils is the father of my two eldest sons; René alone owes his life to Monsieur de Bourneval. I pray to the Master of men and of their destinies to place father and son above social prejudices, to make them love each other until they die, and to love me also in my coffin.

"These are my last thoughts, and my last wish.

"MATHILDE DE CROIXLUCE.

"Monsieur de Courcils had risen, and he cried:
" 'It is the will of a mad woman.'
"Then Monsieur de Bourneval stepped forward and said

in a loud and penetrating voice: 'I, Simon de Bourneval, solemnly declare that this writing contains nothing but the strict truth, and I am ready to prove it by letters which I possess.'

"On hearing that, Monsieur de Courcils went up to him, and I thought that they were going to collar each other. There they stood, both of them, tall, one stout and the other thin, both trembling. My mother's husband stammered out:

" 'You are a worthless wretch!'

"And the other replied in a loud, dry voice:

" 'We will meet somewhere else, Monsieur. I should have already slapped your ugly face, and challenged you a long time ago, if I had not, before all else, thought of the peace of mind of that poor woman whom you made to suffer so much during her lifetime.'

"Then, turning to me, he said:

" 'You are my son; will you come with me? I have no right to take you away, but I shall assume it, if you will allow me.' I shook his hand without replying, and we went out together; I was certainly three parts mad.

"Two days later Monsieur de Bourneval killed Monsieur de Courcils in a duel. My brothers, fearing some terrible scandal, held their tongues. I offered them, and they accepted, half the fortune which my mother had left me. I took my real father's name, renouncing that which the law gave me, but which was not really mine. Monsieur de Bourneval died three years afterward, and I have not consoled myself yet."

He rose from his chair, walked up and down the room, and, standing in front of me, said:

"I maintain that my mother's will was one of the most beautiful and loyal, as well as one of the grandest, acts that a woman could perform. Do you not think so?"

I gave him both my hands:

"Most certainly I do, my friend."

A MÉSALLIANCE

It is a generally acknowledged truth that the prerogatives of the nobility are only maintained at the present time through the weakness of the middle classes. Many of these, who have established themselves and their families by their intellect, industry, and struggles, fall into a state of bliss, which reminds those who see it of intoxication, as soon as they are permitted to enter aristocratic circles, or can be seen in public with barons and counts, and above all, when these treat them in a friendly manner, no matter from what motive, or when they see a prospect of a daughter of theirs driving in a carriage with armorial bearings on the panels.

Many women and girls of the citizen class would not hesitate for a moment to refuse an honorable, good-looking man of their own class, in order to go to the altar with the oldest, ugliest, and stupidest dotard among the aristocracy.

I shall never forget saying in joke, shortly before her marriage, to a young, well-educated girl of a wealthy, middle-class family, who had the figure and the bearing of a queen, not to forget an ermine cloak in her trousseau.

"I know it would suit me capitally," she replied in all seriousness, "and I should certainly have worn one if I had married Baron R——, which I was nearly doing, as you know, but it is not suitable for the wife of a government official."

When a girl of the middle classes wanders from the paths of virtue, her fall may, as a rule, be rightly ascribed to her hankering after the nobility.

In a small German town there lived, some years ago, a tailor whom we will call Löwenfuss, a man who, like all knights of the shears, was equally full of aspirations after culture and liberty. After working for one master for some

191

time as a poor journeyman, he married his daughter, and after his father-in-law's death succeeded to the business. As he was industrious, lucky, and managed it well, he soon grew very well off, and was in a position to give his daughters an education which many a nobleman's children might have envied. They learned not only French and music, but also acquired many more solid branches of knowledge, and as they were both pretty and charming girls, they soon became much thought of and sought after.

Fanny, the elder, was especially her father's pride and a favorite in society. She was of middle height, slim, with a thoroughly maidenly figure, and with an almost Italian face, in which two large, dark eyes seemed to ask for love and submission at the same time. Yet this girl with her plentiful, black hair was not in the least intended to command, for she was one of those romantic women who will give themselves, or even throw themselves, away, but who can never be subjugated. A young physician fell in love with her, and wished to marry her; Fanny returned his love, and her parents gladly accepted him as a son-in-law. But she made it a condition that he should visit her freely and frequently for two years, before she would consent to become his wife, and she declared that she would not go to the altar with him until she was convinced that not only their hearts but also that their characters harmonized. He agreed to her wish, and became a regular visitor at the house of the educated tailor; they were happy hours for the lovers; they played, sang, and read together, and he told the girl some of his medical experiences which excited and moved her.

Just then, an officer went one day to the tailor's shop to order some civilian's clothes. This was not an unusual event in itself, but it was soon to be the cause of one; for accidentally the daughter of *the artist in clothes* came into the shop, just as the officer was leaving it. On seeing her, he paused and asked the tailor who the young lady was.

"My daughter," the tailor said, proudly.

"May I beg you to introduce me to the young lady, Herr Löwenfuss?" said the hussar.

"I feel flattered at the honor you are doing me," the tailor replied, with evident pleasure.

"Fanny, the captain wishes to make your acquaintance; this is my daughter Fanny, Captain—"

"Captain Count Kasimir W——," the hussar interrupted him, as he went up to the pretty girl, and paid her a compliment or two. They were very commonplace, stale, every-day phrases, but in spite of this they pleased the girl, intelligent as she was, because it was a cavalry officer and a Count to boot who addressed them to her. And when at last the captain in the most friendly manner, asked the tailor's permission to be allowed to visit at his house, both father and daughter granted it to him most readily.

The very next day Count W—— paid his visit, in full-dress uniform, and when Frau Löwenfuss made some observations about it, how handsome it was, and how well it became him, he told them that he should not wear it much longer, as he intended to quit the service soon, and to look for a wife in whom birth and wealth were matters of secondary consideration, while a good education and a knowledge of domestic matters were of paramount importance; adding that as soon as he had found one, he meant to retire to his estates.

From that moment, papa and mamma Löwenfuss looked upon the Count as their daughter's suitor. It is certain that he was madly in love with Fanny; he used to go to their house every evening, and made himself so looked for by all of them that the young doctor soon felt himself to be superfluous, and so his visits became rarer and rarer. The Count confessed his love to Fanny on a moonlight night, while they were sitting in an arbor covered with honeysuckle, which formed nearly the whole of Herr Löwenfuss's garden. He swore that he loved, that he adored her, and when at last she lay trembling in his arms he tried to take her by storm. But that bold cavalry exploit did not succeed, and the good-looking hussar found out for the first time in his life that a woman can at the same time be romantic, passionately in love, and virtuous.

The next morning the tailor called on the Count, and

begged him very humbly to state what his intentions with regard to Fanny were. The enamored hussar declared that he was determined to make the tailor's little daughter Countess W——. Herr Löwenfuss was so much overcome by his feelings, that he showed great inclination to embrace his future son-in-law. The Count, however, laid down certain conditions. The whole matter must be kept a profound secret, for he had every prospect of inheriting half-a-million of florins,* on the death of an aunt who was already eighty years old, which he should risk by a *mésalliance*.

When they heard this, the girl's parents certainly hesitated for a time to give their consent to the marriage, but the handsome hussar, whose ardent passion carried Fanny away, at last gained the victory. The doctor received a pretty little note from the tailor's daughter, in which she told him that she gave him back his promise, as she had not found her ideal in him. Fanny then signed a deed, by which she formally renounced all claims to her father's property, in favor of her sister, and left her home and her father's house with the count under cover of the night, in order to accompany him to Poland, where the marriage was to take place in his castle.

Of course malicious tongues declared that the hussar had abducted Fanny. But her parents smiled at such reports, for they knew better, and the moment when their daughter would return as Countess W—— would amply recompense them for everything.

Meanwhile the Polish Count and the romantic German girl were being carried by the train through the dreary plains of Masovia.† They stopped in a large town to make some purchases, and the Count, who was very wealthy and liberal, provided his future wife with everything that befitted a Countess and a girl could fancy, and then they continued their journey. The country grew more picturesque but more melancholy as they went further east; the somber Carpathians rose from the snow-covered plains, and villages, surrounded by white glistening walls and stunted willows

* About $250,000.
† A division of Poland, of which Warsaw is the capital.

stood by the side of the roads; ravens sailed through the white sky, and here and there a small peasants' sledge shot by, drawn by two thin horses.

At last they reached the station. There the Count's steward was waiting for them with a carriage and four, which brought them to their destination almost as swiftly as the iron steed.

The numerous servants were drawn up in the yard of the ancient castle to receive their master and mistress, and gave loud cheers for her, for which she thanked them smilingly. When she went into the dim, arched passages, and the large rooms, for a moment she felt a strange feeling of fear, but she quickly checked it, for was not her most ardent wish to be fulfilled in a couple of hours?

She put on her bridal attire, in which a half-comical, half-sinister looking old woman with a toothless mouth and a nose like an owl's assisted her. Just as she was fixing the myrtle wreath on to her dark curls, the bell began to ring, which summoned her to her wedding. The Count himself, in full uniform, led her to the chapel of the castle, where the priest, with the steward and the castellan as witnesses, and the footmen in grand liveries, were awaiting the handsome young couple.

After the wedding, the marriage certificate was signed in the vestry, and a groom was sent to the station, where he dispatched a telegram to her parents, to the effect that the hussar had kept his word, and that Fanny Löwenfuss had become Countess Faniska W———.

Then the newly-married couple sat down to a beautiful little dinner in company with the chaplain, the steward, and the castellan. The champagne made them all very cheerful, and at last the Count knelt down before his young and beautiful wife, boldly took her white satin slipper off her foot, filled it with wine, and emptied it to her health.

At length night came, a thorough, Polish wedding-night, and Faniska, who had just assumed a demi-toilette, was looking at herself with proud satisfaction in the great mirror that was fastened into the wall, from top to bottom. A white satin train flowed down behind her like rays from the moon, a half-open jacket of bright green velvet, trimmed

with valuable ermine, covered her voluptuous, virgin bust
and her classic arms, only to show them all the more seduc-
tively at the slightest motion, while the wealth of her dark
hair, in which diamonds hung here and there like glitter-
ing dewdrops, fell down her neck and mingled with the
white fur. The Count entered in a red velvet dressing-gown
trimmed with sable; at a sign from him, the old woman
who was waiting on his divinity left the room, and the next
moment he was lying like a slave at the feet of his lovely
young wife, who raised him up and was pressing him to
her heaving bosom, when a noise which she had never heard
before, a wild howling, startled the loving woman in the
midst of her bliss.

"What was that?" she asked, trembling.

The Count went to the window without speaking, and
she with him, her arms round him. She looked half timidly,
half curiously out into the darkness, where large bright spots
were moving about in pairs, in the park at her feet.

"Are they will-o'-the-wisps?" she whispered.

"No, my child, they are wolves," the Count replied,
fetching his double-barreled gun, which he loaded. Then he
went out on the snow-covered balcony, while she drew the
fur more closely over her bosom, and followed him.

"Will you shoot?" the Count asked her in a whisper, and
when she nodded, he said: "Aim straight at the first pair
of bright spots that you see; they are the eyes of those amiable brutes."

Then he handed her the gun and pointed it for her.

"That is the way—are you pointing straight?"

"Yes."

"Then fire."

A flash, a report, which the echo from the hills repeated
four times, and two of the unpleasant looking lights had
vanished.

Then the Count fired, and by that time their people were
all awake; they drove away the wolves with torches and
laid the two large animals, the spoils of a Polish wedding-
night, at the feet of their young mistress.

The days that followed resembled that night. The Count
showed himself a most attentive husband, his wife's knight

and slave, and she felt quite at home in that dull castle. She rode, drove, smoked, read French novels, and beat her servants as well as any Polish Countess could have done. In the course of a few years, she presented the Count with two children, and although he appeared very happy at that, yet like most husbands, he grew continually cooler, more indolent, and neglectful of her. From time to time he left the castle to see after his affairs in the capital, and the intervals between these journeys became continually shorter. Faniska felt that her husband was tired of her, and much as it grieved her, she did not let him notice it; she was always the same.

But at last the Count remained away altogether. At first he used to write, but at last the poor, weeping woman did not even receive letters to comfort her in her unhappy solitude, and his lawyer sent the money that she and the children required.

She conjectured, hoped, doubted, suffered, and wept for more than a year; then she suddenly went to the capital and appeared unexpectedly in his apartments. Painful explanations followed, until at last the Count told her that he no longer loved her, and would not live with her for the future. When she wished to make him do so by legal means, and intrusted her case to a celebrated lawyer, *the Count denied that she was his wife.* She produced her marriage certificate, and lo! the most infamous fraud came to light. A confidential servant of the Count had acted the part of the priest, so that the tailor's beautiful daughter had, as a mather of fact, merely been the Count's mistress, and her children therefore were bastards.

The virtuous woman then saw, when it was too late, that it was *she* who had formed a *mésalliance.* Her parents would have nothing to do with her, and at last it came out that the Count was married long before he knew her, but that he did not live with his wife.

Then Fanny applied to the police magistrates; she wanted to appeal to justice; but was dissuaded from taking criminal proceedings; for although they would certainly lead to the punishment of her daring seducer, they would also bring about her own ruin.

At last, however, her lawyer effected a settlement between them, which was favorable to Fanny, and which she accepted for the sake of her children. The Count paid her a considerable sum down, and gave her the gloomy castle to live in. Thither she returned with a broken heart, and from that time lived alone, a sullen misanthrope, a fierce despot.

From time to time, you may meet wandering through the Carpathians a pale woman of almost unearthly beauty, wearing a magnificent sable-skin jacket and carrying a gun over her shoulder, in the forest, or in the winter in a sledge, driving her foaming horses until they nearly drop from fatigue, while the harness bells utter a melancholy sound, and at last die away in the distance, like the weeping of a solitary, deserted human heart.

THE FARMER'S WIFE

One day Baron René du Treilles said to me:

"Will you come and open the hunting season with me in my farmhouse at Marinville? By doing so, my dear fellow, you will give me the greatest pleasure. Besides, I am all alone. This will be a hard hunting-bout, to start with, and the house where I sleep is so primitive that I can only bring my most intimate friends there."

I accepted his invitation. So on Saturday we started by the railway-line running into Normandy, and alighted at the station of Alvimare. Baron René, pointing out to me a country jaunting-car drawn by a restive horse, driven by a big peasant with white hair, said to me:

"Here is our equipage, my dear boy."

The man extended his hand to his landlord, and the Baron pressed it warmly, asking:

"Well, Maître Lebrument, how are you?"

"Aways the same, M'sieu l' Baron."

We jumped into this hencoop suspended and shaken on two immense wheels. The young horse, after a violent swerve, started into a gallop, flinging us into the air like balls. Every fall backward on to the wooden bench gave me the most dreadful pain.

The peasant kept repeating in his calm, monotonous voice:

"There, there! it's all right, all right, Moutard, all right!"

But Moutard scarcely heard and kept scampering along like a goat.

Our two dogs behind us, in the empty part of the hencoop, stood erect and sniffed the air of the plains as if they could smell the game.

The Baron gazed into the distance, with a sad eye. The

199

vast Norman landscape, undulating and melancholy as an immense English park, with farmyards surrounded by two or four rows of trees and full of dwarfed apple-trees which rendered the houses invisible, gave a vista, as far as the eye could see, of old forest-trees, tufts of wood and hedgerows, which artistic gardeners provide for when they are tracing the lines of princely estates.

And René du Treilles suddenly exclaimed:

"I love this soil; I have my very roots in it."

A pure Norman, tall and strong, with the more or less projecting paunch of the old race of adventurers who went to found kingdoms on the shores of every ocean, he was about fifty years of age, ten years less perhaps than the farmer who was driving us. The latter was a lean peasant, all skin and bone, one of those men who live a hundred years.

After two hours' traveling over stony roads, across that green and monotonous plain, the vehicle entered one of those fruit-gardens which adorn the fronts of farmhouses, and drew up before an old structure falling into decay, where an old maid-servant stood waiting at the side of a young fellow who seized the horse's bridle.

We entered the farmhouse. The smoky kitchen was high and spacious. The copper utensils and the earthenware glistened under the reflection of the big fire. A cat lay asleep under the table. Within, you inhaled the odor of milk, of apples, of smoke, that indescribable smell peculiar to old houses where peasants have lived—the odor of the soil, of the walls, of furniture, of stale soup, of washing, and of the old inhabitants, the smell of animals and human being intermingled, of things and of persons, the odor of time and of things that have passed away.

I went out to have a look at the farmyard. It was big, full of old apple-trees dwarfed and crooked, and laden with fruit which fell on the grass around them. In this farmyard the smell of apples was as strong as that of the orange-trees which blossom on the banks of southern rivers.

Four rows of beeches surrounded this inclosure. They were so tall that they seemed to touch the clouds, at this hour of nightfall, and their summits, through which the night winds passed, shook and sang a sad, interminable song.

I re-entered the house. The Baron was warming his feet at the fire and was listening to the farmer's talk about country matters. He talked about marriages, births, and deaths, then about the fall in the price of corn and the latest news about the selling value of cattle. The "Veularde" (as he called a cow that had been bought at the fair of Veules) had calved in the middle of June. The cider had not been first-class last year. The apricot-apples were almost disappearing from the country.

Then we had dinner. It was a good rustic meal, simple and abundant, long and tranquil. And while we were dining, I noticed the special kind of friendly familiarity between the Baron and the peasant which had struck me from the start.

Without, the beeches continued sobbing in the night-wind, and our two dogs shut up in a shed were whining and howling in uncanny fashion. The fire was dying out in the big gate. The maid-servant had gone to bed. Maître Lebrument said in his turn:

"If you don't mind, M'sieu l' Baron, I'm going to bed. I am not used to staying up late."

The Baron extended his hand toward him and said: "Go, my friend." in so cordial a tone that I said, as soon as the man had disappeared:

"He is devoted to you, this farmer?"

"Better than that, my dear fellow! It is a drama, an old drama, simple and very sad, that attaches him to me. Here is the story:

"You know my father was a colonel in a cavalry regiment. His orderly was this young fellow, now an old man, the son of a farmer. Then, when my father retired from the army, he took this retired soldier, then about forty, as his servant. I was at that time about thirty. We lived then in our old château of Valrenne near Caudebec-in-Caux.

"At this period, my mother's chambermaid was one of the prettiest girls you could see, fair-haired, slender, and sprightly in manner, a genuine specimen of the fascinating

Abigail, such as we scarcely ever find nowadays. Today these creatures spring up into hussies before their time. Paris, with the aid of the railways, attracts them, calls them, takes hold of them as soon as they are bursting into womanhood—these little wenches, who, in old times, remained simple maid-servants. Every man passing by, as long ago recruiting sergeants did with conscripts, entices and debauches them—foolish lassies—till now we have only the scum of the female sex for servant-maids, all that is dull, nasty, common, and ill-formed, too ugly even for gallantry.

"Well, this girl was charming, and I often gave her a kiss in dark corners—nothing more, I swear to you! She was virtuous, besides; and I had some respect for my mother's house, which is more than can be said of the blackguards of the present day.

"Now it happened that my father's man-servant, the exsoldier, the old farmer you have just seen, fell in love with this girl, but in an unusual sort of way. The first thing we noticed was that his memory was affected; he did not pay attention to anything.

"My father was incessantly saying: 'Look here, Jean! What's the matter with you? Are you unwell?'

" 'No, no, M'sieu l' Baron. There's nothing the matter with me.'

"Jean got thin. Then, when serving at table, he broke glasses and let plates fall. We thought he must have been attacked by some nervous malady, and we sent for the doctor, who thought he could detect symptoms of spinal disease. Then my father, full of anxiety about his faithful man-servant, decided to place him in a private hospital. When the poor fellow heard of my father's intentions, he made a clean breast of it.

" 'M'sieu l' Baron—'

" 'Well, my boy?'

" 'You see, the thing I want is not physic.'

" 'Ha! what is it, then?'

" 'It's marriage!'

"My father turned round and stared at him in astonishment.

" 'What's that you say—eh?'

" 'It's marriage.'

" 'Marriage? So then, you donkey, you're in love.'

" 'That's how it is, M'sieu l' Baron.'

"And my father began to laugh in such an immoderate fashion that my mother called through the wall of the next room:

" 'What in the name of goodness is the matter with you, Gontran?'

"My father replied:

" 'Come here, Catherine.'

"And when she came in, he told, with tears in his eyes from sheer laughter, that his idiot of a servant-man was love-sick.

"But my mother, instead of laughing, was deeply affected.

" 'Who is it that you have fallen in love with, my poor fellow?' she asked.

"He answered, without hesitation:

" 'With Louise, Madame la Baronne.'

"My mother said with the utmost gravity: 'We must try to arrange the matter the best way we can.'

"So Louise was sent for, and questioned by my mother. She said in reply that she knew all about Jean's liking for her, that in fact Jean had spoken to her about it several times, but that she did not want him. She refused to say why.

"And two months elapsed during which my father and mother never ceased to urge this girl to marry Jean. As she declared she was not in love with any other man, she could not give any serious reason for her refusal. My father, at last, overcame her resistance by means of a big present of money, and started the pair of them on a farm on the estate —this very farm. At the end of three years, I learned that Louise had died of consumption. But my father and my mother died, too, in their turn, and it was two years more before I found myself face to face with Jean.

"At last, one autumn day, about the end of October, the idea came into my head to go hunting on this part of my estate, which my tenant had told me was full of game.

"So, one evening, one wet evening, I arrived at this house. I was shocked to find the old soldier who had been my father's servant perfectly white-haired, though he was not more than forty-five or forty-six years of age. I made him dine with me, at the very table where we're now sitting. It was raining hard. We could hear the rain battering at the roof, the walls, and the windows, flowing in a perfect deluge into the farmyard; and my dog was howling in the shed where the other dogs are howling to-night.

"All of a sudden, when the servant-maid had gone to bed, the man said in a timid voice:

" 'M'sieu l' Baron.'

" 'What is it, my dear Jean?'

" 'I have something to tell you.'

" 'Tell it, my dear Jean.'

" 'You remember Louise, my wife?'

" 'Certainly, I do remember her.'

" 'Well, she left me a message for you.'

" 'What was it?'

" 'A—a—well, it was what you might call a confession.'

" 'Ha! And what was it about?'

" 'It was—it was—I'd rather, all the same, tell you nothing about it—but I must—I must. Well, it's this—it wasn't consumption she died of at all. It was grief—well, that's the long and the short of it. As soon as she came to live here, after we were married, she grew thin; she changed so that you wouldn't know her at the end of six months—no, you wouldn't know her, M'sieu l' Baron. It was all just as before I married her, but it was different, too, quite another sort of thing.

" 'I sent for the doctor. He said it was her liver that was affected—he said it was what he called a "hepatic" complaint—I don't know these big words M'sieu l' Baron. Then I bought medicine for her, heaps on heaps of bottles, that cost about three hundred francs. But she'd take none of them; she wouldn't have them; she said: "It's no use, my poor Jean; it wouldn't do me any good." I saw well that she had some hidden trouble; and then I found her one time crying and I didn't know what to do—no, I didn't know what to do. I bought caps and dresses and hair-oil and

earrings for her. No good! And I saw that she was going to
die. And so one night in the end of November, one snowy
night, after remaining the whole day without stirring out of
the bed, she told me to send for the curé. So I went for him.
As soon as he had come, she saw him. Then, she asked him
to let me come into the room and she said to me: "Jean,
I'm going to make a confession to you. I owe it to you, Jean.
I have never been false to you, never!—never, before or
after you married me. M'sieu le Curé is there, and can tell
it is so, and he knows my soul. Well, listen, Jean. If I am
dying, it is because I was not able to console myself for leaving the château—because—I was too—too fond of the young
Baron, Monsieur René—too fond of him, mind you, Jean,—
there was no harm in it! This is the thing that's killing me.
When I could see him no more, I felt that I should die. If
I could only have seen him, I might have lived; only seen
him, nothing more. I wish you'd tell it to him some day, by-
and-by, when I am no longer here. You will tell him—swear
you will, Jean—swear it in the presence of M'sieu le Curé!
It will console me to know that he will know it one day—
that this was the cause of my death! Swear it!"

" 'Well, I gave her my promise, M'sieu l' Baron! and, on
the faith of an honest man, I have kept my word.'

"And then he ceased speaking, his eyes filling with
tears.

"Upon my soul, my dear boy, you can't form any idea of
the emotion that filled me when I heard this poor devil,
whose wife I had caused the death of without knowing it,
telling me this story on that wet night in this very kitchen.

"I exclaimed: 'Ah! my poor Jean! my poor Jean!'

"He murmured: 'Well, that's all, M'sieu l' Baron. I could
do nothing, one way or another—and now it's all over!'

"I caught his hand across the table, and I began to cry.

"He asked: 'Will you come and see her grave?' I nodded
by way of assent, for I couldn't speak. He rose up, lighted
a lantern, and we walked through the blinding rain which,
in the light of the lamp, looked like falling arrows.

"He opened a gate, and I saw some crosses of blackwood.

"Suddenly, he said: 'There it is, in front of a marble slab,' and he flashed the lantern close to it so that I could read the inscription:

> " 'To Louise-Hortense Marinet,
> Wife of *Jean-François Lebrument, farmer.*
> She was a faithful Wife! God rest her Soul!'

"We fell on our knees in the damp grass, he and I, with the lantern between us, and I saw the rain beating on the white marble slab. And I thought of the heart of her sleeping there in her grave. Ah! poor heart! poor heart!

"Since then, I have been coming here every year. And I don't know why, but I feel as if I were guilty of some crime in the presence of this man who always shows that he forgives me!"

MY UNCLE SOSTHENES

My uncle Sosthenes was a Freethinker, like many others are, from pure stupidity, people are very often religious in the same way. The mere sight of a priest threw him into a violent rage; he would shake his fist and grimace at him, and touch a piece of iron when the priest's back was turned, forgetting that the latter action showed a belief after all, the belief in the evil eye.

Now when beliefs are unreasonable one should have all or none at all. I myself am a Freethinker; I revolt at all the dogmas which have invented the fear of death, but I feel no anger toward places of worship, be they Catholic, Apostolic, Roman, Protestant, Greek, Russian, Buddhist, Jewish, or Mohammedan. I have a peculiar manner of looking at them and explaining them. A place of worship represents the homage paid by man to "The Unknown." The more extended our thoughts and our views become the more The Unknown diminishes, and the more places of worship will decay. I, however, in the place of church furniture, in the place of pulpits, reading desks, altars, and so on, would fit them up with telescopes, microscopes, and electrical machines; that is all.

My uncle and I differed on nearly every point. He was a patriot, while I was not—for after all patriotism is a kind of religion; it is the egg from which wars are hatched.

My uncle was a Freemason, and I used to declare that they are stupider than old women devotees. That is my opinion, and I maintain it; if we must have any religion at all the old one is good enough for me.

What is their object? Mutual help to be obtained by tickling the palms of each other's hands. I see no harm in it, for they put into practice the Christian precept: "Do unto others as ye would they should do unto you." The only difference consists in the tickling, but it does not seem worth while to make such a fuss about lending a poor devil half-a-crown.

To all my arguments my uncle's reply used to be:

"We are raising up a religion against a religion; Freethought will kill clericalism. Freemasonry is the headquarters of those who are demolishing all deities."

"Very well, my dear uncle," I would reply (in my heart I felt inclined to say, "You old idiot!"); "it is just that which I am blaming you for. Instead of destroying, you are organizing competition; it is only a case of lowering the prices. And then, if you only admitted Freethinkers among you I could understand it, but you admit anybody. You have a number of Catholics among you, even the leaders of the party. Pius IX. is said to have been one of you before he became Pope. If you call a society with such an organization a bulwark against clericalism, I think it is an extremely weak one."

"My dear boy," my uncle would reply, with a wink, "our most formidable actions are political; slowly and surely we are everywhere undermining the monarchical spirit."

Then I broke out: "Yes, you are very clever! If you tell me that Freemasonry is an election-machine, I will grant it you. I will never deny that it is used as a machine to control candidates of all shades; if you say that it is only used to hoodwink people, to drill them to go to the voting-urn as soldiers are sent under fire, I agree with you; if you declare that it is indispensable to all political ambitions because it changes all its members into electoral agents, I should say to you, 'That is as clear as the sun.' But when you tell me that it serves to undermine the monarchical spirit, I can only laugh in your face.

"Just consider that vast and democratic association which had Prince Napoleon for its Grand Master under the Empire; which has the Crown Prince for its Grand Master in Germany, the Czar's brother in Russia, and to which the Prince of Wales and King Humbert and nearly all the royalists of the globe belong."

"You are quite right," my uncle said; "but all these persons are serving our projects without guessing it."

I felt inclined to tell him he was talking a pack of nonsense.

It was, however, indeed a sight to see my uncle when he had a Freemason to dinner.

On meeting they shook hands in a manner that was irresistibly funny; one could see that they were going through a series of secret mysterious pressures. When I wished to put my uncle in a rage, I had only to tell him that dogs also have a manner which savors very much of Freemasonry, when they greet one another on meeting.

Then my uncle would take his friend into a corner to tell him something important, and at dinner they had a peculiar way of looking at each other, and of drinking to each other, in a manner as if to say: "We know all about it, don't we?"

And to think that there are millions on the face of the globe who are amused at such monkey tricks! I would sooner be a Jesuit.

Now in our town there really was an old Jesuit who was my uncle's detestation. Every time he met him, or if he only saw him at a distance, he used to say: "Go on, you toad!" And then, taking my arm, he would whisper to me:

"Look here, that fellow will play me a trick some day or other, I feel sure of it."

My uncle spoke quite truly, and this was how it happened, through my fault also.

It was close on Holy Week, and my uncle made up his mind to give a dinner on Good Friday, a real dinner with his favorite chitterlings and black puddings. I resisted as much as I could, and said:

"I shall eat meat on that day, but at home, quite by myself. Your *manifestation,* as you call it, is an idiotic idea. Why should you manifest? What does it matter to you if people do not eat any meat?"

But my uncle would not be persuaded. He asked three of his friends to dine with him at one of the best restaurants in the town, and as he was going to pay the bill, I had certainly, after all, no scruples about *manifesting.*

At four o'clock we took a conspicuous place in the most

frequented restaurant in the town, and my uncle ordered dinner in a loud voice, for six o'clock.

We sat down punctually, and at ten o'clock we had not finished. Five of us had drunk eighteen bottles of fine still wines, and four of champagne. Then my uncle proposed what he was in the habit of calling: "The archbishop's feat." Each man put six small glasses in front of him, each of them filled with a different liqueur, and then they had all to be emptied at one gulp, one after another, while one of the waiters counted twenty. It was very stupid, but my uncle thought it was very suitable to the occasion.

At eleven o'clock he was dead drunk. So we had to take him home in a cab and put him to bed, and one could easily foresee that his anti-clerical demonstration would end in a terrible fit of indigestion.

As I was going back to my lodgings, being rather drunk myself, with a cheerful Machiavelian drunkenness which quite satisfied all my instincts of scepticism, an idea struck me.

I arranged my necktie, put on a look of great distress, and went and rang loudly at the old Jesuit's door. As he was deaf he made me wait a longish while, but at length he appeared at his window in a cotton nightcap and asked what I wanted.

I shouted out at the top of my voice:

"Make haste, reverend Sir, and open the door; a poor, despairing, sick man is in need of your spiritual ministrations."

The good, kind man put on his trousers as quickly as he could and came down without his cassock. I told him in a breathless voice that my uncle, the Freethinker, had been taken suddenly ill. Fearing it was going to be something serious he had been seized with a sudden fear of death, and wished to see a priest and talk to him; to have his advice and comfort, to make up with the Church, and to confess, so as to be able to cross the dreaded threshold at peace with himself; and I added in a mocking tone:

"At any rate, he wishes it, and if it does him no good it can do him no harm."

The old Jesuit, who was startled, delighted, and almost trembling, said to me:

"Wait a moment, my son, I will come with you."

But I replied: "Pardon me, reverend Father, if I do not go with you; but my convictions will not allow me to do so. I even refused to come and fetch you, so I beg you not to say that you have seen me, but to declare that you had a presentiment—a sort of revelation of his illness."

The priest consented, and went off quickly, knocked at my uncle's door, was soon let in, and I saw the black cassock disappear within that stronghold of Freethought.

I hid under a neighboring gateway to wait for events. Had he been well, my uncle would have half murdered the Jesuit, but I knew that he would scarcely be able to move an arm, and I asked myself, gleefully, what sort of a scene would take place between these antagonists—what explanation would be given, and what would be the issue of this situation, which my uncle's indignation would render more tragic still?

I laughed till I had to hold my sides, and said to myself, half aloud: "Oh! what a joke, what a joke!"

Meanwhile it was getting very cold. I noticed that the Jesuit stayed a long time, and thought: "They are having an explanation, I suppose."

One, two, three hours passed, and still the reverend Father did not come out. What had happened? Had my uncle died in a fit when he saw him, or had he killed the cassocked gentleman? Perhaps they had mutually devoured each other? This last supposition appeared very unlikely, for I fancied that my uncle was quite incapable of swallowing a grain more nourishment at that moment.

At last the day broke. I was very uneasy, and, not venturing to go into the house myself, I went to one of my friends who lived opposite. I roused him, explained matters to him, much to his amusement and astonishment, and took possession of his window.

At nine o'clock he relieved me and I got a little sleep. At two o'clock I, in my turn, replaced him. We were utterly astonished.

At six o'clock the Jesuit left, with a very happy and satisfied look on his face, and we saw him go away with a quiet step.

Then, timid and ashamed, I went and knocked at my uncle's door. When the servant opened it I did not dare to ask her any questions, but went upstairs without saying a word.

My uncle was lying pale, exhausted, with weary, sorrowful eyes and heavy arms, on his bed. A little religious picture was fastened to one of the bed-curtains with a pin.   .

"Why, uncle," I said, "you in bed still? Are you not well?"

He replied in a feeble voice:

"Oh! my dear boy, I have been very ill; nearly dead."

"How was that, uncle?"

"I don't know; it was most surprising. But what is stranger still is, that the Jesuit priest who has just left—you know, that excellent man whom I have made such fun of—had a divine revelation of my state, and came to see me."

I was seized with an almost uncontrollable desire to laugh, and with difficulty said: "Oh, really!"

"Yes, he came. He heard a Voice telling him to get up and come to me, because I was going to die. It was a revelation."

I pretended to sneeze, so as not to burst out laughing; I felt inclined to roll on the ground with amusement.

In about a minute I managed to say, indignantly: "And you received him, uncle, you? You, a Freethinker, a Freemason? You did not have him thrown out-of-doors?"

He seemed confused, and stammered:

"Listen a moment, it is so astonishing—so astonishing and providential! He also spoke to me about my father; it seems he knew him formerly."

"Your father, uncle? But that is no reason for receiving a Jesuit."

"I know that, but I was very ill, and he looked after me most devotedly all night long. He was perfect; no doubt he saved my life; those men are all more or less doctors."

"Oh! he looked after you all night? But you said just now that he had only been gone a very short time."

"That is quite true; I kept him to breakfast after all his

kindness. He had it at a table by my bedside while I drank a cup of tea."

"And he ate meat?"

My uncle looked vexed, as if I had said something very much out of place, and then added:

"Don't joke, Gaston; such things are out of place at times. He has shown me more devotion than many a relation would have done and I expect to have his convictions respected."

This rather upset me, but I answered, nevertheless: "Very well, uncle; and what did you do after breakfast?"

"We played a game of bézique, and then he repeated his breviary while I read a little book which he happened to have in his pocket, and which was not by any means badly written."

"A religious book, uncle?"

"Yes, and no, or rather—no. It is the history of their missions in Central Africa, and is rather a book of travels and adventures. What these men have done is very grand."

I began to feel that matters were going badly, so I got up. "Well, good-bye, uncle," I said. "I see you are going to leave Freemasonry for religion; you are a renegade."

He was still rather confused and stammered:

"Well, but religion is a sort of Freemasonry."

"When is your Jesuit coming back?" I asked.

"I don't—I don't know exactly; to-morrow, perhaps; but it is not certain."

I went out, altogether overwhelmed.

My joke turned out very badly for me! My uncle became radically converted, and if that had been all I should not have cared so much. Clerical or Freemason, to me it is all the same; six of one and half-a-dozen of the other; but the worst of it is that he has just made his will—yes, made his will—and has disinherited me in favor of that rascally Jesuit!

THE ENGLISHMAN

They made a circle around Judge Bermutier, who was giving his opinion of the mysterious affair that had happened at Saint-Cloud. For a month Paris had doted on this inexplicable crime. No one could understand it at all.

M. Bermutier, standing with his back to the chimney, talked about it, discussed the divers opinions, but came to no conclusions.

Many women had risen and come nearer, remaining standing, with eyes fixed upon the shaven mouth of the magistrate, whence issued these grave words. They shivered and vibrated, crisp through their curious fear, through that eager, insatiable need of terror which haunts their soul, torturing them like a hunger.

One of them, paler than the others, after a silence, said:

"It is frightful. It touches the supernatural. We shall never know anything about it."

The magistrate turned toward her, saying:

"Yes, Madame, it is probable that we never shall know anything about it. As for the word 'supernatural,' when you come to use that, it has no place here. We are in the presence of a crime skillfully conceived, very skillfully executed, and so well enveloped in mystery that we cannot separate the impenetrable circumstances which surround it. But, once in my life, I had to follow an affair which seemed truly to be mixed up with something very unusual. However, it was necessary to give it up, as there was no means of explaining it."

Many of the ladies called out at the same time, so quickly that their voices sounded as one:

"Oh! tell us about it."

M. Bermutier smiled gravely, as judges should, and replied:

"You must not suppose, for an instant, that I, at least, believed there was anything superhuman in the adventure. I believe only in normal causes. And, if in place of using the word 'supernatural' to express what we cannot comprehend we should simply use the word 'inexplicable,' it would be much better. In any case, the surrounding circumstances in the affair I am going to relate to you, as well as the preparatory circumstances, have affected me much. Here are the facts:

"I was then judge of Instruction at Ajaccio, a little white town lying on the border of an admirable gulf that was surrounded on all sides by high mountains.

"What I particularly had to look after there was the affairs of *vendetta*. Some of them were superb; as dramatic as possible, ferocious, and heroic. We find there the most beautiful subjects of vengeance that one could dream of, hatred a century old, appeased for a moment but never extinguished, abominable plots, assassinations becoming massacres and almost glorious battles. For two years I heard of nothing but the price of blood, of the terribly prejudiced Corsican who is bound to avenge all injury upon the person of him who is the cause of it, or upon his nearest descendants. I saw old men and infants, cousins, with their throats cut, and my head was full of these stories.

"One day we learned that an Englishman had rented for some years a little villa at the end of the Gulf. He had brought with him a French domestic, picked up at Marseille on the way.

"Soon everybody was occupied with this singular person, who lived alone in his house, only going out to hunt and fish. He spoke to no one, never came to the town, and, every morning, practiced shooting with a pistol and a rifle for an hour or two.

"Some legends about him were abroad. They pretended that he was a high personage fled from his own country for political reasons; then they affirmed that he was concealing himself after having committed a frightful crime. They even cited some of the particularly horrible details.

"In my capacity of judge, I wished to get some information about this man. But it was impossible to learn anything. He called himself Sir John Rowell.

"I contented myself with watching him closely; although, in reality, there seemed nothing to suspect regarding him.

"Nevertheless, as rumors on his account continued, grew, and became general, I resolved to try and see this stranger myself, and for this purpose began to hunt regularly in the neighborhood of his property.

"I waited long for an occasion. It finally came in the form of a partridge which I shot and killed before the very nose of the Englishman. My dog brought it to me; but, immediately taking it I went and begged Sir John Rowell to accept the dead bird, excusing myself for intrusion.

"He was a tall man with red hair and red beard, very large, a sort of placid, polite Hercules. He had none of the so-called British haughtiness, and heartily thanked me for the delicacy in French, with a beyond-the-Channel accent. At the end of a month we had chatted together five or six times.

"Finally, one evening, as I was passing by his door, I perceived him astride a chair in the garden, smoking his pipe. I saluted him and he asked me in to have a glass of beer. It was not necessary for him to repeat before I accepted.

"He received me with the fastidious courtesy of the English, spoke in praise of France and of Corsica, and declared that he loved that country and that shore.

"Then, with great precaution in the form of a lively interest, I put some questions to him about his life and his projects. He responded without embarrassment, told me that he had traveled much, in Africa, in the Indies, and in America. He added, laughing:

" 'I have had many adventures, oh! yes.'

"I began to talk about hunting, and he gave me many curious details of hunting the hippopotamus, the tiger, the elephant, and even of hunting the gorilla.

"I said: 'All these animals are very formidable.'

"He laughed: 'Oh! no. The worst animal is man.' Then

he began to laugh, with the hearty laugh of a big contented Englishman. He continued:

" 'I have often hunted man, also.'

"He spoke of weapons and asked me to go into his house to see his guns of various makes and kinds.

"His drawing-room was hung in black, in black silk embroidered with gold. There were great yellow flowers running over the somber stuff, shining like fire.

" 'It is Japanese cloth,' he said.

"But in the middle of a large panel, a strange thing attracted my eye. Upon a square of red velvet, a black object was attached. I approached and found it was a hand, the hand of a man. Not a skeleton hand, white and characteristic, but a black, desiccated hand, with yellow joints with the muscles bare and on them traces of old blood, of blood that seemed like a scale, over the bones sharply cut off at about the middle of the fore-arm, as with a blow of a hatchet. About the wrist was an enormous iron chain, riveted, soldered to this unclean member, attaching it to the wall by a ring sufficiently strong to hold an elephant.

"I asked: 'What is that?'

"The Englishman responded tranquilly:

" 'It belonged to my worst enemy. It came from America. It was broken with a saber, cut off with a sharp stone, and dried in the sun for eight days. Oh, very good for me, that was!'

"I touched the human relic, which must have belonged to a colossus. The fingers were immoderately long and attached by enormous tendons that held the straps of skin in place. This dried hand was frightful to see, making one think, naturally, of the vengeance of a savage.

"I said: 'This man must have been very strong.'

"With gentleness the Englishman answered:

" 'Oh! yes; but I was stronger than he. I put this chain on him to hold him.'

"I thought he spoke in jest and replied:

" 'The chain is useless now that the hand cannot escape.'

"Sir John Rowell replied gravely: 'It always wishes to escape. The chain is necessary.'

"With a rapid, questioning glance, I asked myself: 'Is he mad, or is that an unpleasant joke?'

"But the face remained impenetrable, tranquil, and friendly. I spoke of other things and admired the guns.

"Nevertheless, I noticed three loaded revolvers on the pieces of furniture, as if this man lived in constant fear of attack.

"I went there many times after that; then for some time I did not go. We had become accustomed to his presence; he had become indifferent to us.

"A whole year slipped away. Then, one morning, toward the end of November, my domestic awoke me with the announcement that Sir John Rowell had been assassinated in the night.

"A half hour later, I entered the Englishman's house with the central Commissary and the Captain of Police. The servant, lost in despair, was weeping at the door. I suspected him at first, but afterward found that he was innocent.

"The guilty one could never be found.

"Upon entering Sir John's drawing-room, I perceived his dead body stretched out upon its back, in the middle of the room. His waistcoat was torn, a sleeve was hanging, and it was evident that a terrible struggle had taken place.

"The Englishman had been strangled! His frightfully black and swollen face seemed to express an abominable fear; he held something between his set teeth; and his neck, pierced with five holes apparently done with a pointed iron, was covered with blood.

"A doctor joined us. He examined closely the prints of fingers in the flesh and pronounced these strange words:

" 'One would think he had been strangled by a skeleton.'

"A shiver ran down my back and I cast my eyes to the place on the wall where I had seen the horrible, torn-off hand. It was no longer there. The chain was broken and hanging.

"Then I bent over the dead man and found in his mouth a piece of one of the fingers of the missing hand, cut off, or rather sawed off by the teeth exactly at the second joint.

"Then they tried to collect evidence. They could find nothing. No door had been forced, no window opened, or piece of furniture moved. The two watchdogs on the premises had not been aroused.

"Here, in a few words, is the deposition of the servant:

"For a month, his master had seemed agitated. He had received many letters which he had burned immediately. Often, taking a whip, in anger which seemed like dementia, he had struck in fury, this dried hand, fastened to the wall and taken, one knew not how, at the moment of a crime.

"He had retired late and shut himself in with care. He always carried arms. Often in the night he talked out loud, as if he were quarreling with some one. On that night, however, there had been no noise, and it was only on coming to open the windows that the servant had found Sir John assassinated. He suspected no one.

"I communicated what I knew of the death to the magistrates and public officers, and they made minute inquiries upon the whole island. They discovered nothing.

"One night, three months after the crime, I had a frightful nightmare. It seemed to me that I saw that hand, that horrible hand, running like a scorpion or a spider along my curtains and my walls. Three times I awoke, three times I fell asleep and again saw that hideous relic galloping about my room, moving its fingers like paws.

"The next day they brought it to me, found in the cemetery upon the tomb where Sir John Rowell was interred— for they had not been able to find his family. The index finger was missing.

"This, ladies, is my story. I know no more about it."

The ladies were terrified, pale, and shivering. One of them cried:

"But that is not the end, for there was no explanation! We cannot sleep if you do not tell us what was your idea of the reason of it all."

The magistrate smiled with severity, and answered:

"Oh! certainly, ladies, but it will spoil all your terrible dreams. I simply think that the legitimate proprietor of the hand was not dead and that he came for it with the one that remained to him. But I was never able to find out how he did it. It was one kind of revenge."

One of the women murmured:

"No, it could not be thus."

And the Judge of Information, smiling still, concluded:

"I told you in the beginning that my explanation would not satisfy you."

A LUCKY BURGLAR

They were seated in the dining-room of a hotel in Barbizon.

"I tell you, you will not believe it."

"Well, tell it anyhow."

"All right, here goes. But first I must tell you that my story is absolutely true in every respect; even if it does sound improbable." And the old artist commenced:

"We had dined at Soriel's that night. When I say dined, that means that we were all pretty well tipsy. We were three young madcaps. Soriel (poor fellow! he is dead now), Le Poittevin, the marine painter, and myself. Le Poittevin is dead, also.

"We had stretched ourselves on the floor of the little room adjoining the studio and the only one in the crowd who was rational was Le Poittevin. Soriel, who was always the maddest, lay flat on his back, with his feet propped up on a chair, discussing war and the uniforms of the Empire, when, suddenly, he got up, took out of the big wardrobe where he kept his accessories a complete hussar's uniform and put it on. He then took a grenadier's uniform and told Le Poittevin to put it on; but he objected, so we forced him into it. It was so big for him that he was completely lost in it. I arrayed myself as a cuirassier. After we were ready, Soriel made us go through a complicated drill. Then he exclaimed: 'As long as we are troopers let us drink like troopers.'

"The punch-bowl had been brought out and filled for the second time. We were bawling some old camp songs at the top of our voice, when Le Poittevin, who in spite of all the punch had retained his self-control, held up his hand and said: 'Hush! I am sure I heard someone walking in the studio.'

221

" 'A burglar!' said Soriel, staggering to his feet. 'Good luck!' And he began the 'Marseillaise':

" 'To arms, citizens!'

"Then he seized several weapons from the wall and equipped us according to our uniforms. I received a musket and a saber. Le Poittevin was handed an enormous gun with a bayonet attached. Soriel, not finding just what he wanted, seized a pistol, stuck it in his belt, and brandishing a battle-axe in one hand, he opened the studio door cautiously. The army advanced. Having reached the middle of the room, Soriel said:

" 'I am general. You [pointing to me], the cuirassiers, will keep the enemy from retreating—that is, lock the door. You [pointing to Le Poittevin], the grenadiers, will be my escort.'

"I executed my orders and rejoined the troops, who were behind a large screen reconnoitering. Just as I reached it I heard a terrible noise. I rushed up with the candle to investigate the cause of it and this is what I saw. Le Poittevin was piercing the dummy's breast with his bayonet and Soriel was splitting his head open with his axe! When the mistake had been discovered the General commanded: 'Be cautious!'

"We had explored every nook and corner of the studio for the past twenty minutes without success, when Le Poittevin thought he would look in the cupboard. As it was quite deep and very dark, I advanced with the candle and looked in. I drew back stupefied. A man, a real live man this time, stood there looking at me! I quickly recovered myself, however, and locked the cupboard door. We then retired a few paces to hold a council.

"Opinions were divided. Soriel wanted to smoke the burglar out; Le Poittevin suggested starvation, and I proposed to blow him up with dynamite. Le Poittevin's idea being finally accepted as the best, we proceeded to bring the punch and pipes into the studio, while Le Poittevin kept guard with his big gun on his shoulder, and settling ourselves in front of the cupboard we drank the prisoner's health. We had done this repeatedly, when Soriel suggested that we bring out the prisoner and take a look at him.

" 'Hooray!' cried I. We picked up our weapons and made a mad rush for the cupboard door. It was finally opened, and Soriel, cocking his pistol which was not loaded, rushed in first. Le Poittevin and I followed yelling like lunatics and, after a mad scramble in the dark, we at last brought out the burglar. He was a haggard-looking, white-haired old bandit, with shabby, ragged clothes. We bound him hand and foot and dropped him in an armchair. He said nothing.

" 'We will try this wretch' said Soriel, whom the punch had made very solemn. I was so far gone that it seemed to me quite a natural thing. Le Poittevin was named for the defense and I for the prosecution. The prisoner was condemned to death by all except his counsel.

" 'We will now execute him,' said Soriel. 'Still, this man cannot die without repenting,' he added, feeling somewhat scrupulous. 'Let us send for a priest.'

"I objected that it was too late, so he proposed that I officiate and forthwith told the prisoner to confess his sins to me. The old man was terrified. He wondered what kind of wretches we were and for the first time he spoke. His voice was hollow and cracked:

" 'Say, you don't mean it, do you?'

"Soriel forced him to his knees, and for fear he had not been baptized, poured a glass of rum over his head, saying: 'Confess your sins; your last hour has come!'

" 'Help! Help!' screamed the old man rolling himself on the floor and kicking everything that came his way. For fear he should wake the neighbors we gagged him.

" 'Come, let us end this'; said Soriel impatiently. He pointed his pistol at the old man and pressed the trigger. I followed his example, but as neither of our guns were loaded we made very little noise. Le Poittevin, who had been looking on said:

" 'Have we really the right to kill this man?'

" 'We have condemned him to death!' said Soriel.

" 'Yes, but we have no right to shoot a civilian. Let us take him to the station-house.'

"We agreed with him, and as the old man could not walk we tied him to a board, and Le Poittevin and I carried him, while Soriel kept guard in the rear. We arrived at the station-house. The chief, who knew us and was well acquainted with our manner of joking, thought it was a great lark and laughingly refused to take our prisoner in. Soriel insisted, but the chief told us very sternly to quit our fooling and go home and be quiet. There was nothing else to do but to take him back to Soriel's.

" 'What are we going to do with him?' I asked.

" 'The poor man must be awfully tired!' said Le Poittevin, sympathizingly.

"He did look half dead, and in my turn I felt a sudden pity for him (the punch, no doubt), and I relieved him of his gag.

" 'How do you feel old man?' I asked.

" 'By Jingo! I have enough of this,' he groaned.

"Then Soriel softened. He unbound him and treated him as a long-lost friend. The three of us immediately brewed a fresh bowl of punch. As soon as it was ready we handed a glass to the prisoner, who quaffed it without flinching. Toast followed toast. The old man could drink more than the three of us put together; but as daylight appeared, he got up and calmly said: 'I shall be obliged to leave you; I must get home now.'

"We begged him not to go, but he positively refused to stay any longer. We were awfully sorry and took him to the door, while Soriel held the candle above his head saying: 'Look out for the last step.' "